# The Amazon Shaman

The story of spiritual development through shamanism, in the midst of a struggle to protect the ecology of the Amazon Forest.

# Roberto Lima Netto

Roberto Lima Netto

**The Amazon Shaman**

LN Edition, 2012

Copyright © 2012 by Roberto Lima Netto

ISBN-13: 978-1467915298
ISBN-10: 1467915297

Title in Portuguese:

"O Xamã Dourado"

Ed. Ediouro, 2002

Copyright © 2002 by Roberto Lima Netto

ISBN 85-00-01289-7

**Key words**: Amazon, forest, Shaman, Jung, spiritual journey, shamanic training, medicinal herbs, ecology, sustainable exploration of the forest, drug war.

# Contents

Foreword ............................................................................................. 5
Chapter 1 – William's Crash ................................................................ 7
Chapter 2 – Tsiipré, the bright Indian Boy ........................................... 9
Chapter 3 – John, the Bad Boy ........................................................... 15
Chapter 4 – Courting Disaster ............................................................. 19
Chapter 5 – Tsiipré, the shaman to be ................................................. 23
Chapter 6 – John, the son of darkness ................................................. 31
Chapter 7 - Lost in the Way to Heaven ............................................... 41
Chapter 8 - John's Revenge ................................................................. 49
Chapter 9 - The Shaman ...................................................................... 59
Chapter 10 – After the trees ................................................................. 69
Chapter 11 – In the heart of the jungle ................................................ 75
Chapter 12 - Tsiipré's Dream ............................................................... 87
Chapter 13 - The Black Hole ............................................................... 101
Chapter 14 - The Shaman's Apprentice ............................................... 113
Chapter 15 - The Gold Cave ................................................................ 125
Chapter 16 – A Rich Man .................................................................... 137
Chapter 17 - The Objects of Power ..................................................... 143
Chapter 18 - The Face of Danger ........................................................ 151
Chapter 19 - A dangerous game .......................................................... 163
Chapter 20 – It's show time ................................................................. 173
Chapter 21 – Visiting the lion´s cage .................................................. 179
Chapter 22 – Tension in the air ........................................................... 185
Chapter 23 – The divine song .............................................................. 195
Chapter 24 - Kauaí-Açú ....................................................................... 201
Chapter 25 – Gold, Always Gold ........................................................ 209
Chapter 26 – Talking to the father ...................................................... 219
Chapter 27 – The Flood ....................................................................... 225
Chapter 28 - The Enemy ..................................................................... 237
Chapter 29 – Light again ..................................................................... 245
Chapter 30 - The Gates of Hell ........................................................... 255
Chapter 31 – Victory thwarted ............................................................ 263
Chapter 32 - Saving the forest ............................................................ 267
Chapter 33 – The Last Battle .............................................................. 275

**Roberto Lima Netto**

## Foreword
### by Walter Boechat (*)

Adventure and spiritual transformation. This new book by Roberto Lima Netto addresses a topic of many meanings: Shamanism. The story occurs in the Amazon rain forest, when a young man's plane crashes and he meets a local shaman who instructs him in the ancient wisdom of his tribe.

The book covers several themes cleverly intertwined: adventure, ecology, biodiversity, psychology, anthropology and religion, all this in an harmonious whole in which the question of shamanism appears centralizing the plot.

But what after all is shamanism? The scholar of comparative religions Mircea Eliade summarized the definition of shamanism in his well-known book "Shamanism: a technique of ecstasy.": 'The shaman differs from other healers and medicine men of tribal societies because he performs the cures with ecstasy; he heals during altered states of consciousness.'

Ecstasy can be achieved through several means: the ayahuasca wine (tribe Huni Kuin of Acre), dances, rhythms and sacred chants accompanied by ceremonial rattle-rattle using the maraca. Among the Siberians, the drum used as an instrument of ecstasy is deified and worshiped, getting even ritual sacrifices. The maraca is thought to be sacred among the Amazon Indians as a great mediator of ecstasy. The ritual pipe is also common as an agent of ecstasy between our shamans. Puffs of smoke are present during ecstasy or accompanying the healing process.

**Roberto Lima Netto**

The shaman is an important element in his tribe, being the guardian of the myths and ancestral memory. The figure of the shaman thus becomes essential for preserving the memory and identity of indigenous groups, many of them threatened of extinction. This ancestral memory is an important part of the Brazilian identity.

The reader of "The Amazon Shaman" is led to know the themes of shamanism by contacting a reality that many Brazilians are unaware of: the natural richness of the Brazilian Amazon, its indigenous peoples, their myths and traditions.

*Medical Doctor, Jungian analyst, graduate of the CG Jung Institute in Zurich, Founder and President of the Jungian Association of Brazil and author of "Myths and Archetypes of Contemporary Man. Director of the Executive Committee of the IAAP - International Association for Analytical Psychology" in Zurich.

# The Amazon Shaman

> Life is a journey towards growth. If you deviate from your path, the Lord sends you gentle signs. If such signs are disregarded, He may throw you in the midst of the desert.
>
> Roberto Lima Netto
> The Little Prince for Grown-ups

## Chapter 1 – William's Crash

Pooofff! Poooooff Pooooooff. My engines are failing. Below, a dense carpet of green. The Amazon jungle. I feel a tightening on my neck muscles. My heart is dancing samba inside me, and my chest is the drum. I look down trying to find some landing alternative, a less risky one. Far away, I see a lake in the direction of the setting sun.

The last pooofff. I have to glide. Have to avoid the tops of the trees. Losing altitude. Will I get there? I won't make it. The green canopies stretch out their arms towards my plane for a deadly embrace. My God!

My life flashes before me. My first job, my fast professional success, moving from the low middle class suburbs in Rio de Janeiro to the classy Ipanema. The good feeling of having, for the first time in my life, money to spend. I thought I could overcome loneliness with a hectic life of parties. With going to bed with a million women. My life turning into a whirlwind: working hard, partying much, and sleeping only on weekends, if possible.

Everything changed when I met Valerie. She was different from any other woman. She was special. Two blackberries for eyes and a birthmark above her right eyebrow. Without it, she would be too perfect. I was flying in my small airplane to her farm, to meet her. I shouldn´t have gone to last night´s party.

These images flashed through my mind in seconds. The trees were already embracing the plane. My last thought was to God. Not a supplication, not a prayer, just God!

I am flying in the bright blue sky. Thousands of birds flock around me. White, red, blue, green, many-colored birds. A magnificent show. I need no plane to fly. My Guide is beside me. It is a pleasant feeling. I am weightless. I am transported to heaven; never been so happy in my life.

But ... something goes wrong. The birds become uneasy. They seem to be trying to say something. They fly in all directions. I look up and see a hawk diving straight at me. It's going to attack me. I try to change direction, but I fail. It bites me hard on my forehead. It hurts. I cover my face with my hands. I'm dizzy. I'm falling, falling, falling. I look down, and see only the sky. I look up. Again, the sky. I am in a merry-go-round. I'm giddy, confused!

 I hear a lovely music. It seems to go through all my body. It is both loud and soft. It enters my skin and floods my body. It penetrates my soul. Heaven! Is this heaven?

> As against Freud's view that the dream is essentially wish fulfillment, I hold that the dream is a spontaneous self-portrait, in symbolic form, of the actual situation in the unconscious.
>
> C. G. Jung
> General Aspects of Dream Psychology – Collected Works 8

## Chapter 2 – Tsiipré, the bright Indian Boy

Our people, the Kauauá, lived near the village of Formoso. Actually, I would say that the people in the village lived near us, because we were there long before the white people had settled in the region. But they soon outnumbered us. When I was seven, we were less than two hundred.

This proximity to the village was a problem. With the white people came disease to which we were not resistant. Those of us who survived assimilated the white culture and our traditions were gradually disappearing. Our elders did not like that, and kept insisting we should move away to guarantee our survival.

One day, as I was getting ready to leave our hut, I heard my mother call: "Tsiipré, Chief Kautá wants to talk to you. Go to him right now."

I was curious. "What does he want?"

"I don't know. Go and find out."

Curiosity soon changed into apprehension: "Could you please come with me?"

My mother was firm: "It's you he wants to talk to . He didn't call me."

Chief Kautá was my father. And this was the first time he called me to his hut. Until then, I was considered to be a mother's boy. Of course I was proud to be summoned by the chief. But I was also concerned. What on earth did he want from me?

My father looked sad and was sitting by the white priest of the village. He turned to me: "Father Justin wants you to live among the white people, and study their sciences and religion."

I couldn't hide my lack of enthusiasm. The curiosity smile I had disappeared from my face.

I think Father Justin noticed my reluctance. He tried to argue: "You will study in our school, and learn many things."

I would not dare contradict our Chief. The decision had been made. Whether I liked it or not, I had to go. Father Justin tried hard to make things look better for me: "Perhaps you could become the first Catholic priest of the Kauauá."

I froze, terrified at this idea. Father Justin kept a close eye at me: "It will be very good for you. This is the wisest step to take, trust me."

Chief Kautá added: "When you come back, you will be of great help to our people."

I never questioned my father's decision. What else would you expect from a seven years old boy, be it Indian or white?

A few days later, Father Justin came to pick me up. Classes were about to start.


Adjusting to the white man's school was hard. I was not used to sitting quietly at a desk, listening to the teacher. It took me a long time to adapt to their ways. But I soon discovered how easy it was to learn. About one month later, I was called to Father Justin's office. As I walked into his room, I was shaking. I already knew he used to call the problem-boys, and scold them. I tried to remember some nasty thing I might have done, but I couldn't think of anything. This didn't help. It only added anxiety to my fear. Why was I being called?

"I would like to congratulate you," I thought I heard him say. "Your teacher told me that you learn very quickly. I want you to study with me in the afternoon, after your regular classes." Praise had never crossed my mind!

From that day on, Father Justin kept me under his care, and became like a second father to me. I remember fondly the contrast between that tall, thin, stern figure, and his golden heart. When the classes were over, he would take me to his office and teach me more advanced things. I became proficient in reading long before my schoolmates. I loved books and would spend hours in the monastery library.

When I was ten, Father Justin took me to see my father. He was in front of his hut. Several of the old Indians were present. Their faces showed curiosity. Naturally, I was the most curious of all, as the Father hadn't given me any hints about the purpose of our visit. This time I was sure I had done nothing wrong. On the contrary, I was doing well at school.

If the reason for the meeting was to return me to my people, I confess that by now, I would have mixed feelings. I loved the life in the tribe, and loved going back to my people on vacations. But I also wanted to learn to be important to my tribe some day. I had no doubt I wanted to return to help my people. But first, I wanted to learn all I could from the white man.

Chief Kautá signaled to Father Justin to sit in front of him and calmly waited for him to begin talking:

"Chief Kautá, I want to tell you that your son is very intelligent. He is the brightest student I've ever had."

Kautá was trying to seem unemotional, but I saw pride all over his face.

Father Justin continued: "Tsiipré is making great progress. I want to continue supervising his studies, but I'll soon be transferred to Manaus."

"Would this mean that Tsiipré has to quit studying?" Now, my father couldn't hide his concern.

"On the other way around. I want to take him with me, and I am asking for your permission."

Kautá wasn´t sure. Father Justin went on: "He will be able to come back on his vacations. This way, he is not going to lose contact with his people."

Kautá was quiet for a long time before I heard him say: "I agree. I know that, in the future, we will need Tsiipré's knowledge."

That settled the issue. I was to stay with my people for a week, and then go to Manaus with Father Justin.

The small village of Formoso was nothing compared to Manaus. Manaus was a big, noisy place. Cars, motorcycles, movie theaters, and wide, tree-lined streets. But of all the attractive places I came in contact with, the Public Library was the best. Pure joy! I became familiar with classical writers and learned a great deal from them.

I was twelve when I realized I would be a Shaman. This knowledge came to me in a dream. I was enjoying my holidays with the Kauauá when I had my first mystical experience. I was strolling in the forest when I tripped and fell to the ground. I hit my head on a stone and fainted.

I stood in the middle of a very wide clearing, a circle over three hundred feet in diameter surrounded by huge trees. The largest tree in the area rose in the middle. It was so huge it would take eight men to embrace its trunk. It was a magic tree; it brought peace to whoever touched it.

In the clearing, there were Indian men, women and children, as well as animals and birds. They were all in peace. A jaguar and a deer were talking and their puppies were having fun together. The sun was shining. The air was filled with the scent of thousands of flowers. Happiness was in full bloom.

Suddenly, the weather began to change. Clouds hid the bright sun. A strong wind started to blow the leaves off the trees. The air was filled with dust. All the animals went to the forest. The birds flew away. Only the Indians remained in the clearing. But they also began to disappear as if sucked by the air. The clearing grew wider and wider and the surrounding forest soon turned into a large desert. I stood alone in the midst of it. Only the gigantic tree remained, but having lost most of its leaves. I was feeling lonely. Scared. I started to pray.

In a short time, the wind stopped and it began to rain heavily. I was soaked, but noticed that the soil was turning green again. The vegetation was coming back. The trees were growing. The reason: I had called God in my prayer. Then, the rain stopped as suddenly as it had started. The animals returned. The birds flew back to the tops of the trees and started singing as if they were praising God. My Indian brothers also appeared. They were all around me again. I looked up and saw, high above the tree, a golden figure giving me instructions.

Under a kind of a spell, I organized the birds and the animals. In the south I put all the land animals: snakes, jaguars, deer, cows, bulls, horses. Despite their differences, they were peacefully together. To the north I assigned the people of the air: birds and butterflies. I did not put the hawk there. Living closer to the sun, the father of fire, I assigned the hawk to the east. I placed the fish, capybaras and otters in the lake in the west. Harmony reigned over the clearing and I heard a soft music coming from the central tree.

I was so happy I forgot to keep praying. At that moment, a white man appeared. Havoc was installed. My dream had turned into a nightmare again.

I woke up worried. On that day I knew I was being summoned by God to become a shaman.

> As many as 4% of the population are conscienceless sociopaths who have no empathy or affectionate feelings for humans or animals.
>
> A sociopath is defined as someone who displays at least three of seven distinguishing characteristics, such as deceitfulness, impulsivity and a lack of remorse.
>
> The Sociopath Next Door
> Martha Stout, Ph.D.

## Chapter 3 – John, the Bad Boy

I'm John. I know what it is to be poor, to be discriminated for having an Indian mother and for not knowing who my father is. I also know that I am much more intelligent than any of my pals. As for being poor, I don't care. I'll soon be very rich and powerful. Perhaps I might even become the Governor of the Amazon State.

At thirteen, my life wasn't a happy one. I lived with my mother in Formoso, a small village on the banks of the Rio Grande. But my world was much smaller. It revolved around some ten children, more or less my age. The other boys feared me, not because I was strong, but because I was clever. Like most boys, bullying was a common practice among us, and I was the best at it.

One day, I was walking down the street, and ran into a group of younger boys who were playing with a ball. I picked it up and kicked it far away into the woods.

"Why did you do that, John?" Asked one of the boys.

"Because I wanted to. You're looking for a fight, aren't you?"

They were all smaller than me, of course. One of them was about to retrieve the ball, when I said: "Be careful. I saw a big snake around there."

He hesitated. I hadn't seen any snake. All I wanted was to scare him. At that moment, Peter showed up. One of the boys said: "Peter, John kicked the ball into the woods."

"Why did you do that?" he asked.

"For nothing. Just for fun."

"OK, then go and get the ball for them."

I couldn't argue with him. He was stronger and could beat me up, so I obeyed. But I promised myself I would get even with him when the time came. Peter was the pharmacist's son, and the boys in the village had a lot of respect for him. His father was important because he had more money than all the other boys´ parents. Peter was strong, and hard to beat in a fight. He liked to tease me, saying that my mother was an Indian, and should stay in the jungle. He organized our soccer games -- the ball belonged to him. So, I could only play when he allowed me to. And I loved to play. The problem was that, whenever I scored against his team, he would throw me out of the game.

I kept waiting for my chance to give Peter what he deserved. Since I couldn't beat him with my fists, I had to use my brains. The occasion finally arrived. We had been playing for about two hours. It was hot and we were getting tired. I suggested: "Hey, everybody, let's go for a swim?"

They all agreed, and we went to a pond near the village. As usual, we left our clothes on the ground, by the water. I was the first to get out. As I was getting dressed, I saw a snake winding its way around the bushes. I knew how to handle snakes, and grabbed this one by the neck, so it wouldn't bite me. With a line and a fishing hook I happened to see lying around, I caught the snake by its tail and dropped it in Peter's clothes.

As Peter picked them up, the snake stung him. The boys were extremely alarmed.

"A snake! Help! A snake in Peter's clothes!"

## The Amazon Shaman

"Watch out, there may be others around."

"Call my father," said Peter.

"Catch that snake," said one of the boys.

No one knew what to do, except myself. Very calmly, I said: "Get Peter to the pharmacy right away. He needs a shot against the poison. I'll try to catch the snake. We have to find out what kind it is. This will help to choose the right antidote.

All the boys went away, taking Peter along, and I was left to myself. I looked for the snake, which I found easily because of the fishing line I had tied to its tail. I killed it and took it to the pharmacy, where it was identified as a very poisonous Urutu.

I told them quite a story: "It was hiding under a fallen tree and, when I lifted a branch, the snake jumped at me, but I stepped back and it missed me by a few inches."

"Terrific, John! How brave!" said Peter's father.

"Peter is my friend," I said. "I had to do it for him. After all, I am the one to blame, because I suggested the swimming."

"No, that's no reason to be blamed for. It was an accident" said Peter's father.

"Peter is my friend." I repeated.

I was proud of myself. They all believed my story and Peter's father, who was important because he was rich, thanked me warmly. Well, he could be wealthy, but I was smart.

Peter was properly treated, and after a few days he was in good shape. After the snake episode, I never had any problems with him again. From then on, he always picked me to play in his team. But I didn't really intend to be his friend. I went on just pretending. Whenever I could, I would play a trick or two on him, being careful not to be caught. My motto was -- my enemy once, my enemy forever, preferably without his knowing it. A friend is a friend, and an enemy, an enemy.

Actually, I didn't have any friends, except my mother. She was the only person who understood me and saw my qualities. I was her only son, and I had my mother all to myself. She was not married. My father? I had always wanted to know who he was, but Mother wouldn't tell me.

> "The stars of thine own fate lie in thy breast," says Seni to Wallenstein – a dictum that should satisfy all astrologers if we knew even a little about the secrets of the hearth. But for this, so far, men have had little understanding.
>
> C. G. Jung
> Archetypes of the Collective Unconscious – Collected Works 9.1

## Chapter 4 – Courting Disaster

"William, your transits are not good. You will go through a difficult period of your life."

I had left the house of an astrologer, and these words kept coming back to my mind. I wish I had a crystal ball to know what was in store for me. What could I do to escape my fate? Maybe I shouldn't attempt that. One should never question the designs of the Lord.

Worried, but happy, I was driving along Atlântica Avenue in Rio de Janeiro to Gordon's party. The sidewalk was teeming with people, tourists enjoying the fair weather in Copacabana. It was my last day at work before my vacations, and I had just left the office, looking forward to my free days. I wouldn´t let the worrying predictions of the astrologer bother me.

All of a sudden, a car bumped into mine, but the driver didn't stop. The damage was small, but enough to upset me. I had just bought my new BMW. There was nothing I could do at the moment, so I went ahead.

I left the Copacabana beachfront, looking for a place to park. I knew it was going to take me some time, but after a few minutes I found one. I was preparing to get into the space, when a young woman pulled up in front of me and parked her Beetle before I could even turn my wheel. Though she was cute, I complained. She just dismissed me with a slight gesture, locked her car and swung past me in her high heels with a defiant smile.

Boy, was I angry! I had to do something. But I saw another parking place a few yards ahead and didn't want to waste time. I parked my car, got out, walked towards the beach, and arrived at Gordon's building. After identifying myself to the doorman, I stepped into the elevator. From the tenth floor, his apartment offered a beautiful, clean and peaceful postcard view of the Copacabana beach.

"Hello, William! Thought you weren't coming anymore! Oh my, oh my, always in blue. Are you trying to match the color of your eyes?"

"Happy Birthday, Gordon. I would never miss your party. You know how I like to fly, to get lost in the infinite space. So, blue reminds me of the sky. How old are you today?"

"Cut it out. Let's forget age. Why didn't Valerie come with you? You're not having problems again, are you?"

"No, no, Gordon. Valerie is at her parents' farm, and I'm flying there early tomorrow. Actually, I shouldn't have come, but I couldn't let you down."

"Great! Then relax and enjoy yourself. It's the first time in ages I don't see Valerie keeping you under control."

The party was in full swing. Lots of familiar faces. I joined a group, reminding myself not to drink too much. Phillip was there, talking about his experience with the Indians. He had lived for more than twenty years among them, working for FUNAI, the Indian Affairs Agency.

"Did you like it?" asked J.J.

"It's quite a different life. We can learn a lot with the Indians."

"I must say that I wouldn't mind living some time among the Indians, learning some of their customs," I said.

J.J. remarked: "Our lives are full of surprises, William. Who knows? You may still have your wishes fulfilled."

I couldn't help laughing. I had told J.J. about my conversation with the astrologer, and he was teasing me. He knew perfectly well that I'm a city guy. No matter how interesting life in the wilderness might be, I was an urban animal and would never consider living in the jungle.

Gordon called me. He was still at the door, receiving guests. He discreetly pointed to a corner of the room, and said: "Do you see that brunette?"

"Which one?"

"The one near the window, talking to Susan."

"Ah, yes, she is really attractive. What a coincidence! She is the driver of the Beetle that stole my parking place."

"She has her eyes on you."

"Well, she had her eyes on my parking place, yes."

"See how she is staring in this direction?"

I was still very angry at that arrogant prick, and I didn't want to be unfaithful to Valerie. Until a short time ago, I didn't think that way. Now, after having met Valerie, I had lost my interest in other women.

Gordon was still at it: "When you came in, she asked me who you were. I think she likes blond, blue-eyed, strong men, who look like movie stars. Her boyfriend has your looks. But you shouldn't worry. Right now he is traveling. Have fun."

Gordon winked and then turned his attention to a couple who was arriving. Drinks were being served. The music was loud. Too loud, actually. A few guests were even louder than the music. The brunette of the parking space was coming closer. She smelled of French perfume and cannabis, and smiled. "Hi, I'm Irene, and you?"

"William. You can call me Bill."

"I think I've already seen you."

"Sure you've seen me … and my car! You took my parking space."

"Are you the BMW guy?"

"Yes! No hard feelings."

"What a coincidence! What's this perfume you're using?

"Fahrenheit. Yours is also very pleasant, but it has a kind of grassy smell to it."

Irene gave me a sly smile, and asked me to dance with her. Somehow I sensed that her talk would hardly interest me. Dancing, you don't have to talk much. That was an advantage. She pressed her body sensually against mine. On the dancing floor she was terrific.

After all, it turned out to be a great evening, indeed. I left Irene's bed at about seven in the morning the following day, feeling very, very tired. I thought of Valerie and felt guilty. I was planning to take off at six, but now I wouldn't be able to do it before nine. I went home to change my clothes, reeking of a wild night. I took a cold shower and relaxed a bit before going to the airport.

> Shamanism is a paradigm of the individuation process, which is a central feature of Jungian psychology.
>
> Walter Boechat, M.D., Ph.D.
> Shamanism and Psycoterapy

## Chapter 5 – Tsiipré, the shaman to be

"Tsiipré, you will be one of us," I heard the old Shaman say after I told him my vision.

From that day on, I tried to learn all I could about religion - all kinds of religions. In Manaus, I learned about macumba, a kind of voodooism brought by the African slaves to Brazil a long time ago. I also studied the Eastern religions. I was careful not to let Father Justin know about my readings. He wouldn´t approve of my interest for other religions. He was a devout Catholic.

My vacations were spent helping our old Shaman. His health was failing.

One day, Kautá called the Council of the Wise Old Men to discuss his proposal of moving the tribe to a new location, far away from the white people. "Brothers, we were a happy people before the white man´s arrival. We had our crops, our fishing, our hunting grounds, and we lived a healthy life. The white man came with gifts. They brought us steel knives, shotguns, and many utensils. They won the Indians' goodwill that way. But they also brought along their diseases and their strong beverages. The Indians do not have the same resistance to measles as the white people do. A simple cold can be lethal to us."

Chief Kautá paused to watch carefully the reaction of the Wise Men. He went on: "We cannot go on living like that. We risk having our tribe extinguished. It is time we moved to another area, far away from the white. If we wait longer, there may not be any of us to continue our traditions. I suggest we send a party to find another place for us to settle, to build our huts, to raise our children far away from the white man."

One of the Wise Men replied: "If we move, we will lose our crops. All the hard work we put into this land to build our huts, to plant our crops, will be gone."

Chief Kautá listened to the arguments of the old man: "Our brother Uirike said sensible words. The effort to build our houses, to plant our crops was great, and has to be taken into account. But we also have to consider the fact that our young people are being destroyed by the white man's way of life. Some of our warriors are always drunk. Many of our girls are being sold in exchange for money to buy liquor. Working hard has never been a problem for the Kauauá. I prefer that to see our people being corrupted by the white people. Let's work hard, build new huts, plant new crops, and live proudly as a Kauauá tribe."

The Wise Men seemed to be convinced. But Uirike still insisted: "I do not want to leave our sacred grounds, where the bodies of our ancestors lie. I do not think that Kauaí-Açú would approve of that."

Kauaí-Açú is our name for God. Of course, Father Justin would not approve of that. But that was not my problem.

Kautá replied: "Kauaí-Açú wants our people to live happy and proud. He doesn´t want the Kauauá killed by the white man's diseases. He doesn´t want our traditions to be forgotten. He doesn´t want the degradation of our customs. If we abandon our traditions, we will be like rootless trees, and the vices are an escape for this lack of structure. When we get to our new grounds, our Shaman will perform some rituals to get Kauaí-Açú to help us."

"I do not think moving is necessary. We could forbid our young people to go into the white man's village," said Uirike.

"Forbidding is not going to work. Many of our people are used to the white men's vices. Let's not forget that. Take drinking for example. It is difficult to resist. We were not used to it and we drink in excess. We have other serious problems. Our young are suffering from venereal diseases and prostitution is widespread."

The discussion continued for several hours. The Council finally approved Kautá's proposal, allowing the ones that wanted to stay in the present grounds to do so. At that time, our group consisted of some two hundred Indians of all ages.

Initially, a party of eight went up the Rio Grande in two canoes, looking for a good place to build our village. Our Shaman was invited to go with them. Since he was ill, he appointed me to go in his place. We rowed up the river for five days until we got to the mouth of the Rio Bonito. We turned right, paddling inside this river, and traveled for a few more minutes. We arrived in a remote place, far from any contact with the white, at the side of a beautiful lake. That was the site we chose.

We left behind four Indians of our group, to start clearing the land and building the village and we returned to pick up more movers. The next group came in ten canoes, all the ones we had. Even so, we needed to make two more trips to bring to the new place all the brothers who wanted to come with their belongings.

A small group decided to stay near Formoso. The others followed Chief Kautá looking for a better place to live. In less than a month, our village was practically built in the heart of the Amazon forest. Our huts were near the Silver Lake, our beautiful lagoon that fed us with fish, and was an ideal place for bathing. Silver Lake – what a perfect name! When the moonlight reflected on its water, the lake looked like a silver plate. The reflected color of the light, especially in full moon nights is something to be seen. A clear water creek coming down from the northern mountains feeds the Silver Lake. From it, the water goes south, as far as the Bonito River, a tributary of the Rio Grande, the big water course that runs about two kilometers downstream. These two rivers, Bonito and Grande, are the main waterways near our area. The Bonito is smaller, and flows in a half-circle, on the west side of our village.

The Rio Grande is about a thirty minute walk to the south, but our lake is quite close. Our village is composed of a large hut, in which the single men sleep, surrounded by a number of small thatched huts for families with small children. In front of the large hut, there is a yard where the festivities of our people and the meetings of the Council of the Wise Old Men take place.

One day, Father Justin called me to his office, where I was introduced to Mr. King, an American missionary. He had moved recently to Manaus. He was a huge man, as tall as I had never seen before. He looked like a Viking warrior I had seen in a book, but was a gentle fellow. I liked him from the very first moment we talked.

"I want to learn the language and the traditions of the Brazilian Indians. Can you help me?" he said.

"We have several Indian groups in Brazil and almost as many different languages and traditions."

"What is your tribe's name?"

"I'm a Kauauá."

"Could you teach me the Kauauá language?"

"Yes. Glad to."

"When can we start?"

"Today, tomorrow. Any time you like. Could you also teach me English in exchange?"

"I will, but not in exchange. I want to pay for your teaching."

"Then, I would have to pay you for the English."

"No! That's my gift to you. After all, I'm happy that a Brazilian Indian wants to learn my language. In the future, I could take you to some lectures in the States. The Americans would be curious to hear about the life of the

Amazonian Indians, and the ecological situation of the forest directly from an Indian."

I was able to train Mr. King on the essentials of our language, enabling him to communicate with our people. At the same time, I applied myself very hard to learning English. It didn't take long for me to start speaking, and reading books in English. A new horizon opened for me. Now I could read lots of new books borrowed from Mr. King.

Mr. King met Father Justin and I overheard their conversation.

Mr. King said: "Tsiipré's progress in English is amazing. I'm learning his language at a fast pace. But he is learning at an astounding speed, and with a perfect accent. You wouldn't believe how fast he can learn." Since I was in the next room and the door was open, I couldn't avoid hearing this conversation.

"I had an equal reaction some time ago. But now that I know him, I don't think anything is impossible for him," said Father Justin. "He has done very well in his classes. All his teachers praise him."

"He already read all the novels I have. And, I tell you, I have many. Now he wants to begin reading Shakespeare. And he is only fourteen."

Father Justin replied: "In the beginning, I was as amazed as you are now. I'm not surprised anymore."

In my conversations with Mr. King, I learned the divisions of the Christian churches. Mr. King was a Methodist Father. As such, he believed in Christ, but not in the various saints.

"How can we believe in a monotheistic religion and adore so many saints?" he used to say. That was one of his points.

For me, this made no difference. In fact, whatever the religion, the Lord is one and the same. Call Him Yahweh,

Allah, the name you prefer. For our tribe, his name is Kauaí-Açú.

My vocation to be a shaman led me to study the eastern religions, a subject about which I found very little in the local library, and none in the priest's library. I used the money I earned from my lessons to Mr. King to buy some of these books. I read about Buddhism, especially the Tibetan, and Hinduism. The life and teachings of Yogananda fascinated me. The methods of meditation of Hinduism, using mantras, had a lot to do with the chants the Kauauá shamans always used to help them to go into a trance.

While some eastern religions agree that there may be various ways to enlightenment, the Catholics postulate that there is no salvation outside the Church. I know this has a much broader interpretation today, but it wasn't so in my time. Although Father Justin kept a good relationship with Mr. King, he would certainly not have approved of my interest in other religions.


Life with Father Justin was not always peaceful. I remember the occasion when I was caught stealing some of the wine used for the mass. I did that together with some other of my classmates. To tell the truth, I did it more to follow the other boys, not wanting to be different. I was sixteen then, and Father Justin called me to his office. I was scared to death of the punishment I might get. I had been in his office many times to study, but now Father Justin did not motion to me to sit down. I just stood there, in front of his desk, and he kept reading a book, without looking at me. The usual treatment for the students about to be chastised was to be taken to his office. The longer I stood there, the more nervous I became. Finally, after what seemed a long time to me, Father Justin lifted his eyes and spoke in a cold and formal tone: "Mr. Tsiipré, do you think what you have done is right?"

How could I justify it? I was thinking of something, perhaps to promise I would never do it again. However, when I was about to speak, he gestured for me to be quiet. He left me standing there a little longer, and then dismissed me. That was all. No preaching, no punishment. But to me, the silent reproach was even worse, as it made me terribly ashamed, and I swore never to disappoint Father Justin for the rest of my life.

During school vacations, I always went back to my people with a stack of books. However, I also used my time there to learn from our old Shaman certain arts that were not approved by Father Justin and his colleagues. The knowledge that I gained from our Shaman was at the core of the strong bond created between our community and myself. Every time I ran into our Shaman, he would start our talks by saying: "Don't ever forget that Tsiipré is an Indian."

I think he feared I wouldn't want to rejoin our people. Yet, although I was enjoying my education with the white people, the idea of abandoning my people had never crossed my mind. In fact, it is difficult to be attracted by the white man's way of life. The violence in the big cities, the hectic life. I cannot understand how this can attract anybody.

Father Justin thought I should go to college in Rio de Janeiro, and tried to get me a scholarship. But at sixteen, no college accepted me, despite the fact that I was considered exceptionally well endowed, with a very high I.Q., and familiar with great authors. Unable to study in Rio, I began to sit in on some classes at the University of Amazonas. The other students probably thought it was strange, an Indian boy seated in the back of the classroom. However, since I never opened my mouth, they just forgot me.

One of the things I learned from our old Shaman was how to prepare herbs to make medicines. Back in Manaus, I used to read everything that was published about natural medicines, thus rounding out my practical lessons from our Shaman.

I made a practice of meditating regularly, even when I was in Manaus. Of course, I never told Father Justin exactly what I was doing. I used to tell him that I was praying, and I was not lying. After all, meditation is like a prayer in that it is also a way of getting closer to God.

> Since the evil (person), deep down, feel themselves to be faultless, it is inevitable that when they are in conflict with the world they will invariably perceive the conflict as the world's fault. Since they must deny their own badness, they must perceive others as bad. They project their own evil onto the world.
>
> M. Scott Peck, M.D.
> People of the Lie

## Chapter 6 – John, the son of darkness

"John, come now. Your mother wants you."

The only person in the world that I loved was dying. I didn't quite understand what death was. Like other boys, I had killed some small animals, hit some birds with a slingshot, and had seen pigs and cows being slaughtered. I had seen dead parents and grandparents of schoolmates. I always tried to understand their grief, but now, for the first time, I was feeling it myself.

My mother had never been sick, but one day she began to feel ill, and during the following two months she became increasingly weak. I overheard the priest talking with Aunt Agnes, our neighbor:

"Yes, Miss Agnes, it is serious. The poor creature has got cancer. And it seems to be in an advanced stage."

Cancer? What is that? I thought. The way they talked, it seemed to be a very bad thing. Our village didn't have a doctor. Few towns in the area had one. The pharmacist helped us as best he could. He substituted for a doctor.

"If she dies, what about John? He is only thirteen and has no relatives that we know of," said Miss Agnes.

"The Lord knows what He does. There will be a way; he will be all right. He is a good boy."

"Sometimes, father, I wonder if the Lord really knows what He is doing. You'll forgive me, but with so much suffering in the world, is the Lord really paying any attention to us?"

"Don´t say this, Miss Agnes, it´s blasphemy. The fact that we cannot understand God's designs doesn´t mean that He doesn´t care for us."

"I hope you're right, father."

That talk made me worry. I didn't want my mother to die, and I didn't know what might happen to me. I didn't know the meaning of cancer, and people talked about it in whispers. I decided to find out, and went to see my teacher. She already knew that my mother was sick. In small communities, everybody knows about everybody else's life. She gave me an explanation, trying to disguise the seriousness of the disease. But I'm no fool, and the conversation with the priest had alerted me.

A few days later, the priest returned to my home, carrying clothes and other objects, as if for a mass. Again, by overhearing the conversation of the grownups, I learned that the priest had come to give the extreme unction to my mother, and that was done for people who were about to die.

The skies were pouring that afternoon, when my mother called me for a serious talk. She couldn't have been more explicit. "My son, I'm going to die." As I started to cry, she said. "We are all going to die. Now, my time has come. Save your tears for later, because we have to talk. You´ve always wanted to know who your father is."

"That's right. Why did you always make a secret of his name?"

"Your father is Colonel Casemiro."

"The Colonel?" I was struck by the news. I never thought I could be the son of such a rich person. Maybe this was the reason I felt, deep inside, that I was superior to the other boys. More intelligent and smarter than all my classmates. Like father, like son.

"Then, we are rich," I said.

Mother gave me a sad smile and said: "When I was young, he bought me from my father, a Kauauá Indian. Our village wasn't far from here. The white men were destroying our people with liquor and diseases. To buy alcohol, many Indians sold their wives and daughters. I was considered very pretty. Your father bought me, and we lived happily for a few years. Your father was poor, but hard working and intelligent."

That statement was a clue to my superiority.

My mother went on: "He began to make money buying things in Manaus, and selling them to the people who lived in the villages along the Rio Grande."

"Why didn't he stay with us? Didn't he like you? Didn't he like me?"

"It wasn't that, my son. Life is not that simple. Your father is an ambitious man. He was rich already, but he wanted to be richer and richer. Formoso became too small a place for him."

"I think he's right. Only money counts. The poor aren't worth anything."

My mother shook her head: "No, no, my son, don't think that money is all there is."

I couldn't agree with her, but kept quiet. She was speaking with urgency: "Your father was a handsome man. In one of his trips to Manaus, he met a rich white girl. She liked him, and they got married."

My mother rested a little and continued: "Your father left us when you were two years old. I seldom saw him after that. But he is a good man. He doesn't visit us anymore, but his employees always bring food and some money for us. After I die, I want you to go and see him. I'm sure he'll help you."

Of course, I'm going to look him up, I thought. I am going to live in Manaus and I'll be rich too. I started dreaming about my new life. Does he have a big house? Does he have a boat? Will he give me a new hunting rifle? I kept thinking about these things, and was quite sure of the answer.

That same night my mother died. I cried all night, and the consolation was to think of my new life as the son of a wealthy man. I already saw myself with my new clothes, hunting boots, all fishing and hunting gear imported from the United States.

The funeral took place the next day, as is the custom in our land. A simple burial in the small local graveyard. The priest said a few words to which I paid no attention. How can someone be sad and glad at the same time? That's how I was feeling.

I spent the time waiting for the FSTC's boat. FSTC was my father's company: Formoso Shipping and Trading Co. The other boys called me to play ball, but I wouldn't go; they called me to go swimming in the river, I wouldn't go. All I wanted was to be left alone, thinking of my future, my new life as a rich man, my new fishing gear, and my imported boots.

Two days later, one of the colonel's boats came to our village. The captain knew me, and when I told him my mother had died, and one of her last requests was for me to go and see the Colonel in Manaus, he made room for me on the boat. The trip took five days. I hardly thought about my mother. After all, the death of a loved one didn't seem so painful. Mother was right when she said that in a few months I would smile again. I started smiling within a few days, and this strengthened my feeling of superiority.

Those were the first nights I had ever slept out of my home, without my mother's protecting presence. But this didn't bother me. I knew I was different, and better than anyone.

"So, you're going to see the Colonel?" asked the Captain.

"Yes," I answered confidently. "He is my father."

The Captain laughed. He sounded as if everybody knew it. After all, the Colonel had lived a few years with my mother, and I was born during that time. But he added: "Don't count too much on that, boy. The Colonel is a tough guy. You may be disappointed."

"Does he have another son?"

"So far, only daughters. Very pretty girls."

The idea of coming to Manaus, to speak to someone I didn't know, who was my father, didn't worry me a bit. I was sure he would welcome me with open arms. If I had any doubts, they disappeared when the Captain said that he had only daughters. I would be his only male heir, and would run the business in my father's old age. I scarcely enjoyed the boat trip, something that, as a boy, I longed to do. I was dreaming awake most of the time, and didn't care to look at the scenery. I was impressed only when we reached the Amazon River. I had never imagined there could be such a large and magnificent river.

I arrived in Manaus early in an afternoon, shortly after two o'clock. A cloudless sky, shining sun, hot and stuffy weather. I left the boat and went looking for the Colonel. His office was in a central location, and a tall, strong man, who screened the visitors, guarded the entrance.

He looked at me. "What do you want, boy?"

"Is this Colonel Casemiro's office?" I almost added, my father, to impress the giant, but decided not to.

"Yes," he said dryly, looking at me as if I were a beggar of whom he had to get rid quickly.

"I want to speak to him," I said with a firm voice.

He measured me up, and even though I was wearing my Sunday church clothes, he didn't seem to be impressed. "What's your name, boy?"

"John."

"John? That doesn't mean anything. It's a very common name."

I was about to say I was the Colonel's son, but decided against it again. The guard might laugh at me and not let me in. "I'm John, Candinha's son. She knew the Colonel and asked me to come see him. She died eight days ago."

When I mentioned death, he seemed to soften. He called his helper, a small boy of around my age, and told him to take me to see the Colonel's secretary. We went up in an elevator. This was my first time in one, and I almost couldn't control my fear when that box closed on me and started going up. But I didn't let the boy at my side perceive my panic. The elevator stopped at a beautiful place, such as I had never seen. A lady was at a reception desk.

"This boy wants to speak with the Colonel," said the boy.

He left, and I was alone with the lady, who seemed to be a kind person, and I began to feel at ease. I stood in front of her desk, and when she finished a long telephone conversation, she asked me: "What do you want to see the Colonel for?"

I didn't expect that question and hesitated, so she insisted: "What do you want to speak with the Colonel about? May I take your message? I'm his secretary."

I felt I shouldn't tell her I was the Colonel's son either. "My mother was Candinha, an acquaintance of the Colonel's. She told me to look him up, before dying a few days ago." I noticed again that the mention of death could soften grownups. I had to keep this in mind.

A bell rang, the lady got up hurriedly, and went into the next room. After a few minutes she came back, and told me to sit down on a sofa near her desk. It was the softest sofa I had ever sat on, but I was too uneasy to enjoy the comforts of that moment. After a brief phone call, she called me and told me the Colonel was ready to see me.

## The Amazon Shaman

I entered a large room. A middle-aged man was sitting behind a desk and talking on the telephone. He didn't even look at me. A luxurious office, with beautiful colored carpets. Persian rugs, I learned later. Looking at that powerful man, owner of a company that filled a whole building, my heart was full of pride. That was my father. In a few minutes I was going to speak to him, he would give a big smile and I would be the owner of all that wealth. No doubt, in seconds he would embrace his only male son, and his eyes would fill with tears. I didn't even think that he hadn't visited me or my mother for the past ten years, so busy was my mind with my vision of the fortune that awaited me.

When the man finished the phone call, he motioned to me to come closer. "So, you are Candinha's son? How many brothers do you have?"

"I'm her only son, Colonel.

"And what brings you up to Manaus?"

"My mother died, and she told me to look you up."

He didn't show any emotion when I told him about my mother's death, and this upset me. But I was still possessed by my dreams: "She told me that you are my father."

He showed some emotion for the first time, but in an unexpected way. He became irritated. "Candinha has a son and tells everybody that he's my son."

"No, sir, she told it only to me, and just before dying."

"That's better. If all my lady friends said the sons they bore were mine, I could have enough votes to be a candidate for governor."

That observation hurt me. I never felt as angry in my life as I was before the Colonel at that moment. It wasn't kind to speak like that about my mother, who had only nice words about him. At the proper time, I'll take my revenge on this shitting Colonel. Who the hell does he thinks he is. Owner of the world? I'll make this Colonel pay dearly for being such a scoundrel. He had only to wait for my sweet revenge.

The Colonel continued: "What do you intend to do with your life? How are you going to live?"

"I don't know, sir."

"By the way, how old are you?"

"Thirteen, Colonel."

"Can you read?"

"Yes, I studied up to the seventh grade at Formosos's school. I was a good student."

"That's enough, unless you want to be a doctor."

"What I want is to make money, Colonel."

"I'm going to get you a job in one of my companies. But if I ever hear you repeating this foolishness about being my son, you'll be fired and will get a good spanking."

The Colonel called his secretary and told her to get me a job in the river trade company.

When I went out the door where I had met the big guard, it was raining heavily, one of those common afternoon showers in the Amazon. While I waited for the rain to stop, I had time to think about all my collapsed dreams. A beautiful house, expensive clothes, boots, hunting guns, pleasure boats. In a few minutes all my dreams had exploded like a punctured balloon.

I was about to go out in the rain, when I saw a big white car park in front of the building. I overheard the guard remark to someone that it was a Mercedes 600, a car that only the very wealthy could afford, and that it belonged to the Colonel. A uniformed driver got out holding an umbrella, and opened the rear door for a beautiful lady, who walked towards the building under the umbrella, while the driver got all wet. As she entered the building, an obsequious guard greeted her: "Good afternoon, Madame."

She didn't even look at him, and he remarked to someone at his side: "The Colonel's wife. She's snobbish."

## The Amazon Shaman

So, that was the woman who had taken my mother's place. Because of her, I was a fatherless son. I instantly resented her. The rain had stopped. I was leaving when I spotted a broken bottle of Scotch on the ground, near the car of the woman that had stolen my father. On an impulse, I picked the broken bottle up, and placed it quickly in front of a rear wheel tire. When starting the car, the broken glass would surely puncture the tire. It was a small revenge, but made me feel good. Others would follow.

**Roberto Lima Netto**

> Try to realize you are a divine traveler. You are here only for a little while, then depart for a dissimilar and fascinating world. Do not limit your thoughts to one brief life and one small Earth. Remember the vastness of the Spirit that dwells within you.
>
> Sayings of Paramahansa Yogananda

## Chapter 7 - Lost in the Way to Heaven

Nine a.m. in Rio. I climbed onto the Golden Eagle and took my pilot's seat, going carefully through the usual checking procedures. I felt comfortable on that seat, relishing the odors inside the plane. Valerie also enjoyed flying, and she used to spray the cabin with exotic scents. I was cleared to taxi and take-off, and in less than one minute the Golden Eagle was airborne.

It was a gorgeous morning with a cloudless, bright blue sky. My hands felt good at the controls, as the plane was rapidly gaining altitude. On such occasions, I was overpowered by a sensation of freedom and bliss.

Golden Eagle was the name Valerie and I had chosen for our plane, a well-equipped Piper Seneca with autopilot and all modern avionics. Its normal cruising speed at 3.000 meters is about 330 km/h. It would take me around three hours to get to Brasília, depending on the winds. That might be my only refueling stop, as the Seneca has a range of 1.500 km, or about five hours, and the rest of the flight to the farm shouldn't take more than four hours.

Although it would be a long trip after Gordon's party and all, it would be restful. Having faced a headwind, the trip took me about three and a half hours, a little longer than usual. I arrived in Brasília for the refueling stop. The sun was well past noon. I should have departed earlier from Rio, but I had to rest a bit because of the wild night. My head was feeling heavy.

The sound of the engines, which for many is merely a noise, is a sweet tune for me, a relaxing purring. I shut my eyes and many thoughts came to keep me company.

I have been giving a lot of thought about where life is leading me. I have a good job. Electronics is an expanding field. Valerie is beautiful, sensible and intelligent. All you can wish in a companion for the rest of your life. I know she loves me very much. Do I love her just as much? In the words of the Brazilian poet Vinícius de Moraes, author of the famous song "The Girl from Ipanema": "love is eternal while it lasts." But I wish I could have an eternal ... eternal love. I don´t want to have five wives in a row like Vinícius. I didn't think that way six months ago. However, the idea of a different woman every night was a thing of the past. Should I marry Valerie? All my friends believe that during my visit to the farm we'll become engaged. So do I.

I put the plane in automatic pilot, and took advantage of the peace inside the plane to talk to my Guide. I relax, get into alpha, come down mentally to my laboratory, my virtual forest, and call my Guide. ShuoKua is an old Chinese sage, with deep black eyes, having always a friendly smile showing tranquility. His face is one of someone who lived enough to know many things of this world. He carried centuries of life lessons. ShuoKua was the grandfather many would like to have. In a sense, I had him now. I started mentally talking to him: "ShuoKua, I love Valerie. My life was empty before meeting her. Knowing her makes me feel much better. I am thinking of asking her to marry me. What does the Master think?"

"To cross a river, it's advisable to come to its banks. Otherwise, you cannot get your feet wet."

"Metaphors, metaphors. But please, answer me with words I can understand. Should I marry Valerie?"

"Always rational. You still have to learn that two and two may not be four. I will give you an objective answer. I think you had better wait for a while. You need some spiritual growth."

"But I can continue to grow after the marriage. I'll be arriving at the farm within a few hours and I would like to ask her this evening, at dinner time."

"You have your free will. If you have already decided, why do you ask me?"

"Well, it' a long trip, and I wanted to talk to you about something. It's always nice to have your company."

"Especially when you have nothing else to do, isn't it? If you want to talk, let us do it. How can you be so sure you are going to see Valerie today?"

That question surprises me. I cannot understand what is behind it. Probably, some other enigma. ShouKua is a Chinese. He thinks differently from us. "I'm flying to Valerie's farm. In a few hours I'll be arriving there."

"Life is more complex than you think."

"No metaphors, please. What are you trying to say?"

"Exactly what I´ve said. It's time you pay attention to your spiritual growth."

"But I've changed now. I admit that I was living an empty life, from party to party. That's the reason I want to change it. Marrying Valerie will help this process."

"Are you telling me that you have quit your life of dissipation? Since when? Since yesterday?"

I felt embarrassed by that remark. "Yesterday I was careless. After all, you can't be always perfect."

"Perfect?" ShuoKua could be thorny when he got you.

I said: "I'm coming to see Valerie today and I'll ask her to marry me. That's my decision, and you just said that I have a free will."

"Again, very rational. Suppose God may have different plans."

"What plans?"

"He may toss some surprise at you, to hasten your development."

"What kind of surprise? You're worrying me. Looks like the astrologer. I don't like surprises. I'd better have everything planned."

"Here is the engineer again. I've told you not to expect rationality from life. The Lord usually puts some hurdles on our way, which force us to grow."

"If I marry Valerie, I'll be starting a new life."

"There are people with ears that hear less than the deaf. I want to leave a thought for your meditation: the eagle soars so high because it knows how to land."

"Do you mean the Golden Eagle, my plane?"

"That is up to you to interpret. Like a modern painting, it can be viewed from different angles."

"But you didn't answer my question."

"I tried to talk to you in a western way, but it didn't help. So, I'll get back to my own way. To cross a river, you must get to its bank."

"You've said that before."

"And you didn't listen."

At that moment, my attention was distracted by the turbulence of flying through a cloud. When I turned back to my Guide, he was gone. I kept on thinking about my life, and what ShuoKua had said. Surprises and uncertainties were not to my liking.

I'm looking forward to spending some time in the countryside. It makes a good contrast with the hectic life of the big city. I want to get there quickly and take a nap. Why did I go out with Irene after the party? Now I have to keep struggling against falling asleep ... and the soft purring of the engines doesn't help.

I'm in the heart of the jungle. The earth is being destroyed. The human race will be annihilated. To save it, I must find a very wise and powerful Shaman, who will put things in good order. But there are terrible forces which want to stop me. The demons wish to kill me and dominate the earth.

I walk back and forth. I don't know what to do to find a savior, to help the earth. A big black jaguar comes in my direction. I am afraid. He wants to talk to me. "You must save the earth."

"Me? Why me?"

"You have to act quickly. They will do away first with the good people. Only the bad will survive. And, before being destroyed, they will kill all the animals of the jungle."

I was distressed, desperate. I repeated my question: "Why me? What can I do?"

"You must find the Wise Man."

"Where can I find him?"

"Follow me. I'll take you to him."

We entered the jungle. Big trees surrounded us. They were looking at me, a white man, with accusing eyes. After walking through the forest for some hours, we came to a hut in a clearing. It was circled by some of the biggest trees I'd ever seen. They looked like a powerful army, distributed around the house, as if protecting their leader.

The hut was cylinder shaped, with thatched roof. It had an otherworldly look, with smoke coming out of its top and going in an almost straight tube reaching heaven. A lot of smoke came also out of its door. I heard the noise. A rattling one. There were people inside. The jaguar stopped and, turning to me, he said: "This is the end of the trail for me. You go in."

"What's inside? What should I do?"

"You are a white man; you are responsible for the destruction of the earth. Do whatever you can."

"All right. But help me."

At that moment, without letting me argue further, the jaguar turned into a beautiful golden bird, and flew away toward the sun. I tried to walk to the hut. A strong wind was coming out of it, holding me back. The more I forced my legs to take me to the door, the stronger the wind blew me out. It was impossible for me to get close to the hut.

The world depended on me. I knew I had to try my best. I crawled, and started getting near the hut. Suddenly, the wind stopped and I went in. A middle-aged Indian was sitting close to the circular axis that held the roof. He seemed to be in a trance. He was singing a monotonous song, and shaking his maraca, an instrument made of a fruit shaped like the body of a very fat woman. It was full of beads, the origin of the rattling noise when shaken. It took me a few minutes to get accustomed to the lack of light inside the hut. The smoke filled the place completely. I noticed a strong scent of herbs.

The Indian looked at me and, without speaking, put his hands together in a kind of oriental salute. I spoke to him. Our dialogue wasn't in words. I was getting his thoughts inside my head. "I need your help."

"I know you do."

"The earth is being destroyed. Only a very wise and powerful Shaman can aid me." He paused for a while, looking straight at me. So far, he was voiceless. A kind of telepathy. This changed, and he started singing his words. In a very melodious tone, he said: "The earth is being destroyed by the white man. Only the white man can save the earth. We Indians have been wiped out long ago. I'm a dream, a mirage."

As if to show that he was telling the truth, he started turning into smoke and fading. His legs and part of his body where already gone. I tried to grab him, to avoid his disappearance. No way. I was stunned. I shouted to him: "Do I have to save the earth alone? What can I do to rescue the earth?"

He continued fading out, as if I did not exist. I tried again: "Come back, give us a chance."

"It is you, white man, who should give us one more chance. The earth will be destroyed if you fail to change the white man's mind."

"And what should I do?"

"Since material wealth is more important than the survival of the planet, no one will be able to save our earth."

In desperation I continued to shout, almost crying: "Help me! What should I do to convince humanity that it's more important to care for the preservation of the earth than to make money?"

"To convince humanity, first you have to convince yourself. Save yourself, then you can think of saving the earth."

"What shall I do? What? You have to tell me. You are the wise man."

Now, only the head was visible. My anguish was useless. I had no answer. The Indian completed his transformation into smoke, and vanished into the skies, leaving through the top of his hut. I was alone, feeling as distressed as I'd never been in my whole life. Save the earth? Oh Lord! I was in real trouble!

I wake up with the loud buzzing of the fuel alarm. I slept too much. I'm afraid I may be in danger. I have about thirty minutes of gasoline left. The GPS shows that I have long overshot my destination. Strong tail winds, still going on at the moment. Not enough fuel to return. Down there, only the thick jungle.

Lord! What have I done to myself!? Why did I have to go to that party? Why did I have to spend the night with Irene? Now, I am in real trouble, flying over the Amazon jungle. There have been so many planes lost in the forest, never to be seen again. I try radio contact, with no avail.

I look for a place to land, and I spot a large lake in the distance. I turn the plane towards its direction and make the approach. At the last minute, I change my mind. I remembered a case of a pilot eaten by piranhas when landing in a lake in the Amazon. There may be piranhas in that lake too. If I'm hurt and bleeding, that's the end. I've seen in the Zoo how piranhas attack bloody meat. I push the throttles and climb back, using up some of my precious fuel.

I keep flying around and far on my right I see what seems to be another lake, a much smaller one. Maybe this is safer. Suppose I land close to its banks. If I´m able to escape fast, it might lessen my risk. The lake is well to the west. My fuel is at the end. Will I get there? I have to try.

> Hell has not been created by anyone, but when a man does evil, he lights the fires of hell and burns in his own fire.
>
> Mahommed
> Quoted in "The Eternal Wisdom" a publication of the Sri Aurobindo Ashram

## Chapter 8 - John's Revenge

I was walking to the address where I was supposed to go, asking for directions on the way. I had resigned myself, not without anger, to the fact that my great wealth would have to wait a little longer. I wasn't the heir of a rich father, as I had thought a short time ago. My rage at the Colonel had not diminished, even with the little revenge I had planted. I'm sure they were already changing the torn tire, and this thought gave me a small pleasure.

I would be living in Manaus with a job in the FSTC, the shipping and commercial company of the Colonel, that dirty bastard. He would probably expect me to thank him for the job. On the contrary, every time I remembered the way he had talked about my mother, my anger increased. I promised myself to think up a sweet revenge. But first, I had to become rich. I was only thirteen, but I already knew that money is power, and I would need a lot of it to face the Colonel.

When I arrived at my destination, I saw an enormous warehouse, with the four letters FSTC painted on the front wall --Formoso Shipping and Trading Company. At least in the name of his company, the rascal acknowledged the city where his fortune began. I looked for a man named Xavier. He was fat, with a kind bearing, and didn't seem to work very hard.

"Mister Xavier, I'm here on orders from the Colonel, to get a job."

He looked at me suspiciously and said: "Yes, I got a phone call from his secretary." And after pondering for a minute, caressing his chin with his right hand, he asked. "How did you happen to know the Colonel?"

"I didn't know him. My mother did. They were sort of relatives."

"Ahhh! I understand. Must have been one of his affairs."

I had to hold back my rage again. I pretended not to understand, but I added him to my revenge list, which was growing rapidly. I didn't mind that. I must admit I liked revenges.

I started working the next day, as a helper in the stockroom. During my first year on the job, I found out some strange things. Could Xavier be cheating the company? In fact, Xavier, together with the chief stock clerk, were overpaying for the goods purchased, taking part of the price for themselves as a commission. I wondered how a smart man like the Colonel didn't suspect something was going on. The fact was that he no longer paid much attention to the FSTC. The company had helped him earn his first few millions, but the Colonel's main business now was real estate. Everybody could make good money in Manaus with real estate. The prosperity arising out of the Free Trade Zone of Manaus was a blessing to this region. People who invested in it reaped good profits. For this reason, the FSTC had become a sideline for the Colonel, and its business was declining. The Colonel was milking the company, and Xavier was doing his part, helping the company to go under. All of the profits that FSTC generated, the Colonel invested in real estate. The company's boats did not have proper maintenance and were decaying.

I wanted to become rich, to make money quickly. I decided to make a risky move. I spent a few months feigning a familiarity with the Colonel that I actually didn't have. After meeting Xavier on my very first day in Manaus, I was careful to go back to the office and ask to see Joan, the Colonel's secretary. I thanked her for the job, as if she was the one responsible for it. Afterwards, I often used to come to see her in the main office. I always brought a little gift, and Joan became my friend. To Xavier, I would hint that I was being called by the Colonel.

After paving the way for some time, and putting together a dossier that would leave Xavier in a very bad light, I thought that the time had arrived for my final play. I had just turned seventeen, and felt an adult. After almost three years on the job, I was able to do all the administrative work in the company by myself. The man in charge was not very active, and when he saw that I could handle all the work, he was only too glad to leave everything in my hands. He kept to himself only the transactions that involved Xavier's graft, which needed the complicity of the stockroom clerk. I decided to go for all or nothing. I went to see Xavier. "Mr. Xavier, you know that I am a friend of the Colonel's. I also know that the FSTC is no longer important to him, and that you work very hard to keep things in good order. For this reason, I think that your salary is ridiculous."

Xavier was surprised, probably wondering where the Colonel's protégé was leading him to. I went on: "That's why I didn't say anything to the Colonel about the commissions that you are getting."

When I mentioned the commissions, Xavier's face turned purple from surprise and fear. I continued my play: "Please don't worry. I'm not about to mention anything to the Colonel. I think it's all right that you do some justice yourself, getting your commissions on the purchases. It's small pay for everything you do for the company. If it weren't for you, the FSTC would already be out of business."

Even with this kind of talk, he didn't seem to relax. So I played the final hand. "I'm also working hard here in the company. I think I should share this division. After all, just because I'm a friend of the Colonel's, it doesn't mean that I should work for him for free."

Xavier's face opened up. Now that he understood what I wanted, he felt on solid ground. Even so, he tried to argue. "I don't get any commissions! This must have something to do with my helper."

"Well, if that's the case, I won't have to keep from telling it to the Colonel. I just wanted to protect you, because I like you. But if the culprit is your helper, I'll take the evidence right away to the Colonel." As I said that, I took the copies of the documents I had and spread them on the table. Xavier paled and began to stammer.

"Well, well …. The Colonel is going to blame me …. I am the manager of the company."

Out of tactics, I stopped calling him Mister. "You are right, Xavier. If I show these papers to the Colonel, things will get tough for you. They show that you're also involved. But as I said, I think you should get more than the Colonel is paying you. My salary is also very low and the Colonel is equally taking advantage on me."

"That's true." Xavier said. "Let's correct that. I'll raise your salary immediately."

"No, Xavier. Let's be smart. A salary raise will catch somebody's attention in the main office. I'd rather share in the commissions. I can carry out this operation in a much safer way than that incompetent helper of yours."

"But I can't fire him. He knows all."

"Who said anything about firing? He'll continue to receive his share; forty percent for you, forty percent for me, and twenty percent for him."

"Forty for you?"

"Only from now on. What you've cashed so far, your past gains, you don't have to share with me."

Xavier looked discouraged: "Your share equal to mine? Am I not the chief?"

"Well, I run the greater risk. Because I'm the Colonel's friend, if he finds out, he'll never forgive me. You know how tough he is. He may even send some of his thugs do away with me."

After this arrangement, things improved considerably for me. The stockroom chief was about to retire, and with the guarantee that he would continue to share in the commissions, he decided to leave right away. Over time, I took on additional functions in the company, and became deputy manager. Only Xavier had more authority, but he almost didn't get involved. Being lazy, he avoided work and was happy to use my efforts and brains. The value of the commissions he received had increased a lot.

During those years, I also attended short courses on financial management, all I could find.

On the day of my eighteenth birthday, I assessed my career. I had already amassed a considerable amount of money, but I was not rich enough to be compared with the Colonel. To carry out my revenge, I had first to become really rich. The Company was going from bad to worse. With the drain of our commissions and the Colonel's neglect, who continued to milk it, the situation was deteriorating fast. I had to do something to prevent the death of my cash cow. At first, I thought of suggesting to the Colonel to buy the company. But if I did that, he would suspect that I was cheating him. Where else would I get the money to buy the company? I decided to be more ingenious. I went to see Joan. "Joan, I've got to talk to the Colonel."

"He'll want to know the subject."

"Tell him it's about some very serious things that are happening at the FSTC. Out of gratitude for giving me my first job, I feel it's my duty to give him a report on the whole thing."

Joan was shocked: "I'll take care of that. He is traveling today, but as soon as he gets back, I'll get you an appointment with him."

Next day, she called me setting a meeting for the following Thursday. On that day I wore a clean but very modest suit. I bought a little gift for Joan, and went to the interview armed with the various reports I made about the financial situation of the FSTC. When the Colonel saw me, he was surprised at my size. He hadn't seen me since our first and only meeting.

I started the conversation in a very professional manner: "Colonel, I'm grateful to you for giving me my first job. I've worked hard to be worthy of your trust, and as a result, Xavier made me deputy manager. But things are not going well at the company. I thought many times of coming to see you, but I didn't want to go over Xavier's authority. I have always insisted that he should talk to you about the condition of the company, but it seems that he's afraid to tell you the truth."

I paused to see his reaction. The Colonel was relaxed in his chair, but after I said that, he moved forward, giving me his full attention. "But now things have come to a critical point. I'm aware that your main interests are now concentrated on the real estate business, and that the FSTC is no longer your main company. But if we don't take drastic measures, it will go bankrupt."

The Colonel was taken aback by that revelation, and looked at me in disbelief. I produced from my briefcase the reports I had prepared for the occasion. With them, I was able to confirm what I had just said about the real condition of the company. He seemed surprised at my professional and competent approach.

"How could the company come to such a situation without Xavier ever telling me about it?"

## The Amazon Shaman

"For the past several months I have been urging him to do so, but I believe he's afraid to face you with such bad news."

"But ... what can we do now?"

"The FSTC today is practically worthless. The two remaining boats are in a very poor condition. To rebuild them would be too costly. Perhaps the best thing to do would be to let the company go bankrupt. However, since I know that the Colonel has political ambitions, and the FSTC is too small a business among your other interests, I don't dare to suggest that. Maybe another option is to look for somebody that would be willing to buy the company."

"Do you think the FSTC could be sold? How much could I get?"

"In its present condition, you would get nothing. The company is practically bankrupt. My feeling is that, at the beginning, you might have to advance some money to the new owner, because the financial situation of the company is awful."

"Give away the FSTC and pay to whoever gets its shares?"

I made a pause, rose from the chair, locked my eyes with his, and in a very professorial tone, I answered "In the present condition of the company, that's the option I´d recommend. The other option is bankruptcy, which may adversely affect your name on the market, as well as your political dreams."

"I never thought the situation was so critical."

"I know! If Xavier had given you an alert earlier, I believe I myself could have found a better solution for you. Even so, in view of the gratitude I owe you, I couldn't let it go on like this without warning you. From now on, the situation tends to get from bad to worse."

The Colonel seemed astonished to hear this. He took a few minutes examining carefully the financial projections. While reading, he passed his right hand on his hair several times, twisting his right ear frantically. He looked as if he couldn't believe what he saw. Finally, he said in a low voice, resembling a lament: "Why didn't you come to see me before?"

I was standing in front of him with the palms of my hands on his desk, looking at his eyes from above. Keeping my calm tone of voice, I said: "Xavier is your trusted manager. Whenever I mentioned the need to speak to you, he would say he was getting prepared to do so. As time passed by, I've decided to come by myself." I made a small pause to let my words sink into his head. "The only thing I ask is that you don't tell him I've come here. I don't want to seem disloyal to him."

The Colonel took some time looking at the ceiling before going on. "Yes, I really cannot let the company fail. It would be a disaster for my political plans and, of course, for my credit in the market."

"Furthermore, Colonel, a well-run FSTC can be a good instrument to get votes. It serves a large part of the population along the Amazon River and the Rio Grande. I would like to go on working for whoever you put in charge of the company, so that I can help you on the political side. I've received some good offers to change job, but I feel I have to return the help you gave me when I came to Manaus as a boy with no alternatives."

"I want to thank you for your zeal. I'll review these reports and I'll call you again. And my congratulations for the amount and quality of the information they provide. Even before examining them in greater detail, I can see that they are well prepared. I wouldn't imagine you made so much progress."

"Again, I want to ask you not to mention my report or our meeting to Xavier."

"Don't worry, I'm going to fire that incompetent right away."

"If I may say so, I wouldn't do that, Colonel."

He looked startled at me and asked: "Why not?"

"You intend to get into politics, don´t you? So why make needless enemies?"

"What do you mean by needless! He is a thief."

"So what? Leave that to the new owner. That´ll be his problem."

The Colonel thought for a minute and then said: "You're right. Thinking politically, a quarrel isn´t worthwhile, even with a thief. I see your capabilities cover more than financing. You have a knack for politics too. I'll follow your advice, and leave this problem for the new owner. You are a lot smarter than you look. Congratulations."

On my way out, I stopped for a chat with my good friend Joan, whom I knew to have some influence on the Colonel. At least she had his ear. "Joan, do you know that the FSTC is going under and the Colonel will have to invest some money and give it away?"

"My goodness! Is the situation that bad?"

"Much worse than you imagine. I've been saying that to Xavier for quite a while, but he didn't have the guts to tell the Colonel, so the situation has been deteriorating. I decided to put the cards on the table before the Colonel. My concern now is that I may lose my job under a new owner, and it's not easy to get another one. If the Colonel is really going to give the company away …

"Give the FSTC away? I can't believe it. No, it isn´t possible things have come to this point."

"Yes, they have.

"And to transfer the company to somebody else, the Colonel will have to put money in it?"

"Yes, or else is will go bankrupt."

"That's awful."

"I'm afraid I'll lose my job. It's a paradox that by telling the truth to the Colonel and opening his eyes, I may find myself out of a job."

"Why would a new owner dismiss you?"

"He may want to have someone he trusts in command."

"Yes, that's true. But what can I do to help you?"

"If the Colonel is really going to give the company away, I wish he would give it to me, but I don't have the nerve to say that to him."

"At your young age, are you brave enough to undertake such a responsibility?"

"I've got the courage and the desire to. I dream of owning the FSTC."

"Leave it to me, kid. I'll see what I can do."

Joan always called me kid. She was especially kind to me. I liked her because she reminded me of my mother. I knew that she would be my best advocate before the Colonel.

> If you can comprehend God, you shall comprehend the Beautiful and the Good, the pure radiance, the incomparable beauty, the good that has not it's like.
>
> Hermes
> Quoted in: "The Eternal Wisdom," a publication of the Sri Aurobindo Ashram.

## Chapter 9 - The Shaman

"Tsiipré, hurry up. Father Justin is dying."

I was twenty-two when Father Justin died. I felt a terrible grief. He was like a father to me. In fact, he was more of a father to me than Kautá, my own father. I had spent most of my life under his guidance; more time than with Chief Kautá.

After Father Justin's death, I decided to leave Manaus, and go back to my tribe. I was to stay with our old Shaman, my mentor, since I had already been appointed his substitute. Our hut was a little farther away, apart from the center of the village. As a Shaman, dealing with spirits and demons, the people preferred us at some safe distance from the other village huts, somewhere in the forest.

I was convinced we should take advantage of the good things I had learned during my stay among the white people. We must preserve our culture, without avoiding what was good in the white civilization. I felt it was important to prepare ourselves for the day -- hopefully distant -- when it would not be possible to stay away from the white man.

One day, I went to see Kautá. He was old and about to retire and pass on his chieftaincy to my older brother

Kaniuá, who was also present. "Chief, I think that we should take advantage of the white people´s good things."

He answered, while Kaniuá listened intently: "Our customs must be preserved. If we lose our roots, the Indians will be destroyed."

"I would like to prepare our brothers for the day when contact with the white people becomes inevitable."

"Contact with white men is always bad."

"My father, today we are avoiding such contacts, but this cannot go on forever. The day will come, perhaps not in your time nor in mine, when our people will have nowhere to go."

"What is Tsiipré's idea?"

"I propose that we set up a school for our boys and girls. A bilingual school, in which our brothers will learn to write both in our language and in Portuguese. Also, they should receive instructions in mathematics and in music, which is good for the development of their thinking abilities."

"Will this make our children forget our way of life?"

"No, by no means. The school will pass on to the young people our legends and customs, so that they will learn the meaning and value of our roots."

Kautá reflected for a moment, and then said: "I shall convene the Council of the Wise Old Men, to discuss your idea."

Despite my younger age, he asked me to present my idea to the Council. The tribe knew I would succeed our old Shaman. I had already won the respect of some of the old councilmen for other ideas I had submitted before. Even so, there was much discussion at the meeting; however, the Council reached a favorable decision, with the support of my father. Having accepted my idea, the Council put me in charge of its implementation. In the beginning, I was the only a teacher, but the school was a success and many former students turned instructors. Thanks to the school, our youngsters are now much better prepared to deal with the white people, if and when this becomes inevitable.

I vowed to devote my life to help saving the Kauauá. The first action should be to seek the demarcation of our new land. This would be essential for our legal protection against any white man invasion. A federal law enacted in 1973 provided for the demarcation of all Indian territories within ten years, but it has not been effectively enforced, and many Indian tribes, like ours, still do not have this basic right. To this day, after more than three decades, little has been done.

"Tsiipré, the Chief is looking for you."

Now, after my father Kautá's passing, the new Chief was my brother Kaniuá. Although I am twenty years younger, I am now the Shaman and he always seeks my advice. Our tribe, the Kauauá, has lived happily for over two decades. But things aren't always flowers in paradise, and one day trouble began to rise in the horizon. And our problems are always brought by the white man.

I walked the two hundred yards that separated my hut from the village, and met Chief Kaniuá.

"Tsiipré, there are some important matters I want to have your opinion about. John insists in talking to me."

"Are you willing to talk to him?"

"Not yet. The least contact we have with his people the best. I was hoping he would give up."

"Not likely. Not John.

"That's the problem. What would you suggest?"

Now, after more than two decades of separation from the white man, two happy decades of relative tranquility, things would start all over. It was clear to me that we could not keep running away into the forest. To wage war against the white people was not a solution either. How long could this last?

I got very worried after that conversation with the Chief. We needed further discussion. After talking to some of our people in the village, and learning more about John's moves, I went to see the chief again: "Chief Kaniuá, I'm worried about the way things are going. The white man is getting closer and closer to our area."

"It is good that you brought up this matter again. Kaniuá is concerned. John is saying that he will get our trees one way or the other."

The cutting of trees had been banned by the Government, except with a special permit, difficult to get. But the white man does not bother with that. He wants timber at any cost. Government inspectors make it difficult to cut trees near the cities, so the lumbermen are moving farther inside the forest, where inspection is more difficult. They are already getting near our land. I heard of men in our lands.

I went immediately to talk to the Chief: "Chief Kaniuá, I came to see you because there was trouble yesterday. Uakaú saw white men walking around our land."

"What were they doing?" asked the Chief.

"Apparently, they were looking for the best trees in the area. Uakaú drove them out."

"He already told me that. Do you know who they are?"

"Not for sure. Most probably, John's thugs. They were trying to set up camp in our land."

"Did they fight?"

"Being few, there was no resistance. They were afraid of Uakaú, and left. I bet they will return in force."

"Well," said the Chief, "it is not going to be always that easy."

"I think we should call the Council of the Wise Old men to discuss this matter. I'm afraid the situation will get worse quickly."

"Good idea, brother Tsiipré. I don't know what to do. Good to listen to old men. Good to listen to the voice of experience."

On that very night the Council held a sitting. The night was glorious. The heat of the day was dissipating and the temperature was mild. The full moon was high in the sky, lighting our meeting and dimming the brightness of the stars, even of the most radiant ones. We could feel the scent of the forest in the air. There were ten of us in a circle. I took my place, as the Shaman, to the right of Chief Kaniuá, who began to speak: "Brothers. I have a serious matter to discuss. Kaniuá is concerned. Our tribe's life may be in jeopardy. The white man is getting nearer and nearer."

A murmur went around the circle. They were old enough to remember the problems of the past. Even so, the Chief decided to refresh their memories, recalling things that had happened more than twenty years ago.

Kaniuá concluded: "If it were not for my father's firmness, now we could very well be beggars in the city of the white people, if alcohol had let us live."

I said: "Yes! We cannot forget that those members of the tribe who did not leave have mostly died of drinking or are living a wretched life. The group that moved away had some initial difficulties in settling down here, but we are happy today. Our success has attracted some brothers, who had opposed the move. We have increased our population here and nowadays we are a group of more than two hundred people."

There was a shaking of heads in agreement. In that group of old people, many had faced problems with the white men. Today, all agreed that the decision to get away from the white people, and to move to a remote place inside the jungle, had been a wise one.

Kaniuá went on: "The white man wants our timber. He has destroyed the forests near their cities, and is now moving inland. The other day, a group of men tried to settle down in our area. Uakaú forced them out. They did not resist because they were few, but they may come back with more people. In fact, we can expect that they will try again."

One of the wise men, old Pokrã, who as a young man had been a great hunter and warrior, spoke: "Pokrã already knows about the conflict. There is a lot of gossip in the tribe. Pokrã is worried. What should we do?"

During the long discussion that followed, almost all the wise men spoke. But the only two options proposed involved either fighting a war against the white man or moving farther away into the forest. Both were difficult solutions. We were at a loss as to what to do.

Kaniuá recommended: "I think we should wait for a while. Perhaps the white men will give up. Everyone must be alert. Also, let us keep thinking about other possible actions."

Kaniuá ended the meeting by saying: "If we have no better idea, there would be only the two options already raised: either moving the whole tribe farther inside the forest again, or driving the white man away by fighting for our land.

I joined the discussion once more. As I began to speak, they were all most attentive, even though, at forty four, I was younger than all of those wise ones. "None of these two options is a good solution. If we fight, we can gain some time, but we will lose many young warriors. If we move, we will lose our crops and will have to start all over. And, once more, we shall leave the grounds where some of our ancestors have been recently buried."

I noticed the concern of the old men, as they shook their heads in approval of my reasoning. I went on: "Maybe some will want to stay, like in the past. Now, we are a large group. If we move, our tribe will be split again. I think Kaniuá is right. We should keep trying to find a better idea, and wait for a while. If we are lucky, the white man may go somewhere else, and leave us alone."

Kaniuá closed the meeting asking everyone to watch for any sign of the white man's presence in the area. Although I had suggested that the white man might leave us alone, I didn't really believe it. I said that just to appease the Council. Yet, knowing the white man as well as I did, I thought it unlikely that the lumbermen would back off so easily. In the case of John, this would be even more unlikely.

Our village was located near the Rio Grande, a natural outlet for carrying the logs downriver. Bonito, a tributary to the Rio Grande, would also be used to carry the logs to it. All that, plus the fact that we were sufficiently far from the white settlements not to call the attention of the Government inspectors made our area ideal for a safe and relatively inexpensive exploitation of the timber.

I felt responsible for devising a way out of our plight, other than the fight or flight. I had a different view from the group, since I had gone to white people's schools, had shared their company and learned their way of thinking. Maybe Kauaí-Açú could help me with a bright idea to get us out of that predicament.

**Roberto Lima Netto**

## CHIEF SEATTLE'S LETTER (*)

"The President in Washington sends word that he wishes to buy our land. But how can you buy or sell the sky? the land? The idea is strange to us. If we do not own the freshness of the air and the sparkle of the water, how can you buy them?

Every part of the earth is sacred to my people. Every shining pine needle, every sandy shore, every mist in the dark woods, every meadow, every humming insect. All are holy in the memory and experience of my people.

We know the sap which courses through the trees as we know the blood that courses through our veins. We are part of the earth and it is part of us. The perfumed flowers are our sisters. The bear, the deer, the great eagle, these are our brothers. The rocky crests, the dew in the meadow, the body heat of the pony, and man all belong to the same family.

The shining water that moves in the streams and rivers is not just water, but the blood of our ancestors. If we sell you our land, you must remember that it is sacred. Each glossy reflection in the clear waters of the lakes tells of events and memories in the life of my people. The water's murmur is the voice of my father's father.

The rivers are our brothers. They quench our thirst. They carry our canoes and feed our children. So you must give the rivers the kindness that you would give any brother.

If we sell you our land, remember that the air is precious to us, that the air shares its spirit with all the life that it supports. The wind that gave our grandfather his first breath also received his last sigh. The wind also gives our children the spirit of life. So if we sell our land, you must keep it apart and sacred, as a place where man can go to taste the wind that is sweetened by the meadow flowers.

Will you teach your children what we have taught our children? That the earth is our mother? What befalls the earth befalls all the sons of the earth.

This we know: the earth does not belong to man, man belongs to the earth. All things are connected like the blood that unites us all. Man did not weave the web of life, he is merely a strand in it. Whatever he does to the web, he does to himself.

One thing we know: our God is also your God. The earth is precious to him and to harm the earth is to heap contempt on its creator.

Your destiny is a mystery to us. What will happen when the buffalo are all slaughtered? The wild horses tamed? What will happen when the secret corners of the forest are heavy with the scent of many men and the view of the ripe hills is blotted with talking wires? Where will the thicket be? Gone! Where will the eagle be? Gone! And what is to say goodbye to the swift pony and then hunt? The end of living and the beginning of survival.

When the last red man has vanished with this wilderness, and his memory is only the shadow of a cloud moving across the prairie, will these shores and forests still be here? Will there be any of the spirit of my people left?

We love this earth as a newborn loves its mother's heartbeat. So, if we sell you our land, love it as we have loved it. Care for it, as we have cared for it. Hold in your mind the memory of the land as it is when you receive it. Preserve the land for all children, and love it, as God loves us.

> As we are part of the land, you too are part of the land. This earth is precious to us. It is also precious to you.
>
> One thing we know - there is only one God. No man, be he Red man or White man, can be apart. We are all brothers after all."
>
> (*) The authorship of this letter is questioned, but the contents are to the point.

## Chapter 10 – After the trees

Two days later, John showed up in the village, and asked to speak to Kaniuá. It was a very hot, overcast day, a predictor of the afternoon rain. John was sweating abundantly, his shirt all wet, sticking to his body. Before seeing him, Kaniuá sent for me. He usually heeded my advice, and after my father's death, he always called me to discuss the more important matters.

He said to me: "I want Tsiipré with me in the meeting with John. I do not like him, even knowing that his mother was a Kauauá."

"What does he want?"

"I don't know. But I am sure it has to do with the timber."

At that moment, John came closer to us, sat on the ground in the Indian manner, and began to talk, trying to be nice to us: "Great Chief Kaniuá, my wise friend Tsiipré.

I looked at Kaniuá and he understood my look. I knew John disliked me because at many other times I had opposed his plans and proposals. In almost all his attempts to befriend the Kauauá, I had been the one to thwart them.

John went on: "The other day, your brave warriors expelled from your land some men who work for me. They came peacefully, and did not mean any harm to the Kauauá."

"Your men arrived without asking our permission," said the Chief. "This is our tribe's land."

"They came just to appraise the trees in this area. But I don't want to steal your timber. I want to buy the land where the trees are, and I can pay you well."

"This land is not for sale. It belongs to Kauaí-Açú, the Great Spirit that protects our people and the Kauauá are the keepers. How can I sell Kauaí-Açú's land?"

"I can leave the land for the tribe and buy only the timber. I pay good money for each tree."

"The trees, like the animals, are our sisters. How can I sell my sisters?"

"I can pay a lot of money. The Kauauá will be rich."

"We do not want any money. The Kauauá do not want any business with the white people. Kaniuá does not want to sell the trees. They are like our brothers and sisters. Not for sale."

"If the great Chief doesn't want money, I can bring knives, machetes, hoes, and even guns. I exchange timber for anything the Indians may need. Don't you need medicines?"

"Kaniuá wants nothing from the white people. We want only to live in peace."

"Great Chief, I'm here as a friend. I thought of paying the Indians very well to help me remove the trees. But I can also take the timber without involving the Indians."

"How would you cut trees without the Indians?"

"I'll bring men from outside. And I'll even protect your peace. When other white men looking for timber know that this is John's area, they'll stay away."

"This is not John's area. It belongs to the Kauaí-Açú. The Kauauá are its guardians."

"If John is not here, other lumbermen may come. And they are bad people. They think that it's better to eliminate the

Indians right away, to avoid problems. They will shoot their way in, and kill many Indians."

That argument made Kaniuá stop and think. That's when I joined the conversation: "The Kauauá are good warriors. We know the area well. We will kill many white men if they want to fight." I said that to impress John, but I was sure that a war would have the worst outcome for us.

John got up and spoke as he left: "I think the Great Chief Kaniuá may change his mind. If you want to talk, just send word to me."

On his way out, John saw a group of warriors in conversation. An Indian that John knew, named Pinuim, was among them. John called Pinuim and they walked together to the river. I didn't like that. I knew Pinuim wanted to be chief of the tribe and marry Tatainim, Kaniuá's daughter. But I don't believe she was interested in him.


The next day, I ran into Pinuim in the village and took the chance to ask: "What did John want from you?"

"John wants Pinuim to work on timber with him. He offered me many gifts."

"Did you accept them?"

"No. I told him that our people are ruled by the Chief and the Council of the Wise Old Men. Whatever they decide, Pinuim will do."

"And what did he say?"

"He said that Kaniuá is very old to be the Chief. He will not be chief forever. There is already the Council of the Wise Old Men, so the chief should be young to make up for the elderly. John thinks that Pinuim would be a better chief than Kaniuá."

That conversation worried me, and I decided to observe Pinuim on the following days. If John was planning to split the tribe, he would surely try to entice Pinuim to his side.

Pinuim was not a bad character, but he was very naïve, and anything but bright. John could easily deceive him. I went to my hut thinking about the meeting. On the way, I ran into Uakaú, followed by many children, coming back from fishing. As we got near each other, he said: "Tsiipré, I'm glad to see you. I've got a fish for you."

I was quite fond of Uakaú. If I had children of my own, I would like him to be one of them. He was always in high spirits, playing and teaching the children. However, in our village, there was some rivalry between Uakaú and Pinuim. Uakaú was a good hunter and a skillful wrestler. He was tall, strong, capable of going alone for several days into the forest, and coming back with enough game to share with the members of his clan. He also took care of his field crops, chiefly cassava and bananas. Uakaú had great empathy with children. They liked one another, and usually went out together to fish in the lake, or learn from Uakaú how to hunt small game. Pinuim was not as tall as Uakaú, but he was stronger. He used to win most of the wrestling contests in the village, and was also regarded as the best hunter of the tribe. But unlike Uakaú, Pinuim was introvert and distant. He didn't care for children, and was not interested in working in the fields. He preferred to hunt. He was sort of taciturn.

I remembered a conversation I had had with Kaniuá, when we talked about preparing his successor, in which I said: "Of all the young men in the village, only two seem qualified to be the chief of our people. I think that a preparation should begin as soon as possible, and I would like to discuss this matter before you take it up with the Council."

"Tsiipré speaks of Uakaú and Pinuim, am I right?"

"Exactly. I believe either one of them can be a good chief. Both are good hunters, respected by the other young men, and they have a leadership spirit."

"But they are very different. Pinuim is feared. A Chief has to be so. This is good," said Kaniuá.

## The Amazon Shaman

"I believe Uakaú would have a different style, but he also can be a good chief. People follow him naturally, while they follow Pinuim out of respect."

"In a crisis, respect is more important. If there is no crisis, anybody will do."

"But Uakaú also knows how to be respected, when needed."

"Let us prepare Pinuim and Uakaú. The Council will choose one of them at the proper time. Your task."

"Kaniuá is right. Nobody knows what is in store for tomorrow. When the time comes for a decision, the Council will select the best one."

Other Old Men were present at that conversation, and before long the entire village knew about the double choice. But this was not the only possible friction between the two men. Tatainim, Kaniuá's only daughter was a beautiful girl, and I believe both contestants would like to marry her. When she was a child, her father had promised her in marriage to a boy of a friend's family, but he died early, so that Tatainim now was free.

Would Tatainim be thinking about marriage? She was a very intelligent girl, my best student when I started the village school. Today, she is our best instructor. She learned all I could teach her about herbs and their preparation. She was my assistant, and she wanted to be a shaman. It was uncommon for our tribe to have a woman shaman, but not impossible.

Our religion, as well as the religion of the white people believes that God knows what He does. I decided to teach Tatainim all I could, preparing her to take my place, and let Kauaí-Açú do what He thought best. Of course, she would not learn from me all it takes to be a shaman. She would have to go through her own personal experience, her own Call, like all shamans.

Actually, none is chosen to be a shaman just by wishing to be one. The future shaman receives a sign, the Call. Then, whether he wants or not to be one, he has got to be because, if he refuses, he may end up mentally disturbed.

Tatainim has learned how to use the herbs, how to prepare medicines. But, to be a shaman, you need more than that. You must have an inner vision that will guide your life. Your life's aim will be to seek spiritual growth, and that is a hard task. You will be always treading on thin and dangerous ice. That is the price you have to pay for spiritual growth.

Your lifestyle becomes different from that of your social group. Even though having to adapt to it, you cannot be a conformist. Your life is a constant search for new paths, new horizons in a spiritual level. If yours is a successful journey, you'll be rewarded.

Your journey is far from being a sunny one. You suffer with the diseases of the members of your community. The more competent you are, the greater their hope that you will cure them. But some die. You cannot save everybody, and the family always thinks that you have not been devoted enough, that you have been neglectful. This is especially true in the death of a child. The father, and particularly the mother, does not accept the fact that their child may die before them.

To be a shaman is a fate from which only death may release you. On the other hand, everything in life has two sides: you are nearer Kauaí-Açú. You reach states of ecstasy that the common man will never attain. One single occasion in which you feel closer to Kauaí-Açú, or God for the Christians, is enough reward for all labors, all suffering.

After all, what is the reason for life? This question has been haunting people for centuries. And the reason is simple. Life is your opportunity to meet God. If you do not succeed, you will come back thousands of times to live again in this world. You will live again and again, as many lives as necessary, until you reach your objective of meeting God.

> You had to fall in the desert. Every man has to go through this experience."
>
> "But ... there are so many people that throughout all their lives, never get close to a desert," I said.
>
> "A symbolic desert. In fact, you think that you are in a desert, when really it's the desert that is inside you."
>
> Roberto Lima Netto
> The Little Prince for Grown-ups

## Chapter 11 – In the heart of the jungle

I wake up. I'm sitting on the Eagle or, rather, on what was left of it. On the rough landing, I must have hit my forehead somewhere, and I'm bleeding. The Golden Eagle slid over the tops of the trees, breaking the wings and leaving a streak of engine parts and debris of the fuselage, until it came to a stop before a thick trunk of a tall tree.

I feel dizzy, but only for a short time. I check my body. Legs and arms are okay. Except for the bruised forehead, all seems well. How lucky the cockpit is almost intact. My first sensation is the joy of being alive and moving. But a dark thought crosses my mind: those sentenced to death are alive one minute before being shot.

It's about time to take a good look around, and assess my situation. I'm in the midst of the jungle, inside what's left of my Eagle. It was sitting on top of an enormous tree.

I have no idea where I am. I try the radio and the GPS. Disabled. I can see that a few of my belongings are still in the partially destroyed cabin. My handbag with the chocolate bars supply is there. I was taking them to the farm to satisfy my addiction, which is shared by Valerie. I don't know about the baggage compartment. The survival kit and the rescue flares are there. But I cannot get to them, as the plane is unstable on the trees.

There is a strong smell of gasoline. The last remaining supply, which was not used up by the engines, must have spilled out over the place. This smell may serve as a protection, driving away undesirable visitors. Actually, I'm not afraid of animals, except snakes. It's a childhood trauma. Once, I was walking around a ranch, and almost stepped on one. I was saved by my father's shout.

The sun was setting. The birds, saying good bye to the day, were playing a great symphony. The howler monkeys were making the forest resound with their evening choruses. It's an interesting show, but my condition doesn't allow me to enjoy it. Tonight, we'll have a full moon.

In my Boy Scout days, I always wanted to spend a vacation alone in the forest. How ironic the way my wish is coming true. If these forced holidays are not too long, and if I can go back, fine. But let's face it -- to be lost in the jungle, and not having the slightest idea whether you would manage to go back to civilization, is terrifying.

It should have been a smooth flight. The weather was fine and I'm a good pilot. Why did I go to Gordon's party? Why didn't I pay more attention to Wilson's astrological predictions? Why did I stay late? Why did I spend the night with Irene? Why, why, why. Now I'm here, lost in the jungle, and happy to be alive.

The night falls. A beautiful moonlight. Without the city lights to compete with , the stars offer a magnificent spectacle. The birds and monkeys are quiet. It's the time of the toads and the crickets. I'm surrounded by strange sounds, not all of which I'm able to recognize. To tell the truth: I'm scared!

But being optimistic as I am, I try to convince myself that there is a way out for everything. I can't do anything tonight. So I'd better get some sleep, make up for my excesses of yesterday.

## The Amazon Shaman

I try to meditate. I took a course in Transcendental Meditation six months ago. Perhaps for being in a strange place, perhaps for the critical situation in which I found myself, perhaps for fear, I am unable to avoid undesirable thoughts. My mind always comes back to the same question: how to get out of this mess?

I think of ShuoKua. I remember his words and his hints. I couldn't imagine that the surprise he mentioned would be so terrifying. I should have tried to get more out of him. If I had suspected that his remarks might be a foreboding of trouble ahead, I could have been more attentive, more careful, and taken care not to fall asleep in the plane. How can I consider myself a good pilot? I remember again Wilson's astrological prediction: "The transit of Saturn is a serious one. It causes a change in life."

Well, what can't be helped. . . I'll wait for daybreak to take stock of my situation, and plan what to do. Now... go to sleep. The cockpit seat feels comfortable, and I'm tired enough.

I open my eyes as the sun begins to come up from the horizon. The day is waking up. The birds are starting their symphony. The forest canopy resonates with the cries of the monkeys. The weather is warming up, and the insects' whine follows the increase of the temperature.

The smell of the fuel is weaker, and I can scent the morning dew on the leaves surrounding me. As a former boy scout, I have some survival training, but that was in the camping and the woods around Rio. The Amazon jungle is a completely different world.

My first priority will be to find water. The plane – whatever remained of him - is supported by a huge tree, about one hundred and twenty feet from the ground. Its various branches make a natural ladder, which I can use to step down for about sixty feet. To win the last half, and reach the ground, I must use ropes, which I have in the plane.

Except for some slight pains in my muscles, caused by the crash, I feel well. So far, my irresponsible behavior in Gordon's party has been cheap. I put a big chocolate bar in my pocket, get a rope in the plane and begin my descent. This isn't as easy as it seemed. It had rained during the night, and the tree was wet and slippery. I step down carefully, holding on to the small branches.

It is interesting how some trees compete for sunlight, growing tall for several meters without branching out, as if saving strength to reach the top, where they can receive the sun's rays.

For the last sixty feet of my descent I use the rope like mountain climbers do. I fasten it firmly around my waist and keep my feet on the tree trunk, and my legs in an almost horizontal position. I reach the ground easily, but climbing back is going to be hard.

The chirping and singing of the birds fill the air, in a kind of welcome to me. It was a soothing concert in my desperate plight. The day is likely to be hot and stuffy.

When I'm already on the ground, I hear the distant sound of an airplane. I grab the rope and climb back up to the Eagle like a cat. What an emotion! I will be saved! The plane comes in my direction. My God! I have nothing to attract its attention. I wave my arms and shout, uselessly, because the noise of the engine dampens my efforts. The plane passes directly over my head. From the registration letters, I recognize Valerie's father plane.

It's almost disappearing in the horizon, when I see it turning back. My hope is renewed. I know I will be saved! Sure, they saw me. This is my lucky break! The plane makes another pass, now somewhat to my right. I again wave my arms frenetically, and shout as loud as I can. It flies away without a sign that I've been seen. I'm alone again. Anguish! No chance! It's not my day. The Saturn transit. ShuoKua's words. Oh Lord!

## The Amazon Shaman

An air search is conducted by dividing the area into sections. Not having found anything in a segment, they were not likely to cover it again. I tried to find the survival kit in whatever was left of the cockpit. Nothing! Even so, I prepared to light a fire, just in case another plane flew over.

I started my going down the tree again, landing on a cushion of wet and soft leaves. The trees are majestic. They are not hostile, but merely indifferent to the intruder I am. Yet, their stern aspect shows that the struggle for survival in the jungle is no feast. Will I survive?

Despite the beauty of the surroundings, I feel restless. It is a terrible situation for a so-called civilized man to be lost in the Amazon jungle. Again, the words of my guide, and his warnings about surprises, come to my mind. It may be a good time to call him to my help. I am in serious trouble and need his support. I sit on the ground and cross my legs in the oriental posture I use for meditation. After a few minutes, I enter into alpha, look for my virtual lab and call my Guide.

It's an irony of destiny that the spot I had selected for my usual relaxation and meditation was precisely an imaginary forest, as I knew that in the midst of the trees, in virtual contact with nature, I could better relax. Now, my contact was more than virtual. In view of the circumstances, I'd rather not have it so near the nature.

"Good morning, ShuoKua, I'm in trouble and need your help." Looking at my Guide, I recalled a photo that I'd seen once, of an old Amazon Indian who looked a lot like the Shaman of my dream. Could it be that the Chinese and the Indians have a common origin?

"Good morning, son. Every difficulty brings with it an opportunity for growth. You know that the Chinese ideogram for crisis means also opportunity."

"In the critical situation I'm in, your remark is rather theoretical."

"But I'm serious. You are going to have a great chance to learn some life lessons. Now you can understand why I said that our journey is never linear, but keeps many surprises."

"Yes, you did mention surprises. And what a surprise! Couldn't you have got me a lesser-trying experience?"

"Indeed, I also said that you needed an opportunity for spiritual development. Who knows, maybe now you'll have that chance. Do not waste it."

I felt a bit hurt by the way ShuoKua made that remark, with a smile in his face. Was it possible that he considered the situation funny? I didn´t. I confronted him.

"I'm in big trouble, and you seem to be having fun. I'm lost in the jungle. Do you know that very few pilots who crashed in the Amazon came back to tell their stories?"

"Would you rather see me crying? You have to cross the great river. That may be your big chance. Only God knows what´s in store for you. It´s too soon to judge!"

"I remember now what you said about the landing of the eagle. Was that a hint that I might not land well? Unfortunately, I didn't understand you."

"If this teaches you to listen to others, your plight will not be wasted."

" If I survive. Now, I remember how foolish I was talking about free will."

"You do have free will. Perhaps you confused it with full control of your life."

This remark was something I would have to think about in due time. Now, my problems were different. So I asked ShuoKua: "All right, what shall I do now?"

"I've already told you. You have to cross the big river."

I decided not to argue with ShuoKua. I couldn't understand his metaphors, and he knew it. What I needed now was objectivity -- clear instructions on how to proceed.

"ShuoKua, I know that getting out of here isn't going to be easy. I have gone way off the normal air routes because I haven't seen or heard any commercial aircraft flying overhead. Not even the search planes may come this way again."

"Accept your condition as an adventure, as well as a chance to learn, to grow. You are an optimist. That will help you. Be alert. Take advantage of what life is offering you and learn from it."

"Oh Lord! My survival depends on finding water and food. What can I do to get them?"

"Water, food, and hope. You may call it faith, if you prefer. On the first two needs, I can be of help, but hope is up to you."

"If it depends only on hope, I'll be all right. I promise you. Since you will provide water and food, what should I do?"

"Do not put words in my mouth. I will not provide what you need. I may be of some help, if you listen to me, which you have not done so far."

"I'll listen to you. Unfortunately, I can't understand your metaphors."

"Follow your hope. Look upwards."

"Oh, no! Metaphors again. You know that I'm not good at that. Come on, give me some more help."

"Look upwards, follow your hope."

With these last words, ShuoKua disappeared. I couldn't get anything more specific from ShuoKua. For a second, he came back to me, and almost shouted: "LOOK UP!"

I looked up, and noticed that the plane's nose pointed west. That was the direction of the lake I'd seen. Ah! My hope was to get to it.

"Thank you, ShuoKua. I think we'll talk a lot, especially if I learn to decipher your metaphors. Your help will be precious."

The Eagle was poised somewhat below the crown canopies. A rescue flight would have difficulty spotting it. I'll have to manage only by myself. Not quite; by myself and ShuoKua. By myself, ShuoKua and my hope.

My base camp must be the plane. At least I'll be able to sleep, protected by the strange object that is the airplane. I trust that the animals may be less curious and more fearful than people. I must watch out for the monkeys only, because as my relatives, they are curious creatures. The priority now is to get water. Before planning an escape, I must assure my survival.

The sun is shining. I follow in the direction the nose of the Eagle is pointing. I put markings on the trees with my knife, and keep watching for natural signs that may help me on my way back. This is important because my limited food supply is in the plane, and because I feel safe in it.

In the farm, Valerie is certainly worried. The search plane did not find me. They may have lost hope of finding me. Several cases of lost planes in the Amazon came again to my mind. Will they go on looking for me? Where am I? This question keeps popping up, but I'm not going to let it bother me. According to ShuoKua, keeping hope is on me.

The priority is water. I walk for about two hours, always straight west. I hear a soft purl and walk faster. Water! Thanks ShuoKua! Thanks God!

I come to a clear lake, fed by a brook of crystalline water, running on white rocks. A vision of paradise! In the lake, lots of fish of amazing colors swimming around. I have fishing net in the plane. I'll have to recall my old times as a boy scout on how to make fire. Salt? Forget it.

I start walking along the margins of the lake; maybe I'll find someone. After about an hour, I come to another brook which is fed by the lake. Tomorrow I'll follow its course because if there are people living in the area, they would normally be close to some water source. The position of the

## The Amazon Shaman

sun tells me I must go back if I intend to sleep in the plane. The lake is alluring. The temperature is high. I decide to take a splash, even at the risk of going back to the plane with no daylight. The water temperature is just right. Refreshing, without being cold. When I'm about to jump in I think -- would that beautiful and crystal clear lake have piranhas? It is unlikely, but I won't take any chances. Tomorrow I'll test for it.

I'm so absorbed in my thoughts, that I let the time pass. I look at the position of the sun. It should be well past three o'clock. The common daily afternoon rain in the Amazon starts pouring. It's a heavy, but quick shower. I need the remaining daylight to get back home. Home? I mean, the airplane, or what's left of it.

The way back wasn't as easy as I had expected. At various points, I was in doubt about the right direction, but I arrived back at the Eagle tree just before sunset. Climbing up was much harder than descending. I wondered how I had climbed like a cat, when the search plane flew by. The branches were still wet from the afternoon rain, and for a couple of times I almost fell down.

I got into the plane in time to watch the beautiful sunset in the jungle, from the vantage point high up on my tall tree. Despite all the worry, fear, and uncertainty, somehow I was having a little entertainment.

The night noises in the jungle are quite different from those of the day. Since I was already a veteran of one night, I tried to calm myself down. Only someone who has been lost in the Amazon jungle can understand how scary it becomes when the night falls.


Before falling asleep, my dream in the plane came to my mind. This was odd, as I'm not good at remembering dreams. Even when there is a fresh one in my mind when I wake up in the morning, by the time I get out of bed I've forgotten it. Yet, that particular dream remained very clear in my mind. Especially the part on meeting the Wise Shaman. Would I really meet one? Most unlikely! But I certainly could use some help.

The day before my trip I had gone by a bookstore, and a volume had attracted my attention: "The Golden Book of Dreams." I bought it as a gift for Valerie, and it was among the stuff in the Eagle. I had to take a look at it, if I could find it somewhere in the plane. I was curious to know its meaning. At least, by dropping me in the midst of the jungle, the dream had been prophetic. I had heard about premonitory dreams, but I had never really believed it. From now on, I would be less unbelieving. My dream was right about the forest. I could no longer doubt it was prophetic. If now I found a Shaman. . . How to interpret the part in which I shall have to save the earth? I certainly couldn't understand that, except symbolically. Such a message would have to be deciphered. But how? The only way would be to wait, until and if I encountered a shaman.

Probably because I was so tired from the two previous nights, I fell into a heavy, sound sleep.

I wake up the next morning with the glorious symphony of the birds, warbles and trills of hundreds of lovely multi-colored ones. The forest a live orchestra. Macaws, toucans, birds of the most dazzling colors surround my plane-house. A combination of red, blue, yellow, all colors of the rainbow get together to celebrate through the birds the beauty of the morning. Birds, that I had seen before only on TV, are now almost at arm's length. The fragrance of the morning fills the air.

I want to start early. I'm going to fish because my cookies and chocolates won´t last long. I get my fishing net and begin the descent. Now I'm trained and move faster. The branches are slippery, but that's no problem for me. I'm well and being overpowered by my optimism. I have a feeling that, today, something will happen to lessen my plight.

## The Amazon Shaman

Halfway down the tree, I grab something that does not feel like a tree branch. A live branch? It's a snake. The shock makes me lose my balance. I grab the rope which was still hanging from the tree. This is not enough to avoid my fall, but it helps to reduce its speed.

I have my last thoughts. Would I die falling from a tree? Would all that happen after surviving the plane crash? Would I break a leg? Would I be unable to walk for water? For food? Would I die an agonizing death? Would this be in store for me?

No! That can't be! I let out an anguished cry.

**Roberto Lima Netto**

> Native healers say that a spirit influences your state of mind. The usefulness and thus the future of both psychology and shamanism depend upon the coming together of these two disciplines.
>
> Arnold Mindell, M.D.
> The Shaman's Body

## Chapter 12 - Tsiipré's Dream

"Tsiipré, I'm worried about what's happening around here. You know I don't like John. Do you think that we should move our settlement or fight against his men?" asked Uakaú.

"I hope we shall not have to do either," I answered.

I was concerned with the meeting of the Wise Old Men, and also with John's visit. I still believed we could think of an idea to save the situation. A war is the worst option, but some young warriors are eager for a fight. We have been living in peace for over two decades and a few of our young men are eager to have some war experience. Combats were things of the past, told as epic stories to our children. As adults now, they wanted to fight, to show their worth, all those foolish things in the minds of youngsters. It is difficult to explain to them that war is interesting as a tale, but not in the real world.

Moving the tribe to another area isn't a good option either. Some Indians might not agree with the Council's decision, and our people would be split again, as in the past, when we moved away from the community of the white men. Until the process of demarcation of our land is not concluded, we shall live under uncertainty.

I remembered the dream I had about two weeks ago.

The day was dark, with rainy clouds. There was something hostile in the air. I saw a group of white men arriving in our village.

John was the leader. He spoke to me: "We are going to expel all of the Indians from this land. You either leave or die. Your option."

"We are not afraid. You are smaller in numbers. We can defeat you easily."

It is true that we are in much larger numbers. Although I felt bad vibrations, the threat did not worry me.

John said: "When the battle begins, we'll grow, you'll see."

The fight starts. At first, we are winning. But every time a white man touches an Indian, the white man becomes two and the Indian a dwarf.

Kaniuá shouts to me: "Tsiipré, your magical powers! The way things are we'll be defeated."

When a white man touches a tree, it begins to wilt and dies, and the white man multiplies himself, becoming two or three. The fight now turns against us. The situation is desperate.

Kaniuá shouts again: "The magic, Tsiipré, the magic!"

I try all the tricks I know. I do my best to weaken John's group, but nothing works. Kaniuá looks at me in despair. As a last resort, I decide to ask my protective spirits for help. I leave the fighting grounds, come to my hut and sit on the floor, where I start chanting and playing the maraca. In a short time, a friendly spirit appears to me.

"Do not despair, Tsiipré. On orders from Kauaí-Açú, the Higher Spirits will help you."

"We have not got much time. The white men are slaughtering us. Their magic is stronger than ours. Help must come quickly. Save us!"

"Help will come. A Golden Shaman will fall from the sky to your aid."

"A Golden Shaman? He must come right away, while we still have time. If he does not, there will be nobody to save."

"He will not be prepared yet. You have to take care of him, and teach him the things of the spirit."

"To prepare him? How? There is no time for that."

"You forget that time has no place in the world of spirits."

"Why teach him, if he is already a powerful Shaman?"

"He doesn't know that."

"Even if I could train him, we have not got the time. Don't you see how we are being butchered by the white men?"

"I will say it again: the world of Spirit is timeless. Time is not an issue."

"You are asking me a very difficult task!"

"Nothing is easy in this world."

"What should I do?"

"This Golden Shaman was a great Shaman in another life. In this life he does not know himself yet. He's still young, unprepared for life. He thinks happiness can be bought."

"White man's idea."

"You will have a lot of work.

"So I will have to train a white man that does not even know he is a Shaman? Kauaí-Açú is giving me an impossible mission."

"If you think it is impossible, it will be... Nothing is impossible if you have a strong will."

"I know that nothing is impossible for Kauaí-Açú."

"You are right. Everything can be achieved, but he demands total effort and dedication."

"Where shall I find this Shaman that does not know he is a Shaman?"

"He is going to fall from heaven."

Frankly, I was stunned. A fight in full intensity, and here I was waiting for a miracle.

"Fall from heaven? How is that possible?"

"Wait and see."

"How can I make him become a great Shaman again, so powerful that he will save the Kauauá from the white man's claws?"

"Easy, son, don't hurry. Things will happen little by little. When the right time comes, you'll know how to act."

"I am sorry, my friend Spirit. You are right. Kauaí-Açú knows what he is doing. I will devote myself entirely to this task. I will do whatever I can and if I can't, I will ask for your help."

Meanwhile, the fight was going on, but there could be no doubt as to the winner. Some miracle was needed, and fast.


I woke up full of sweat. That vision touched me deeply. I normally have many dreams, but this one was different; its luminosity was charged with energy. A great dream. I thought about it all the time, trying to understand its symbols. A Golden Shaman fallen from the sky? What was the meaning of this dream? It certainly couldn't be interpreted literally. After all, no one would fall from the sky, let alone a Golden Shaman that had to be trained and didn't know he had spiritual powers.

No use to keep thinking about the future. The day would come when we would have to choose among the choices available to us. For the time being, I had work to take care of. My inventory of curative herbs was low, and I was going out with my niece Tatainim, who often helped me gather the herbs. It was early morning, and she was waiting for me at the door of my hut. The sun was rising and the morning was splendid. The gorgeous chorus of birds almost made me forget my dream.

"A beautiful day to walk in the forest, Tatainim. I want to cross the lake, as I know we will find the herbs we need on the opposite side. Let us get on the boat. Take this basket and I will take the other one."

"All right, uncle. I enjoy going with you. I learn a lot with our walks and I'm glad that you haven't found an apprentice for company yet."

"Even if I do, I will always need your help. You have a sharp eye and a good scent to find herbs. It is a pity you cannot be my apprentice. Your father wants you to marry and have children."

"I know, but I'm going to convince him that it will not make me happy. I like your work very much, and I don't intend to get married. I want to go on helping my uncle. If I'm lucky, I hope to receive a call to be a Shaman. And I need your help to change my father's mind."

I knew Tatainin's desire and I hoped she could succeed in persuading her father. After all, times are changing, and even in our traditional society, parents cannot dictate their children's life as easily as in the past. But as to be a Shaman...

"We are not the ones to decide whether you are going to be a Shaman. That depends on a call from Kauaí-Açú. If you get it, not even your father can prevent it."

"He doesn't even want to hear about the idea of my being a Shaman."

"Leave it all in the hands of Kauaí-Açú and don't worry. No use bothering with what does not depend on you."

We got on the boat and began to paddle slowly across the lake. The day was clear and the sun was warming us up. We rowed in silence, just listening to the birds. I never got tired of their melodies. On reaching the opposite margin, I tied the boat down, and we started walking into the forest.

We had been gathering herbs for some time when I heard a scream. I turned quickly, in time to see a man falling from a tree about a hundred feet away. He hit the ground with a thud, and bumped his head on a fallen tree trunk. I was afraid he wouldn't survive the ugly fall and the bump on his head. Tatainim uttered a cry, and we ran toward the man.

"Is he dead, Uncle?"

I felt his pulse.

"No. His left leg has a bad fracture. Look how twisted it is. Let us get some pieces of wood to make a stretcher, and take him home. But first let us straighten his leg and put a splint on it."

He was a white man. I saw he was not from the region because of his clothes. How did he get here? When I looked up and saw the remains of the plane, I understood what had happened.

A Golden Shaman fallen from the sky! I saw the color of his hair and remembered my dream.

We made a stretcher from tree branches and carried the man to the boat. The fracture of the leg was serious, and it would be difficult to mend it. I was sure he would survive. He had to survive -- my dream was becoming real.

When the boat arrived at the village, we got help to carry the man to my hut. The news spread around: there is a stranger among us. Many Indians came to see the white man. His hair drew a lot of attention, because it was the first time that they saw a blond man.

We went to my hut and I put him in a hammock. With Tatainim's help, I prepared a plaster cast with herbs, to stop the bleeding and prevent infection, and placed it on his leg. I had tried to reduce his fracture in the forest, but only now was I successful. All we could do at the moment was to wait and hope that things would turn out well.

The injuries were serious, but because of my dream, I hoped he would be saved. Was it wishful thinking? Was I putting too much weight on my dream? No! I was confident he would be cured.

## The Amazon Shaman

One of my missions as a Shaman was to bring comfort and health to all suffering. My desire was to be able to cure any fellow man in need of help. Although he was unknown to us, I was anxious for his recovery. And not only because of the dream. Something inside me made my desire much stronger, as if I had a special attachment to him. Could I have known him in previous incarnations?

I looked at him closely and he seemed to be an old acquaintance. Yet, I was sure that in this life I had never seen him before. How to explain that sensation of closeness, if not taking into account previous incarnations? That white man seemed to have a strong bond with me, like a son. Maybe he had been one, in another of our lives.

Tatainim came to my hut again for news of the white man. She said: "It's been three days since the white man's fall, uncle, and he remains as if he were dead. Do you think he will survive?"

"To tell you the truth, I don't know, Tatainim. Only Kauaí-Açú knows. But I have a strong feeling that he will survive, and will be of great help to our tribe."

"At least he is not worse. He is always sleeping and sometimes moves a little. My intuition tells me that he will get over this."

"How long can he stay like that, without food or water?"

"Not much longer. If he doesn't wake up, he is going to die."

Tatainim, just like me, was also showing a special interest for the white man. Could she have the same gut feeling? My dream showed that his coming would be of great importance to our tribe. How? I didn't know. I refrained from telling my dream to Tatainim, not to influence her judgment, and that of others, about the man. After all, I didn't know who he was and what he was doing in the area. We would have to wait until his recovery to make a judgment. Was he a good character? Again, my feeling said yes.

I decided to take a more active stand to cure the man. When Tatainim left, I set up a fire and put some green leaves in it. Smoke rapidly filled the hut. I sat down on the floor and started singing my chants of invocation of the spirits, accompanied by the rhythm of my maraca.

In less than ten minutes I got into trance. I, or my spirit, walked out of the hut and entered a hole in the ground, where I began to go down as if in a bottomless pit. It was a long descent, but I soon met the first Jurupari, one of the many demons that guarded the underworld. This one was watching the door to the Valley of Forgetfulness, where I suspected I would find what I was looking for.

It was a gray and gloomy place, with a deafening, dissonant noise resembling the warming up of an orchestra. This Jurupari who guarded the gate had a fierce attitude. I had already met several of them in my long role as a Shaman, but that one was different; its smell of sulphur, normally associated with the demons, was the most intense I had ever scented.

When he saw me, he tried to block my way. "Nobody alive enters here, and dead you are not."

"I'm Tsiipré, assistant to Kauaí-Açú, master of time and space. I have earned my entry in these areas long ago. I have fought with your king, and won. Now, I have a free entry."

The ugly creature hesitated, but finally said: "No free entry with me. You said you have fought with my chief. You'll have to fight with me too.

"He who has defeated your chief, can whip a mere doorman.

That infuriated him, as I intended. The fight was hard, but I was experienced and knew all the tricks to beat a Jurupari. With a last blow that I had learned from our old Shaman, I knocked him down, and he screamed in pain.

"Where is the soul of the white man that arrived a few days ago? Which Jurupari stole his soul?"

He wouldn't say. I hit him again and he screamed louder. Finally, he said: "He went in the direction of the Mountain of Horror, straight in front of you. Let me go, you are hurting me."

"I will let you go. But take a good look at me. The next time I come around here, don´t be so stubborn. I am Kauaí-Açú's assistant. Do not mess with me again. Is that clear?"

"Yes, yes, but let me go."

I released him and he ran after the other Jurupari, to catch him before he reached the mountain. The Mountain of Horror was the dwelling of many Juruparis, and it would be much more difficult to retrieve the soul if I had to go inside.

After walking less than a mile, I saw, at a distance, a Jurupari carrying the soul of the white man. He also noticed me, and increased his pace. But the load was heavy. As I approached, I recognized him. I had fought against him on another occasion and had defeated him. Even so, it wouldn't be easy because the area was full of Juruparis, and I couldn't fight a whole gang.

"Jurupari, Jurupari, I know you. You have already fought with me and you know that you cannot beat me."

"That was once. Now it's another day. I'll win, and get two souls with one stroke."

He didn't sound as confident as he wanted to appear. He was nervous, and I thought this would give me an advantage, which allowed me not to take chances "Jurupari, Jurupari, you know I´m strong, powerful. I fought with your chief and beat him. I have beaten you too, but I don´t want to do this again. I don´t want to take away what you are carrying. Let´s make a deal: I have with me an enchanted gem, as beautiful as any can be.

As I said that, I pulled from my pocket a sparkling green stone, which I had found in the creek that fed our lake. His eyes shone when he saw the stone. I continued: "You give me the soul and I give you this gem. It is valuable. All the other Juruparis will envy you. With it, you will have power over all. Only your chief will be above you."

He thought for a while. Then he said: "I can give you this soul, but I need a proof that I got it. A white man's soul is very rare. I would gain a lot of prestige in the group."

"The proof is this gem. It will mean greater prestige for you. Its green comes from the depths of the ocean, far, far away."

I put the stone near his eyes. I could see the greed in them. Even so, he was resisting.

"The stone does not prove anything. What does it have to do with the white man's soul?"

"The name of the stone is "Great Greed." Take it or leave it. If we fight, I will beat you, and you get no soul and no stone."

Again, the Jurupari hesitated. Then, he said: "I must keep a piece of the soul. I need a proof to show that I got a white man."

"With a missing piece, the white man will not be complete. Something will be lacking."

We had been talking for some time, and I heard a distant noise that might mean the coming of a group of Juruparis. I didn't want to face this. So I decided that, after all, it was a good deal. If the missing piece was an important one, I could come back later to retrieve it. I gave him the stone, took the soul and went on my way. As I passed by the guard, he looked startled when he saw I was returning with a soul.

"Don´t forget I am powerful. Do not ever try to get in my way. Keep in mind that I am an assistant to Kauaí-Açú."

I was almost at the earth's gate when I heard the noise of many Juruparis coming up the road. I hid in the bushes, keeping the wind in my face, so that I wouldn't be given away by my scent. The Juruparis have a good nose for the human odor.

As I was getting up to go on my way, I saw an animal coming toward me. It was a striped jaguar. I was already used to talk to animals, which is something a Shaman must do. You do have to lure your protective animals. You never know when one could be of use. The jaguar had seen me, but it was not hostile. I called and it came near me, waving its tail.

After greetings, I said: "I'll give you a name: Stripes."

It waved its tail more livelily, showing satisfaction.

I said: "Now you are my friend. I can be of assistance to you, if you need, and whenever I call you, you are going to help me."

The jaguar agreed. It's always good to achieve new protective animals. I walked a little farther, followed by Stripes, and came to the gate, the hole in the ground through which I had entered. I said good-bye to my new friend and climbed back to the earth.

I went to my hut and put the soul on the floor. I was tired from the fight and the effort to carry the soul. It was 3 o'clock in the morning. My excursion should have lasted about four hours. The fire was out, but the smoke still filled the shack. I rekindled the fire for more smoke and started again my chanting and playing the maraca.

When I got into trance, I got up, took the soul that was on the floor and threw it on top of the white man's body, who was still in a coma on the hammock. Then, I blew smoke on his chest. Again, we could only wait. Even with the retrieval of his soul, would the white man live? What about the missing part? Was it important?

I spent the rest of the night in trance, asking Kauaí-Açú's help. "Kauaí-Açú, if this is the white man who is going to help us, he cannot die."

"I did not say that I would do everything. It is up to you to cure him and educate him. I will come to your aid, but let me warn you, I am not going to make things easier. Do not forget that the obstacles of life make a person grow."

I was never tired of telling this to my pupils. I was convinced we would save this white man. He would be our Golden Shaman and, for unexplainable reasons, he was there to assist us against the "Johns" of life. I had great faith in that. More than two thousand years ago Jesus Christ said that faith moves mountains.

I laid down and tried to sleep a little before daybreak. My previous dream came back to my mind as a vision.


With the help of the Golden Shaman, now the situation was reversed. John's army was being defeated.

"You are not going to win, John. Retreat while there is still time," I said.

"I'm not dead yet. I have some tricks that you don't know."

"You will never be able to defeat our Golden Shaman."

"Don't be so sure. I'll withdraw today. Tomorrow, I'll be back."

In the same vision I saw John making a pact with the chief of the Juruparis: "Chief Jurupari, I'm in need of your aid," said John.

"Give me a good reason to help a white man."

"No reason. A deal. In exchange for your help, I'll deliver the souls of all Kauauá Indians to you. None will be left alive."

"Including Tsiipré, my worst enemy?"

"Sure. He is the first one I want to destroy."

"How about the Golden Shaman?"

"He'll die, too. You can keep his soul."

"I already have a piece of it. One of my soldiers sold the biggest part for a worthless green stone. Stupid!"

My vision faded. On the hammock, at my side, the white man moved a little, as if he was about to awake. I said a silent prayer to Kauaí-Açú, asking him to keep an eye on everything.

**Roberto Lima Netto**

> The unconscious mind of man sees correctly even when conscious reason is blind and impotent.
>
> C.G.Jung
> Answer to Job – Collected Works 11

## Chapter 13 - The Black Hole

I woke up a little dizzy. The place was full of smoke and I couldn't see anything. There was a smell of burnt green leaves. I felt around with my hands, and it seemed I was lying on a hammock. Trying to move, I felt a sharp pain on my left leg, and I realized that my leg was in a splint. Was my leg broken? I waited for the dizziness to ease off, and asked: "Hello, anybody there?"

Immediately someone came closer and bent over me. He was an Indian of about forty, with deep eyes and a kind smile. I was sure that I already knew him from somewhere. Despite my efforts, I couldn't remember. I had never seen an Indian in person. Had I seen him in a film or a picture?

In perfect Portuguese, he said: "Are you all right, my son?"

The way he spoke, I felt welcomed to wherever I was. "I think so. But I am thirsty and my leg hurts."

"You have been unconscious for three days. You must be hungry too. My name is Tsiipré. What's yours?"

He brought me a calabash full of water, which I drank in a gulp. I tried to think of my name and began to feel certain anguish. I couldn't remember who I was. I couldn't remember where I came from. Did I have a family? I ran my hand over my head and felt a big bump in the back, on the right side near the neck. A sense of despair began to overpower me. I tried to turn on the hammock, but my leg hurt.

My memory. Where was it? Without a past, I wasn't a full man, only half a man. I felt as if I had lost a piece of myself. It took me a long time to answer the Indian. He was waiting patiently, perhaps aware of my affliction. After a few painful minutes, I had to admit: "I don't know, I forgot."

"You suffered a big fall and your head bumped into a tree trunk on the ground. But have no fear. You will get well. Things will clear up in time."

"My memory seems to have been stolen."

I began to be aware of my surroundings, and again became conscious of the strong smell of smoke. The Indian, who gave me his name as Tsiipré, was looking at me with his keen eyes. Would he know more than he was willing to tell? Would I ever recover my memory? How to get out of this place? And where to go, if I didn't even know my own name?

As if reading my mind, Tsiipré spoke: "Your leg is not well. It will be some time before you will be able to walk again."

"How will I be able to get out of here?"

"Get out of here? You will not be able to walk for several months. Where would you like to go?"

I thought for some time, more and more anguished. Tsiipré continued to look at me with his keen eyes. He tried to instill some hope in me.

"To leave here you will have to walk to the river, and row a long distance. Even if you could walk, where would you go? You do not even know your name. We will take good care of you, and you will get better. Do not rush. Time cures almost all."

His voice was full and melodious, inspiring confidence. I felt that there was empathy between us. At that moment, a pretty young Indian, with black shiny hair and bright eyes, came into the hut, and spoke to Tsiipré in a language that I couldn't understand. When she saw that I was awake, she was happy. She also wanted to help me.

She came closer and said in Portuguese: "I'm Tatainim, what's your name?

I looked at Tsiipré for help. He noticed my embarrassment and said: "Tatainim is Chief Kaniuá's daughter , and she is my niece. She saw when you fell from the tree and helped me carry you here. She is also helping me as your nurse." And turning to Tatainim, he said something in a language I didn't understand, which I suspected as meaning I had lost my memory. Tatainim looked at me.

I said: "Thank you for your help. I would certainly have died without it."

"While you don't remember your name, may we call you Eagle? That's what is written on your cap, Golden Eagle," said Tatainim.

"All right, I'll be Eagle for you, for a short time I hope. It's hard to lose all your past."

"You'll recover your memory. Time will help, and Tsiipré is a great Shaman, who knows how to cure like nobody else."

"How did I happen to get here?"

Tatainim answered: "You fell from a tree, banged your head on a log and fainted."

"But...how did I get on top of a tree?"

Noticing my astonishment, she added: "You came on an airplane. It's still there, perched on the tree."

"Maybe I can find my name there, in some document."

"We can try when your leg is all right."

This possibility filled me with hope. If I discovered my name, perhaps I could remember other things about my life, I thought. I asked the Indian: "How long do you think my leg will take to get well?"

"About three months. No less."

"Well, since I'm going to be here with you for at least three months, I'd love to know more about your tribe and about where we are."

Tatainim answered me: "We are the Kauauá, a group of about two hundred Indians."

"Are you in contact with white people in the area?"

"We live away from the white civilization, by our own choice. In the past, we had a very bad experience caused by contacts with the white men, so we feel it's better to stay away from them. We don't dislike white men in general, just some of them."

"Is there any city nearby?"

"The nearest village is Formoso, on the banks of the Rio Grande. We moved from there about twenty years ago. We came up the Rio Grande, some five days from Formoso, which is in the heart of the Amazon region."

In the first few days I felt much pain in the leg, so most of the time I stayed in a hammock, a kind of a hanging bed. I tried moving as little as possible. Tsiipré had made me a pair of wooden clutches, but even with them, it was painful to move around. What was worse was the confusion in which I lived, because of the smoke screen that hid my past. I was feeling as if I were in a black hole, but I decided not to let this worry me for the moment, I had to live in the present, a difficult decision to carry out.

In one of Tatainim's visits, she said: "You are very popular. All the women ask me about you. Especially the old ones. We have never seen a blond man in this area."

"I've noticed that. They don't come into Tsiipré's hut, but they follow me in the few occasions when I go out for my toilet needs. The boys want to touch my hair and so do the women. The more aggressive old women try to pull its threads."

"They mean well."

"I know, they seem to be nice people, and I regret I don't understand what they´re saying to one another. I must learn your language."

"If you wish, I can teach you."

"Sure I do. It's a good way to pass my time. It's boring to have to lie down most of the time, and it's painful to walk. My leg still hurts."

"We can start today, if you feel well and the leg does not bother you."

"Great! Let's go ahead."


Everyone in the village respected Tsiipré, but many kept away from him, perhaps because of his involvement with the spirits. Practically the only people who called on his hut were Chief Kaniuá, Tatainim and a young Indian of about twenty, named Uakaú, who became my friend. I talked a lot with them. With the exception of Kaniuá and the elders, whose Portuguese wasn´t good, the others spoke the language well. No doubt they had studied it.

One day on which Tsiipré was away and I was chatting with Uakaú and Tatainim, I asked: "The young Kauauá speak good Portuguese. So does Tsiipré. But Kaniuá doesn´t . If you have been separated from the white men for twenty years, how can young people like you have learned such good Portuguese?"

"Tsiipré studied in a Jesuit school," said Tatainim. "Although he was opposed to acculturation, Tsiipré convinced Kaniuá to let certain elements of the whites' culture be introduced into the Indian community."

I learned a great deal about the Indians from those conversations. After three months I was able to communicate regularly with them, and I could also understand some of the conversation between them.

Confined to my hammock, I witnessed Tsiipré's sessions and spiritual work. I became extremely curious about it all, and I felt greatly attracted by the rituals.

Tsiipré often got into trance. He would sit on the floor and burn some green leaves, producing a smoke with a pleasing fragrance which filled the entire hut. Then, he would inhale a long and thin cigar prepared with sacred herbs, and begin a monotonous chant, while he played his maraca. After a few minutes, the chanting and the sound of the maraca faded, and Tsiipré got into a deep trance. His whole body seemed to radiate a brilliant light. Sometimes he would meditate for hours, and when he finished, his eyes were shining and he appeared to be in a state of grace.

I became interested in those activities. My interest pleased Tsiipré and he used to encourage me to question him. One day, he invited me to accompany him on his meditation. "I've always been interested in knowing a Shaman's work. I would like to learn it from you, if it is not a secret."

"You really need to learn how to meditate, so that when you are ready, you can retrieve your memory."

Wow! This interested me immediately. I would do anything to have my life back, to free myself from my black hole. "To retrieve my memory? How? When?"

"When you are ready, you will know it. For the time being, concentrate on learning how to get into trance. I will teach you how to meditate."

"First, I'd like to understand a little how it works. If the aim is to bring my memory back, I want to do it right."

"No problem. Ask your questions."

"What's the smoke for?"

"The smoke represents your thoughts and how you have to deal with them. At the beginning, the smoke has a shape; over time, this shape keeps transforming itself and is dispersed. This is the way you deal with your thoughts. When they come to your mind, do not fight them trying to get rid of them. Do not waste energy trying to avoid them. Do not give importance to them. Let them fade away into the air, like the smoke."

"And the sound of the maraca?"

"The maraca represents man, symbolizing your need to be void of ego, but always moving and sounding. However, do not think you are going to learn it all using your rational side. You should strive to enter the other reality. That, you will encounter when you are able to get into trance. It is far from rational."

"When can I begin my training?"

"How about now? I will not ask you to sit on the floor, because of your leg. Stay on the hammock, just as you are."


Tsiipré lit a fire, in which he put some green leaves he'd stored in a corner, and began to chant and play the maraca. That monotonous but pleasing sound made me sleepy. With my eyes shut, I was falling asleep when Tsiipré alerted me: "Don't sleep. We must meditate seated, to overcome sleep. You will have to do this lying down because of your leg; yet, control your sleep. To make it easier, keep your eyes half-open."

"How about the thoughts that keep coming to my mind?"

"Do not struggle with them. Just follow my chanting. If your mind is drawn to something, do not worry. Bring your attention back to the sound of the maraca and to the chanting."

"Is that all? I thought it would be more difficult."

"Do you find it easy? This reminds me of the story of an American who, on a visit to India, asked a great Guru to teach him meditation. He asked the Guru how long it would take for him to achieve enlightenment if he really attained perfect concentration. The Guru answered that if he attained perfect concentration for five uninterrupted minutes, he would get enlightened. Then, with an ironic smile he added: but be careful, do not think of the little monkey."

"And did he achieve enlightenment in five minutes?"

"Of course not; he could not get rid of the little monkey."

I laughed. Tsiipré continued: "In the beginning, it is hard to come to a deep concentration. Every so often your mind escapes, and you find yourself thinking about something else. Stop thinking and bring your attention back to the song. My chant is like a mantra. Mantras are recommended as a way to calm the mind."

I began to follow Tsiipré's chanting and tried not to think of anything else. After a few days, I succeeded in getting to a level of concentration that Tsiipré found to be satisfactory for the initial exercises.

"I think you must have had some familiarity with meditation in the past. Such a rapid progress as yours is not common."

And jokingly he said: "If you go on like this, you will end up as my successor. With your golden hair, you will be known as the Golden Shaman."

Unfortunately, I still didn´t remember anything of my past. Who knows? Perhaps in my black hole there might be some training in meditation. I was very curious, and wanted to learn quickly as much as I could from Tsiipré. The suggestion about retrieving my memory was a strong motivation. As he seemed to have some free time, I continued with my questions: "What is a Shaman?"

"A Shaman is a spiritual warrior who discovers his integration with the universe, his personal power, knows and moves throughout other realms."

"I'm not sure I understand you."

"It doesn´t matter. My answer does not sound easy for a beginner. Besides, a shaman's way is not through the rational side. Time and spiritual growth will help you to understand. Keep this thought and meditate about it calmly."

"The role of the Shaman is to cure the sick, isn't it?"

"It is also to cure the sick. But there is a very important distinction to be made here. The Shaman does not cure. The Shaman is the instrument used by Kauaí-Açú, or God if you prefer, to bring about the cure."

"Wouldn't this be the same thing? If a physician cures with medicines, shall we have to say that the medicines, not he, produce the cure?"

"That is not a valid comparison, God and medicines. I grant that, in a simplified way, people say that a Shaman cures. But remember: the cure comes from God. Even in the case of the white doctor."

"And what else does the Shaman do besides assisting the sick?"

"The Shaman is in charge of preserving the myths, customs and rites of the tribe, for which he is responsible, such as burials, for example."

"Forgive me for saying so, but I think that keeping myths is a waste of time. And I don't mean the Indian myths only, which I don't even know. I mean myths and rituals in general, including those of the white people."

"You are wrong, my son. Myths and rites are important to the Indian communities, such as rites of passage, for example. We have a collective mentality, as opposed to the individualism of the white man. In order to maintain our customs, preserve our roots and traditions, we need our myths and rites. And the rites are simply the representation of such myths."

I scratched my head. Unwillingly I touched the region that I had hurt on my fall and, although it was cured, I still felt some soreness on that spot. "I cannot be sure about the influence of myths for the Indians. As for the white man, I'm convinced we don't need them."

"How wrong you are." Tsiipre rose from his sitting position and went to one side of his hut, where I saw a bookshelf, full of books. He took one and gave it to me. "Do you read English? Try its first paragraph."

I opened the book and red: "History and Anthropology teach us that a human society cannot survive long unless its members are psychologically contained within a central living myth. Such a myth provides the individual with a reason for being." I closed the book and red in the front page: "The Creation of Consciousness by Edward. F. Edinger."

"Edinger was one of the most important disciples of Carl Jung, a great psychologist and thinker of the twentieth century."

I was startled to find, in that end of the world, such a knowledgeable Indian . My surprise kept me quiet for a few minutes. Tsiipré was just looking at me without interrupting my silence. "Getting back to Shamanism, I'm curious to know how you became a Shaman. Could you tell me, if it's not a secret?"

"No, it is not a secret. One of these days I will tell you in detail. I received a call when I was twelve years old."

"Suppose you didn't want to be a Shaman?"

"A person does not choose to be a Shaman. He is called by the Spirit. The Call represents the emergence of inner factors seeking expression. It is a very strong feeling. If you do not respond to the call, you may go out of your mind because you did not make room for these factors. When repressed, they will cause you psychological problems."

"I'm not sure I understand. I guess it's too profound for me. I´ll think it over."

I was impressed by Tsiipré's intelligence and culture. I'm sure nowhere else could I find a better teacher. Tatainim was right in saying that the priests considered him super-endowed.

## The Amazon Shaman

After around three months, I was freed from my clutches and could walk. My legs were still weak, but would become stronger over time. After all, they were my only means of transportation, and I started walking a lot to make up for the time I'd been inactive. Another thing that happened was a change in the interest of the children and the old people. When the news went around that I was studying with Tsiipré, they became a little fearful of me. At least they stopped following and bothering me. Perhaps Tsiipré had deliberately spread the story that I was powerful, so that they would leave me alone.

I walked enough to strengthen my legs to the point of being able to cover long distances normally. I was anxious to get to the place of my crash, to see whether I could retrieve something from the debris of the airplane that would help me uncover something about my past. One day, going out with Tsiiprée and Tatainim to gather herbs, I asked Tsiipré:

"I'd very much like to see the place where my plane is."

"We have not been gathering herbs in that area for some time. I believe that we can walk in that direction. When we found you, we had made an excellent harvest there."

We crossed the lake on the boat and walked slowly for about an hour. On our way, we picked up the plants that Tsiipré needed, and he described their properties to me.

When we came to the place of the crash, Tsiipré pointed to the top of a tree, and I could see what had been left of my plane. A rope was hanging from one of the branches, and I used it to climb up the tree, while Tsiipré and Tatainim were busy gathering their herbs. After climbing the first sixty meters holding on to the rope, I continued going up, using the branches of the tree up to the top, where the airplane was perched. I climbed into the cockpit and sat down.

Suddenly, I felt anguished. I recognized a few things in it, but they didn't help my memory. I looked into the scattered remains and didn't find anything of interest, except a picture of a very beautiful girl. Her face was familiar, but I didn't know who she was. A sister? Did I have one? My girl friend?

After several minutes of this agonizing search through my black hole, I decided to get down and look near the tree for some object that could have fallen on the ground. There were mechanical pieces scattered around, but no documents, nothing personal. I was continuing the search when, suddenly, I saw a snake, ready to spring at me. I jumped back and even knowing I was safe, I was overcome by an abnormal fear. Something I couldn't understand was disturbing me.

I picked up a big stick and was about to kill the snake when Tsiipré stopped me.

"Don't do that. Why kill it?"

"It can be poisonous."

"So what? It will bite you only if threatened."

Tsiipré leaned over and getting close to the snake looked fixedly at it. The snake was nervous, but gradually calmed down and let Tsiipré touch it. "You see? It doesn't want to hurt anybody. Man is always to blame."

"Many people are bitten who don't want to hurt the snakes."

"Snakes and all of the animals and birds are our brothers. We should not kill them."

"But... they can bite us."

"Would you kill your baby brother if he bites you?"

"Of course not."

"That is the attitude we must have with the animals. Trees must also be treated as our daughters. Man is destroying the earth, bringing forth an ecological disaster, because he is not aware of that."

> We will be seen on this stage of life over and over again, until we become such good actors that we can play our parts perfectly according to the Divine Will.
>
> Paramahansa Yogananda
> Spiritual Diary

## Chapter 14 - The Shaman's Apprentice

I used to talk a lot with Tsiipré. I was very curious about his life and his function as a Shaman. "The other day you promised to tell me how you've become a Shaman."

"I was studying in a school of priests in Manaus, and on holidays I used to come home to my people. When I was twelve years old, in one of my holidays, I had a dream, which we Indians call a "Great Dream.""

"How can you tell you've had a Great Dream and not a normal one?"

"The brightness, the strength, the emotion that you feel when you wake up. When you have one, I am sure you will know."

"Was it a dream that indicated your vocation?"

"Yes. Shortly after the dream I had a strong flu and an intense headache. I stayed three days in bed, in a state of half-consciousness. Then, I had three more dreams, one each day I was ill."

Tatainim showed up in Tsiipré's hut, and sat down to listen to our conversation. Before Tsiipré continued with the story, Tatainim turned to me and said: "Tsiipré is the person that best knows the use of the medicinal plants of the Amazon region, in theory and in practice. As a boy, he studied at the University of Manaus, and during the holidays he would take practical lessons with our former Shaman. But go ahead, uncle."

"In my first dream, I fell into a hole on the ground. Fall may not be a good word. I was walking and, all of a sudden, I began to be swallowed by the ground, as if I had stepped on a bottomless pit. I desperately tried to get out, but my efforts were useless. I fell down on a dark corridor, and, after walking for about one hundred yards, I arrived at the center of the earth."

"How did you know it was the center of the earth?" I asked.

"There was a large tree, different from any I had ever seen, growing straight toward heaven. It was so tall that I could not see its canopy. I could see only the thick trunk growing upwards, piercing the clouds, as the axis of the world. Around the tree, as if to prevent my climbing it, I met a reception committee that seemed to be waiting for me. They were Juruparis."

"Juruparis?"

"The catholic call them demons," Tatainim answered.

Tsiipré continued: "These evil spirits, dressed in black, wanted to destroy me. I tried to escape, but they caught me and began to dismember me. I saw myself spread all over the place. Suddenly, another white-claded spirit appeared, got rid of the black ones and started gathering the pieces and putting me together. I finally was whole again. He introduced himself to me and said that he was my Guardian Spirit. I talked to him for some time before he said good bye, and I floated upward in the hole through where I had entered. Then I woke up."

"After that experience you became a Shaman?"

"No! Not yet. That was only the beginning. When I woke up, my body was aching all over, as if I had actually been dismembered. Arimatã, the old Shaman, offered me food. I had not eaten for three days, but I couldn't swallow anything. Only some water. I continued with a high fever and was completely drained, almost in a coma. Then, I had my second dream. Again, I was swallowed by the same hole. The difference now was that when I walked the long, dark corridor and reached the bottom of the earth, my Guardian Spirit was there, waiting for me. We took a tour around the area, and he pointed out to me several animals around, saying that I should conquer them to be my assistants. He promised to help me.

At this point, Uakaú came in and sat on the floor, also listening to Tsiipré's story.

"I woke up again. Arimatã gave me a little more water, and I went back to dreaming. In my third dream, I returned to the bottom of the earth, met my Guardian Spirit and started walking with him in the underworld. Suddenly, an enormous Jurupari approached, smelling of sulphur. It looked terrifying. My Spirit said that I had to fight against him without his help. The Jurupari lurched ahead, shouting toward me, and the fight began. I hardly knew how to defend myself. In an instant that I felt completely lost, I looked at him fixedly between the eyes, and focused my thought with great faith in the idea that I would win. He would not be able to resist my power. After that, the fight began to turn in my favor and the Jurupari collapsed to the floor. A column of smoke formed over his body and he disappeared. I had won the fight. I was feeling proud of myself, when my Spirit spoke.

"You are just beginning. Hold your ego, do not let your pride inflate you, or you may lose the next time. You still have got a lot to learn."

"I woke up without a fever and feeling very well. Arimatã was at my side, and offered me food, which I devoured. I drank a lot of water and got up. From that day on, I became a Shaman's assistant starting my process of initiation. My time as a simple helper was over, and my struggle to improve myself had just begun. I still had to go through various exercises and tests, which I did under Arimatã's guidance. I will not go into details because if you really want to learn from me, you will have to pass through all of them at the proper time."

The following days were sheer delight. Now that I could move around freely, you can imagine how happy I was to spend my holidays in the midst of that luxuriant forest - a paradise on earth. It was early summer. I used to wake up in the morning with the chorus of the birds in my ears, and the scent of the forest in my nostrils. Then I would take my walk through the forest. The lake was a feast of colors, where the poor fish took part in it by being food for that immense flock of hungry birds.

In early summer, the clear blue skies were so bright as to blind you. When I became tired of walking, I would come to the lake, where my arrival caused a turmoil. Thousands of small butterflies, lying on the margin of the lake, organized by color, were the first ones to take flight. They were small butterflies of various colors, but on landing on a tree, promptly organized themselves in groups according to their colors.

Next, the nearest birds would hastily take off, which was the signal for the rest to fly away in droves. Then, the canopies of the trees would be painted with all the colors of the rainbow.

I relaxed by swimming and floating in the tepid waters of the lake. After swimming enough, I would rest my feet on top of a piece of wood and keep myself lying on the water. This ideal holiday program normally lasted for about two hours. I took advantage of the time to think about my life and try to revive my memory. On this, I made no progress and continued frustrated. But my despair was controlled, after Tsiipré's encouraging words. I no longer spent every minute of my time trying to solve my enigma.

Uakaú often invited me to go hunting or fishing. We would usually go in a group of three of four, sometimes joined by a few small boys to whom Uakaú was teaching hunting and fishing. Game and fish were plentiful.

The only thing that disturbed my happiness in that paradise was the black hole of my past, but Tsiipré assured me that the recovery of my memory was only a matter of time. I trusted him and tried not to worry, although this was rather difficult. The thought of my black hole came back to me at least once a day a day, despite my strong decision and my efforts not to pay attention to it. If it weren´t for that, it was a good life, a unique opportunity to have the perfect holidays in an enchanted forest.

In addition to all that, Tsiipré was teaching me his arts. I was a diligent pupil, and greatly enjoyed the spiritual experiences. He said that whenever I was prepared, I would go on a trip to retrieve my memory.

When I became capable to concentrate more fully in my meditation, Tsiipré gave me the first practical training in the preparation to be a Shaman.

"As I have told you, in my case, the initiation began with my first dream, my illness and the three following dreams. Even after receiving this call, I had to perform a series of actions required by my training. Certain practices must be mastered before one can consider oneself a Shaman."

"I haven't received any call."

"Really? Think about it and let us discuss this further."

"Aren't these exercises harmful?"

"I do not think so, because you are in an advanced stage of meditation, and will be doing the exercises under my supervision. I would be worried if you were to do them without guidance. But I cannot guarantee anything. Incursions into the spiritual world can be hazardous for the unprepared person."

"When shall we start"?

"Right now, if you like."

The answer took me by surprise. Although I was anxious to close the black hole of my memory, I hesitated a little, because I didn't feel really prepared. But I made up my mind:

"Well, let's do it, especially if it´ll help me recover my memory."

"It certainly will. My plan is, when you are ready, to go with you in search of your missing piece."

"Where to?"

Tsiipré then told me how, on hearing my cry and finding me unconscious in the forest, he went to the inner world to fetch my soul, and negotiated with the Jurupari that had stolen it. This increased my already great motivation to follow Tsiipré's instructions. It was the only way to close the black hole in my life.

"Your first exercise will be an exploratory journey, to get acquainted with your entry channel into the inner world. Your only mission at this time will be to explore this channel in details."

"How do I get there?"

"You are going to sit down on the floor, shut your eyes, take twelve deep breaths, and accompany me in my chants. When you go into trance, you will imagine yourself seeking an entry to the underground world. Each person has his own individual passage. It can be a tree trunk, a hole on the ground, whatever you choose and your intuition points out as the ideal entry. Are you following me?"

I gave him an affirmative nod.

He continued: "On finding your entry, go through it and pay careful attention to all the details. Follow the tunnel as far as the door to your inner world. Stop, look around carefully, note all details, but do not leave the tunnel. Do not pass through the door. Do not enter the underground world on the first trip. You do not have to run unnecessary risks at this stage. Return by the same way, leave through the same opening and come here. As a start, that is all you have to do."

I sat on the floor, as Tsiipré ordered. The smoke from the burnt leaves already filled the hut. I breathed deeply, twelve times, and concentrated my mind on Tsiipré's chant, repeating them mentally and following the rhythm of the maraca he was playing. In about twenty minutes I attained a good concentration level. I imagined myself leaving the hut and started walking into the woods. In a few more minutes, I came to the entrance of a beautiful cave, which attracted me in a special way. It seemed that it called me in, like a magnet attracts iron particles. I went in. It was enormous. Its walls were inlaid with crystal stones, shining like stars.

I started walking down a steep trail, toward the bottom of the cave. The ground was slippery, the trail was narrow and flanked by a precipice, the bottom of which I couldn't see. I threw a stone into it, and waited long for the return of the sound when it reached the bottom. The hole was really deep. If I slipped and fell in it, I couldn't hope to get out alive.

After following the trail for about a hundred yards, the cave ended, but I felt I hadn´t gone down enough. I was near a small spring of clear water. The water was transparent, but I couldn't see the bottom. Something was telling me that I should dive and try to get to the bottom of it. That's what I did. I took off my clothes and dove in. The water was cold and I felt it biting through my skin. After a few seconds, I started to run out of breath. Even so, I decided to keep going down, and this seemed to give me a new condition of being able to live underwater without breathing.

I finally reached the bottom, went up a few yards through a channel and emerged in a small beach, still inside the cave. Looking to my left, I saw an opening leading to a different world, illuminated by a strong bluish light. The scenario attracted me, and I was almost crossing the cave's opening to enter this magic world, when I remembered Tsiipré's instructions. I checked my impulse and did not leave the cave. I only looked. Dazzled!

The scenery was beautiful. Balls inlaid in the sky, emitting a silver blue light, illuminated the place. I had never seen anything like that. I could have stayed there, looking at it for a long time, so splendid was the new world on whose door I found myself. Again, I wanted to enter that silver blue space, but refrained myself. Obeying Tsiipré's instructions, I paid careful attention to all its details, trying to memorize everything. After being sure that I was able to visualize the whole picture, I sat on a rock to rest.

I relaxed for a short time, and reluctantly started my way back. This was easier, as I no longer needed to worry about breathing. I returned to the hut and entered my body again. Tsiipré was still chanting and playing the maraca. I sat in meditation for a few minutes, before opening my eyes.

Then Tsiipré asked me: "How was it? All well?"

I wanted to tell him everything about my trip, but he said that I must keep it for myself. He only wanted to know if all had been well, and if I liked what I had seen.

"Oh! It was fantastic. Sensational!"

"You did very well in this first stage of your initiation. I want you to repeat this work every day for the next week, before we move on to the second stage of your training. But remember, do not cross the door to the new world, the cave's opening. I say this because I noticed your hesitation. I don't want you to rush, destroying all the work we have done.

As Tsiipré recommended, in the following week I repeated my descent during my daily meditation. Every day I liked it better, discovered new details and became more familiar with the path. I found out that my aquatic channel was entirely inlaid with precious stones of various colors, shining in the dark and giving to the dive a special, surreal luminosity.

My interest in finding out how all this worked also increased, and at every chance I had, I would ask Tsiipré many questions: "When I go into a trance, what happens?"

"What we call a trance may be expressed as an altered state of consciousness, as opposed to the ordinary state in which we spend most of our waking life. With the concentration of your mind, you reach this altered state, which allows you to live another reality, different from the one you know in your normal state."

"Is it like in the Candomblé, the African cult in which the mediums receive the spirits?"

"No, it is completely different. Candomblé is also an altered state of consciousness, but in it, the medium is dominated by the spirit. It is like being the horse of the spirit. Sometimes, when the medium recovers the ordinary state of consciousness, he does not remember what happened when he was in trance. Our way is different. You are not dominated by the spirits, but you become associated with them as your partners. You are going to learn this in the next stages of your initiation process."

"Does this mean that, instead of the passive stance of the Candomblé's mediums, you have an active participation?"

"Exactly. You got the idea. That is the big difference."

Sensing my great curiosity, Tsiipré explained a few more things to me. "The function of Shaman is very old and exists in various cultures throughout all continents: Africa, America, Asia Australia and Europe, sometimes with different names, such as Shaman, Witch Doctor, or even Magician. The name Pajé is more common in South America."

"Is it true that Shamans existed in the old civilizations?"

"Sure! Perhaps this is one of the oldest activities in the world, which exists since the time of hunting and collecting, before the advent of agriculture. The figure of the priest appeared in the agricultural society, but the Shaman already existed."

"In a certain sense, isn't the priest also a Shaman?"

"There is a fundamental difference between the two. The priest represents a religion. He does not necessarily have a direct experience of Kauaí-Açú or, if you like, of God. If you remember your Bible, the Old Testament has several passages where the prophets speak directly to God. Moses is an example. In the New Testament, the communication is through the intermediation of the Church, of a priest."

"How can you explain that?"

"In the first centuries of the Christian era, the Church needed to consolidate itself. It fought vigorously the Gnostics, precisely because they maintained the possibility of direct communication with the Superior Beings, as often occurred in the Old Testament. In assuring the monopoly of direct conversation with God, the Church became much stronger. It was an indispensable intermediary for the people to know what were God's instructions and directions."

"Do the Shamans also speak with God?"

"Not only us, but many sacred men, both in the East and in the West, can also speak with God. Even in the Catholic Church, certain mystics, like Saint John of the Cross, had this privilege. In a state of deep meditation, you establish a direct contact with God. This is the primary objective of meditation."


One morning I woke up, as always with the chorus of birds and squeal of the monkeys. On that day, I decided to go on a longer walk and explore the margins of the Rio Grande. It was a three-hour walk. I´d been there with Uakaú, but never alone.

As I reached the river, I saw a boat approaching with three men. They saw me as well, and rowed to the margin. As we met, the man who seemed to be the chief, spoke to me:

"My name is John. I'm surprised to find a white man in this area. I've never seen you around here. Are you an employee of FUNAI?"

I knew the Kauauá didn't want to have any contact with the so-called civilized man. I decided to fool them. I mentioned the first name that came to my mind. "My name is William. I'm not from FUNAI. I'm an Army lieutenant on a special mission here, living for a while with the Kauauá to get to know the region better. Brasília is very much concerned with the felling of trees. If you know anything about that, please let me know."

The trick worked. When I said I was from the Army, they looked startled. I noticed a certain fear in John's eyes.

"How did you come so far?"

The question disturbed me a little. I said: "In the Army, particularly on special missions, we like to ask, not to answer questions."

After this rebuke, John said good-bye. The men got into their boat and proceeded downriver. I decided to cut short my exploration and go back to the village, to tell Tsiipré the news.

"Tsiipré, I met a certain John today in the Rio Grande."

"This guy is no good. He only wants to cut our trees. His business is illegal lumbering. Be careful, he is a killer."

"I think he is going to respect me, as I said that I was Lieutenant William, from the Army, on a special mission."

"Yes, as long as you do not interfere with his business. Be careful. We must let Kaniuá know this."

We went together to see the Chief, and told him the whole story. Kaniuá was worried.

Tsiipré continued the conversation. "These people are getting nearer and nearer. The authorities are tightening the control over the timber, so the lumbermen are pushing farther inland."

"As I said I am of the Army, maybe they'll stay away from this area.

"Do not count on that. They are bad people and will certainly bring trouble. We must be careful," said Kaniuá.

> Jesus says: The one who seeks should not cease seeking until he finds. And when he finds, he will be dismayed. And when he is dismayed he will be astonished. And he will be king over the All.
>
> The Gospel of Thomas – saying 2

## Chapter 15 - The Gold Cave

After my morning meditation, I looked for Uakaú to take a walk. I couldn't find him, so I decided to go alone. After walking for two hours, I came to the banks of the Rio Grande. I sat on the ground, looking at the flowing water and thinking about my life. When would I be able to retrieve my memory? Whenever I asked Tsiipré, he evaded the question. After sitting there for some time, I decided to go back. I felt like taking a swim, but I had better do it in our lake. The water of the Rio Grande was muddy, and the current strong.

I was on my way back when it started raining heavily, as is common in the region. I ran for shelter under a tree, where I saw a beautiful blue bird, with a bright yellow chest, hiding in a pile of dry woody limbs. Moving closer, I saw that the limbs disguised the entrance to a cave. I went in for cover, and I saw that the cave was illuminated from above, by a sort of natural chimney. In the midst of the cave, there was a small pond, fed by a fountain.

I was surprised by the beauty of this cave, enhanced by the gentle light coming from the top. I leaned against the wall, and felt a spike in my back. As I looked, I was astonished to see that I was leaning against nuggets and lumps of metal.

I had just discovered a gold mine! It should be worth a fortune and might make our village rich. I returned home quickly, anxious to tell Tsiipré about my finding. He was surprised to see me back so soon: "I was not expecting you this early."

"I have some incredible news to tell you. I discovered a gold mine that may make our tribe rich."

"I know about the mine." He said without any emotion. His indifference astonished me. We had a fortune in our hands and Tsiipré was so cool?

"Do you know where it is?" I asked.

"Sure. A cave near the mountain, in the opposite margin of the lake. I found it some time ago."

"But ... why is it not being explored?"

"That's not good. I disguised the entrance of the cavern with some branches."

"It could change the life of our people."

"Change our life? For better or worse?"

"The Kauauá could get rich."

"What would happen to the Kauauá if we were rich?"

"Well ... you could buy an airplane, make a landing field nearby, build a tourist hotel in this lovely area. You can do so many things with money, all you want."

"Not all. But what shall we want? You, yourself, said you feel like in a paradise. Can money make this area a better paradise?"

"Well..."

"What would tourists do here? Many tourists, a lot of hunting, a lot of fishing. To what extent would the paradise remain as such?"

"But..."

"I lived with the white people until I was twenty-two. The priests wanted me to make a career in the church. They thought that I could convert many Indians. However, the life of the white man never attracted me. It is an empty life, with lots of stress. That is why gold is so important to the white people. You will never buy happiness accumulating material goods."

I listened attentively to Tsiipré. I already admired him for his wisdom about life, and there was always something to learn from him.

Tsiipré continued: "How many of us would become adapted to the white man's culture?"

I kept looking at him, without any answer. He went on: "Perhaps I would, if I had no choice, but I can assure you that most of our people would be destroyed. Remember, we had this kind of experience in the past. The old Chief Kautá, my father, brought our group to this remote area to get away from the white civilization that was ruining us. He was himself struggling not to fall victim of some of the white men vices and diseases. He won the battle, got out of the stinking hole, and saved our people. This was not easy, and many fell by the wayside."

"Tsiipré, you have to admit that the white man is getting closer and closer. What shall we do?"

Tsiipré didn't take notice of my remark. He continued: "This reminds me of the story about the American millionaire who used to go every year to a Caribbean island for a holiday of fishing. His Guide and companion was a local fisherman, who became his friend. He thought the fisherman was smart and invited him to come to the United States to work for him. "You come to work for me and you will make a lot of money."

"And what am I going to do with all the money?"

"We'll come here for our holidays and spend one whole month just fishing."

"Today I fish all year round and have fun all year round. Why should I work eleven months so I can fish for one month?"

What Tsiipré was saying made a lot of sense. But I also had a point. Before I could state it, he continued: "And what's more. Do you believe that we would really be owners of the mine? Do you believe that the white men would leave this kind of wealth in the hands of the Indians? Don't you think that the politicians would somehow appropriate the mine for themselves? We would have no choice but to turn the mine over to them, dead or alive."

"If you are rich, you can better protect your land."

"The best protection for our community will be the demarcation of our land. The delimitation of the area was made four years ago but despite my efforts, bureaucracy keeps thwarting the process and we are still waiting for the official act. If it becomes known that there is gold here, we will never get our demarcation approved."

"Well ..."

"I am going to ask you something. Do not mention your finding to anyone here. Just a few Indians know about the mine. Not all see the problem as Kaniuá and I do. Not all have suffered in the hands of the white men. Let us not test them with such a temptation."

That made me think for a moment. I'd been so excited, believing that I would help to improve the life of the Kauauá, and now I found that it may not be quite so. At least Tsiipré had a different opinion, although I was not entirely convinced.

No doubt Tsiipré's reasoning was solid. But was it unquestionable? I agreed with him only in part. The weakness in the argument was that the Indians would not be able to stay away from the white man forever.

Whenever in my walks I went by the mine, I couldn't help but think about all that fortune, lying idle underground, and how it could be used for the benefit of the Kauauá.

I admit I might be oversimplifying the problem, perhaps having a waking dream. But I also reasoned that we wouldn't be rid from the loggers so easily. Maybe with gold, we could get some officials in Brasília to speed our process of land demarcation. I realized that I couldn't persuade the Kauauá to build an ecological lodge without first getting Tsiipré's support. I decided to bring up the idea on another occasion. And this opportunity came up one day on which we were walking in the forest, searching for medicinal herbs.

"Tsiipré, do you remember our conversation the other day?"

"About the gold mine. I thought I had convinced you."

"Well … I think your reasoning was logical, but I see a weak point in it. It is impossible to ensure that we'll be isolated from the white man forever. You've admitted that yourself, in creating the school for the Indians. I would like to get back, and discuss with you a bit more the idea of building an ecological lodge in the lands of the Kauauá, We could accept only selected people as guests. I'm aware I still have a lot to learn about the Indians' problems, and I need to have a better understanding of your objections."

"There are many objections. First, your understanding of selected people is somewhat theoretical. There have been cases where anthropologists created great problems for Indian communities that they intended to help. One thing you will learn with time is that man's mind is a very complicated business, and a university degree neither guarantees a good mind nor a good character. It provides only theoretical knowledge of a higher level."

"But wouldn't an anthropologist be better than a guy without any instruction?"

"That is where you are wrong. Do not be so elitist. There are anthropologists and anthropologists, just as there are uneducated men fully conscious of the Indian problem. Your view is distorted. The ecological hotel has been tried out in the Bananal Island. The hotel was built on the land of the Carajás. It was closed because of the conflicts it brought."

"How to protect ourselves from the loggers? And from the gold diggers? How to ensure that the white men will not invade the lands of the Kauauá?"

"I know that gold is the white man's undoing, but with the demarcation of our land we will at least have the possibility of better protecting ourselves.

One morning, I woke up earlier than usual. Tsiipré was already awake and meditating. When he saw me get out of my hammock, he asked me whether I wanted to start the second stage of my initiation as a Shaman. That was all I wanted. I had already repeated the first training for many days, and was quite familiar with my way to the inner world.

"In this exercise your aim is to find your Protective Spirit, your Guide. You are going to repeat the previous stage until you reach the gate of the lower world. This time you will enter, and take a walk, paying close attention to everything you see."

"Any special recommendation?"

"If you meet any Jurupari, run away or hide. You are not prepared to fight with them yet. After a while, when your intuition guides you, sit down on a pleasant place, and mentally call your Protective Spirit."

I was anxious to do everything right. I had lots of questions in my mind. "When I meet my Protective Spirit, how shall I behave? Will he be able to take me in search of my memory? Can I ask him to do that?"

Tsiipré laughed. He gestured with both hands for me to be patient. "You still have to go over many stages to retrieve your memory. Concentrate on following the instructions carefully, and do not think about anything else. Everything will come on its time. When your Guide arrives, greet him, and ask for his help."

"Help to find my memory?"

"No! No! Again, do not be so anxious. Ask help for your spiritual development. Stay with him as long as you wish, and afterwards, come back.

I followed Tsiipré's instructions. I started my meditation, walked to the cave, dove through the spring, crossed the entrance and began to wander in the inner world. Looking up I again saw the sky full of balls, shining like stars, emitting a strong silver blue light. A divine music, chanted by angels, delighted my ears. I scented a fragrance of the rose, but there was something extra that made it even better.

After walking for a while in the inner world, and admiring its beauty, I sat under a big tree near a lake and called my Protective Spirit. An old man with the face of a Chinese appeared before me.

"Good morning. I'm Eagle."

"I'm ShuoKua, and I came to help you. But I will not call you Eagle. For me, you are William."

"Is this my real name?

"Yes, it is."

I was happy to eventually know my real name. Exactly the very first that occurred to me when I met John, in the banks of the Rio Grande.

I looked carefully at ShuoKua. I had the immediate impression that I knew him in other lives. His name was also familiar. I searched my memory but to my dismay, I couldn't cross my black hole.

He looked at me deep in the eyes, a kind and piercing look. I liked him instantly, and felt that I could trust him. I didn't remember my grandfather, but if I could choose, ShuoKua would be my choice. I couldn't resist asking the question that was my torment. "You know I've lost my memory. Can you help me find it?"

"I also know that Tsiipré told you not to be so anxious. I am going to help you find your memory when you are prepared for it."

"Very well. I think I am. Shall we try it now?"

"Be calm, my son. I will help you when the time comes. When you are well prepared. And one of your preparations is to learn how to be calm. Your anxiety will lead you nowhere."

"It's quite difficult trying to live with a black hole in your life."

"Do you believe in God's designs?"

"Sure."

"Then, think that your woes may have a purpose. You cannot cross a river before you arrive at its margins."

Metaphors. Something buried deep down into my mind wanted to tell me something about metaphors, but I didn't know what it was. After we talked for a while, he stood up and suggested that it was time for me to go back. I thanked him for his presence, and said that I would be in great need of his help and guidance. I bowed with my hands together, in the oriental way, and returned to the entrance of the cave. When I arrived at the hut, Tsiipré was there and asked me how the exercise had come out.

"It was fine. I met my Guide and we had a very good rapport."

"Splendid! I am glad you have had such good results right at the first meeting."

"My Guide is a great person. He must have a lot to teach me, and he promised to help retrieve my memory."

"You will continue in your daily meditations to go back to your inner world and talk to your Guide. But I repeat: the only important recommendation is that if you meet a Jurupari, run away from him. You are not prepared for a confrontation yet. That day will come."

"Since you are saying that I've done well, can we advance to the next stage?"

"Easy! If you do not want to listen to me, at least follow your Guide's advice. Be calm! You want everything in haste."

"Well ... You know, my black hole!"

"Learn to live with it, being completely aware that you are working to solve your problem. Go on meeting with your Protective Spirit. I want you to do that every day, during your meditation. At the right time, you will move to the next stage. In the meantime, talk as much as you can with your Guide."

"That will be fine with me, I liked him very much."

"Then listen to his advice. I know that it is difficult for you to control your anxiety. You must have been born in Aries."

"Are you also familiar with astrology?"

"I have studied it a little. As you are hasty, I think you were born under Aries."

I had to laugh. "I don't mean to press you, Tsiipré, but when you think I'm ready, I'd like to go ahead. My black hole hurts. I'm willing to run the risks."

With a mocking tone, Tsiipré said: "You do not mean to press me? Is this not a little pressure?" And turning serious, he continued: "You are going to run the risks, sure, but only the ones that are necessary."

"By the way, call me William from now on. ShuoKua told me that's my real name."

"Very good! Some progress."

I continued to pay my daily visits to the inner world, and to meet with ShuoKua. I was very happy with my meditation, and I was eager to learn whatever would bring me nearer the objective of retrieving my memory.

In one of my fishing trips with Uakaú, we were walking towards the Rio Grande. It was a beautiful morning and the temperature was mild. We had the company of four children. Uakaú was fond of children, and four of them, aged between eight and twelve, were fishing with us. I turned to Uakaú and said: "This was a fruitful day. We caught many fishes, and the children had a good time. The village will eat a lot of fish today."

"Look!" said Katu, pointing ahead.

I saw two white men. We were going to speak to them, but when they saw us, they got their guns, and fired at us.

Uakaú shouted: "Back to the trees."

The bullet hit the smallest boy, the grandson of Pokrã, one of the Wise Old Men of the tribe.

Uakaú shot an arrow. The man who fired the gun was hit, and fell down. The other man fired his gun. Uakaú sent another arrow that hit his left arm.

Seeing his companion lying on the ground, as if dead, the man ran into the woods and escaped. I wanted to go after him, but Uakaú stopped me. "Let's be careful. He may be around. We will go after him, but very cautiously."

We waited a while, to make sure that the man wasn't ambushing us. Uakaú said: "Wait here." I was not armed and Uakaú asked me to watch over the boys. Uakaú was the first to get near the fallen man. He quickly found out that the man wasn't breathing.

The boy was bleeding in the stomach. Uakaú took him in his arms and went racing to the village. I tried to follow him as fast as I could. The other boys followed us.

When I met Tsiipré, he had already started to examine the boy. I saw in his face that the case was difficult. "The wound looks bad. The bullet hit the belly and the bleeding must be stopped," Tsiipré said.

While Tsiipré was busy with the hurt boy, I returned with Uakaú to the site of the shooting. "Why would they want to attack us?" I asked.

"I do not understand their attitude either. It is not common to meet white men in our area. We do not like to be close to them, but we never get to the point of shooting at each other. Very strange, indeed."

## The Amazon Shaman

"What could they be doing around here?"

"I don't know. Let us take a look at the dead man. I believe I have seen him with John. Maybe we can get some clue to solve this mystery."

We went back to the place of the encounter. When we examined the body, all became clear. His pockets were full of gold nuggets. Surely, they did not want us to know they had found the gold mine. If we had gotten nearer, we could have seen their stuffed pockets.

"What shall we do with the body?" I asked.

"I think we should hide it. It will be difficult to explain this accident without letting many others know about the gold."

"If we do not mention the gold nuggets, how to explain the reaction of the white men?"

"Let us not worry about this now. We will talk to Tsiipré later. Let us take care of the body."

"Should we bury him?"

"We are near the Rio Grande. If we throw the body into the river, the piranhas will take care of it. The bones will sink the bottom."

We emptied the pockets of the corpse, and returned the nuggets to the gold cave. Then, we dragged the body to the Rio Grande, put it on a boat, and rowed as far as the spot where Uakaú knew there were many piranhas. Before dumping the corpse in the river, Uakaú made a deep cut in one of its legs. The corpse had been in the sun, and was still warm because of the high temperature. It started bleeding. As soon as it was put into the water, a swarm of piranhas, attracted by the scent of blood, attacked it, and before long there were only the bones on their way to the river bottom.

We returned to the village, anxious to know whether Tsiipré had been successful with the boy. On our way home we went talking about the other man that had escaped. "He must also have taken some nuggets," I said. "Shouldn't we try to go after him?"

"Too late." said Uakaú. "We will not catch him. He has a good head start.

"This bandit that escaped can cause a big problem. The news of gold in the lands of the Kauauá will spread like fire in dry grass."

I went looking for Tsiipré. The boy was not doing well, and he was busy taking care of him. He suggested that we discussed the case latter.

The village was in total chaos. Everybody wanted to know what happened. Kaniuá called the Council of the Wise Old Men, and practically the entire Kauauá population was present to hear the news.

> For the love of money is the root of all evil: which while some coveted after, they have erred from the faith, and pierced themselves through with many sorrows.
>
> But thou, O man of God, flee these things; and follow after righteousness, godliness, faith, love, patience, meekness.
>
> Paul, apostle - 1 Timothy Chapter 6-10-11

## Chapter 16 – A Rich Man

My God! I barely escaped. This pain in my arm... but I'm alive. It was really tough to pull out the arrow. The bandage I made with my shirt helps to stop the bleeding. Now, I have to get the hell out of here, before these Indians get to me. Poor Jake! Just now that he was going to be rich. Why did those Indians have to show up right at that time? Why did Jake shoot the Indians? If he hadn't done this stupid thing, they wouldn't have suspected we found a gold mine. I'll have to think up a good explanation for my wound when I arrive in Formoso. But at the moment, that's not my problem; now, I must get away before those damn Indians catch me.

I walked fast, in a roundabout way to sidetrack them, and reached the safety of the Rio Grande, where we had hidden John's boat. The pain on my left arm was unbearable. The boat was faster going downstream, and I got at Formoso more quickly to get help.

In the village, before caring for my arm, I went by my house, dug a hole in the backyard, and hid the nuggets. The pain in my arm made it difficult, but I had to do it. My wife didn't see anything. Then, I went to see Joseph, the pharmacist.

He said: "Ben, man, what's this that you got for me now?"

"The Indians are mad at us. John wants to take timber from their land, and they have been shooting at any white man they see around there."

"This is something new. These Indians have never been aggressive."

"Times are changing."

As we spoke, Joseph was cleaning and disinfecting my wound, and suturing it. I stood firm. When the pain increased, I would think of my gold mine, and the rich man I would be.

Joseph said: "John spends most of his time in Manaus. When he comes here, I'm going to talk to him. I think he should not provoke the Kauauá. There are many other places for logging."

"But don't tell him I've been wounded. To tell the truth, I went over there without asking his permission. I just wanted to have an idea of the kinds of trees that existed in the area."

"Didn't you go with Jake?"

This question caught me by surprise. Maybe Joseph noticed my hesitation. I said: "I left Jake not far from here, a little up river. I thought he had already returned."

"What was he doing there?"

"I don't know. He said he was looking for land to plant some crops."

"Funny! He has a large backyard at his home, and does not cultivate anything."

I thought it would be better to keep quiet, not to complicate matters even more. I just shrugged, indicating that it was none of my business, and that was the end of our talk.

I'll have to be extra careful now. Go to Manaus and sell a few nuggets, not many, to avoid curiosity. Luckily, there's a boat going down tomorrow.

I'd never sold any gold. I'd always lived with the miserable wage John paid me. But luck had decided that I should be rich, and I couldn't miss this opportunity. I didn't even know

## The Amazon Shaman

where to sell the gold, and, on the boat, I struck up a conversation with the captain.

"Some guys are really lucky. Can you imagine? A friend of mine just found some gold nuggets. He wants to sell them, to make some money, and is waiting for John to come up to Formoso."

"Is that right? Where did he find the gold?"

"He doesn't say. He just mentioned some place very far away, close to the border of Colombia. He was very vague. If he found a mine, he wouldn't tell anyone where it was."

"John is going to cheat him, no doubt. He bargains hard with everybody," said the Captain.

"But where could he sell his nuggets?"

"The Colonel likes to buy gold, and he's got more money than John. He's made John's fortune, giving him the FSTC for free."

"In Formoso, people say that the Colonel is John's father."

"It makes sense. Only that can explain the Colonel's kindness. He has never given anything to anyone."

Arriving in Manaus, I went straight to the Colonel's office, a large building in the center of the city. A tall negro stopped me at the door. I was wearing my best suit. Even so, he gave me a hard look, as if not quite approving what he saw, and asked: "What do you want here?"

I didn't want to let the man know that I had gold in my pocket. But if I didn't, he wouldn't let me in. I decided to take the risk. I showed him one of the nuggets, and said: "I've heard that the Colonel likes to buy gold."

He opened his eyes wide, with amazement and greed. Then, he grabbed a telephone on the counter, and spoke to someone, but I couldn't hear what he said. He called a boy, and told him to take me to the Colonel's office.

We went up the elevator. The boy asked me to wait on a sofa, and spoke to a lady in a front desk.

What a luxurious place! How can one have so much money! And people say he was poor when he started. With my gold mine, I would also be rich. It's a pity that Jake has died. He was a nice guy and we were good partners. His family was big, five small children, and this gold would be important to them. As soon as I put my hands on some money, I'll help his family. They will think it odd, but I have to help them. How to explain my gesture without talking about the mine? I don't know, but I will find a way. After all, Jake was in this business with me. It is fair to give a generous portion of my gains to his family.

The lady called me and asked me to go in. I had never met the Colonel, only knew him by reputation. I entered his room, still dazed by the sumptuous place.

He asked me: "I understand you want to sell gold."

"Yes, Mister Colonel."

I had with me two nuggets, and when I drew them from my pocket his eyes shone.

"Where did you find these?"

"A friend of mine asked me to sell them for him. He didn't say where he got them."

"Ah! And where does he live?"

"In Formoso."

"I lived there many years ago. I never knew that there was gold around there."

"I didn't know either. My friend said that he brought them from far away. Close to the Colombian border."

"Has he got more?"

"He said that maybe he would get a few more next week."

The Colonel took a small scale from a cabinet, weighed the nuggets and said: "I can pay ten thousand dollars for them."

Never in my life had I dreamed of so much money. John used to pay me fifty dollars a month. This was low, even below the legal minimum wage. Since I had no other job opportunity, I had to accept John's trickery. Take it or leave it. Now, in one shot, I was getting a fortune, something like two hundred monthly salaries.

I knew that the Colonel would try to take advantage of me. So I answered: "Colonel, these nuggets are worth a lot more. I would like to sell them to you, because I know you are a serious businessman. I may have more of them in a few days, and I want to do business with someone I trust, like you. But I would not sell them for less than the triple of what you are offering me. Otherwise, my friend, the owner of the gold, would be mad at me."

The Colonel thought for a while, and said: "The price of gold has declined in the international market."

"Well, maybe I should offer this gold to John. He has become very rich since he got your company."

I noticed that the Colonel didn't like my mentioning John. The rumor around was that he had stolen the FSTC from the Colonel. He thought for an instant and gave in.

"All right. I'll pay you twenty thousand because I'm interested in establishing a commercial relationship with you. I want you to bring me all the gold your friend can get."

I knew that if I bargained harder, I could get more. But it was enough money already. I was about to put my hands on more than three years salary, and I had a lot more gold in my backyard, not including the mine. I was a rich man, and I wanted to be in good terms with the Colonel. So I accepted his offer.

"Do you want to be paid in dollars or reals?"

"For this first batch, reals."

The Colonel moved a painting in the wall, opened a safe behind it and gave me the money. I tried to act businesslike but I could hardly contain my joy. The money I had just received represented my freedom from having to work for John. I stood up to leave, and the Colonel added: "Your friend seems to have found a gold mine that can be very valuable. But he will need capital to explore it efficiently. Tell him I'm willing to form an association with him, to explore the mine. I'll provide the capital, and we'll share the results fifty-fifty.

This could be an interesting proposal. But I was afraid that after knowing the location of the mine, the Colonel might betray me, or even kill me. I shouldn´t be too ambitious. Why want more, if only two nuggets gave me so much money? Better not risk it. I said: "I'll talk to him about your proposal, Colonel, and I'll give you an answer when I return to Manaus, possibly one week from today."

Leaving the Colonel's office with that bundle of money, I felt like floating in the clouds. What would I do with so much money? Better clothes for myself, my wife and my son and also gifts for them. Maybe a large fridge for my wife. She would love it. And a big-screen color television.

First, I set aside some money to give to Jake's wife. Then, I went to some fashionable stores in the city, where I had never been before. I bought a lot of things, yet spent very little of my new fortune.

A FSTC boat was to depart the next day up the Rio Grande. I bought tickets for myself and my cargo. During the trip, I was thinking hard about the story I would have to tell in Formoso.

> The Self is a part of you, it is within you. It is the divine inside you. As you absorb additional material, as you become conscious of more parts of the Self, you are in the process of getting conscious of yourself. You are in your journey of getting to know yourself.
>
> Roberto Lima Netto
> The Little Prince for Grown-ups.

## Chapter 17 - The Objects of Power

The meeting was to start in a few minutes. The members of the Council were arriving, and practically all the people of the tribe converged to the place. They were all curious about the matter to be discussed.

Before the meeting started, I called Uakaú aside and said: "I think we shouldn't mention the gold."

"I can't tell a lie to the Council."

"I'm not suggesting that you lie. Just skip this part for a while."

"This is an indirect lie."

"Think about this. If we mention the gold, everybody will know about the mine, and that is what Tsiipré is trying to avoid."

Uakaú didn't seem convinced, but finally he agreed, especially because Tsiipré was taking care of the boy, and would not be present at the meeting. We didn't have time to speak to him, so I managed to convince Uakaú.

Uakaú told the case in almost all the details, skipping only the part about the gold. Without it, the councilmen didn't understand the white men's reaction. I saw that Kaniuá looked suspicious about our story. I think he guessed that there was more to it. Addressing Uakaú, he asked: "Why would they shoot at you?"

Uakaú was momentarily uneasy, and I answered: "Maybe they thought we were going to shoot at them. They probably know that the Kauauá do not want the white man to take our timber."

"Did you make some aggressive move?"

"Absolutely not. As soon as they saw us, they started shooting."

"Very strange, indeed," said Kaniuá.

Kaniuá was the most worried one. He was not buying our story, but we could not tell it in full not to alarm the community. Even without mentioning the gold, the incident was bad enough. Nobody could understand the reason for the white men's attitude.

It was night when the meeting ended. Uakaú and I walked to Tsiipré's hut and asked him to go for a walk with us. He wouldn't be away from his hut because the boy was in critical condition, under Tatainim's care.

Uakaú repeated what he had reported to the Council, and Tsiipré said: "I have a feeling that there is more to this than you have told. My guess is that we have a bigger problem in our hands."

"You're right, Tsiipré. We are going to tell you the whole story, and you will understand why it was not presented in full to the Council. Let's go where we can have some privacy. I do not want to risk being overheard on what we have to tell you."

"I have to stay nearby, because the boy's situation is difficult. Shall we walk in the direction of the lake, where we will be isolated, but not too far away?"

Near the lake, we sat on some rocks, and I said: "The two white men found the mine. Their pockets were full of golden nuggets."

Tsiipré was startled: "That explains their aggressive reaction."

"Exactly, but they were two. One is dead, but the other escaped. And he knows about the mine."

"It will be difficult to keep the gold mine in secrecy." said Tsiipré.

"We have to worry about the man who escaped," I said. "He might have leaked our secret and before long, a lot of white people will know about the Kauauá's gold."

The moonlight on Tsiipré's face showed his concern. He spoke: "Gold, always gold. Man's doom."

I said: "We are sitting on a powder keg. If those two found the mine, others may also find it."

"Since the mine was discovered, I've had nightmares because of this situation. I think we will have to leave it in the hands of Kauaí-Açú," said Tsiipré.

"What shall we do now? We have to tell Kaniuá the full story," said Uakaú, who had been quiet so far, probably feeling sort of guilty for not having told the whole truth to the Council.

"Of course we will tell Kaniuá. But let us think a bit more before we do that. The white man who escaped had his pockets full of nuggets. It's only natural that he will want to get another supply. Therefore, he will likely keep quiet about the location of the mine."

"You're right, Tsiipré."

"But let's not get excited" continued Tsiipré, "This does not solve our problem. Such a secret is hard to keep for long. Think about it. He will probably take the nuggets to sell in Manaus. If he is smart, he will sell one or two nuggets at a time. Even so, when he comes back, the people at the village will see that he has plenty of money. Will he keep quiet about the secret on his first drinking spree?"

"Your reasoning is perfect. Our problem remains serious, but we'll have a few days before things blow up. In the meantime, we´ll have to work out a solution," I said.

"If there is one," said Uakaú.

We continued our conversation, each one with their suggestions, trying to minimize the problem. I said: "I think we should build a stone wall, blocking the entry to the mine. The man who escaped probably has not had a clear view of the entrance of the mine. After all, it may be the first time he got there."

"A wall will be more visible than the foliage cover we have there. You are a city man, who doesn't know how to recognize tracks and signs. It would be easy for those who live in the forest to spot the wall and suspect that it was hiding something valuable."

"Is our single option to rely on our luck, which, in this case, is not helping?" I asked. I couldn't agree that there was nothing to do. So, I suggested: "How about putting sentries in the entrance to the mine?"

"You don't know the Indians. They are not a disciplined army, and in a short time they would lose interest. Besides, a sentry attracts even more attention. Relax. Leave it in the hands of Kauaí-Açú."

"And look!" said Uakaú, "If we use sentries, the next day the whole tribe will know about the mine."

Next day, after sleeping over the problem, I went to see Tsiipré. "Tsiipré, I have an idea that I think you'll like."

Tsiipré was not inclined to talk. The boy was worse, and this was his concern at the moment. I went to see Uakaú. He had problems, too. Pinuim had spread the rumor that Uakaú was to blame for the boy´s injury. He was telling everyone that Uakaú should take better care of the little Indians.

## The Amazon Shaman

The parents of the boy were furious at Uakaú. Pokrã, the grandfather, was trying to calm them down, but he also thought that Uakaú was to blame for what happened.

Only at the end of the day I, had a chance to talk to Tsiipré. I was very anxious to tell him about my new idea to protect the mine. In the evening, I managed to take him for a walk by the lake, together with Uakaú. I said: "I think I have an idea on how to hide the mine."

"With the boy in a critical condition, this is a minor problem for me at the moment," answered Tsiipré.

"Since there is nothing Uakaú and I can do for the boy, we'll try to solve the other problem, if you approve the idea."

"All right," Tsiipré sighed, "what is the idea?"

"First, we'll take all visible nuggets off the walls of the cave, and hide them in a hole to be dug inside the mine. Second, we'll cover with clay all the veins that are still apparent."

"Sounds like a good idea," said Tsiipré.

"There's more. Most important of all is to cover, with tree branches, the chimney through which the sunlight enters the cave. This way, whoever goes into the cave won't see much. Without a torch or a flashlight, no one can see anything. Even so, the artificial light is not as good as natural light," I said.

"I think it's a good idea. You and Uakaú could take care of this task."

Next day, we went out early to the mine. The chorus of the birds filled my ears. The sun was rising. We entered the mine, and found several nuggets already extracted and piled up on the ground of the cave. The rogues had extracted much more than they could carry, and this would make our work easier.

Pulling out the more apparent nuggets was easy. We made a hole at the end of the cave, filled it with those nuggets and with all the ones that we had found piled in the cave. We buried a small fortune that day. Disguising the gold veins was more difficult, but we did it by making a clay mixture with water from the small pond inside the cave, and carefully plastering the veins. Then, we covered the chimney with dry branches to block the light. The whole job was quite satisfactory. Of course, all this work would not protect the mine from the white man who had already been there. We could only hope that God, or Kauaí-Açú in Tsiipré's words, would watch over us.

We worked hard without stopping until late, and I was very tired.

I asked Tsiipré to move to the next stage of my initiation. I had already made several incursions into the inner world, always with success. That night, Tsiipré said that next morning we would be starting the third stage. . He asked me to wake up before daybreak. I was anxious, and it took me a long time to fall asleep.

The next day I was up before sunrise. Tsiipré spoke: "The objective of this stage of your initiation is to increase your personal power. For this purpose, you will seek objects of power. You will go out alone through the forest, without eating and will grab whatever object that catches your attention and that you think can be of help to you. Pick them up and put them in a bag. They should not be big objects. The purpose is to fill a small bag that you can wear as an amulet tied to your neck. Following Tsiipré's instructions, I rambled all day through the forest, eating nothing, drinking only water, and gathering objects that attracted me, such as stones, shells, and small pieces of roots with strange shapes. Tsiipré had given me a bag made of the skin of a jaguatirica, a small leopard cat, native of the Amazon forest. As I picked the objects up, I put them in the bag. I arrived home late, very hungry and feeling weak. But Tsiipré didn't let me eat. He told me to sit down and start meditating. He sat beside me, and helped me by chanting his mantra and playing the maraca.

According to his instructions, as soon as I went into trance, I should return to my inner world, call my Protecting Spirit and, together with him, select the objects, among the ones I had gathered in the forest, that were to compose my amulet.

I returned by the road with which I was so familiar, went to the place where I used to meet my Guide, sat cross-legged on the floor and called him.

ShuoKua appeared: "You want my help to select your amulets, don´t you?"

"It's difficult to hide anything from you."

"Of course. I already told you that I live within you."

I didn't quite understand that statement, but made a note of it in my memory, to clear it up in the future. I wanted to proceed with the selection of the objects, following ShuoKua's instructions. It took longer than I expected.

ShuoKua said: "You must concentrate on each object at a time, trying to feel its vibration."

I spent some time choosing about half of the objects and discarding the others. I went back to the hut and told Tsiipré what I had done. He was very satisfied, but although I was hungry, he suggested I shouldn´t eat, and should spend the night in meditation.

My empty stomach was uncomfortable, but as I went deeper into trance, I no longer felt hungry, and I reached a very deep trance, one that I had not attained in previous attempts.

**Roberto Lima Netto**

> It is not your passing inspiration or brilliant ideas so much as your everyday mental habits that control your life.
>
> Paramahansa Yogananda
> Spiritual Diary

## Chapter 18 - The Face of Danger

As I awoke that morning, I found Tsiipré worried.

"How is the boy doing?" I asked him.

"Not well. I cannot seem to make him get better. I am afraid to lose him."

"How about his parents? Are they calmer?"

"No. The family is not only blaming Uakaú, but is also unhappy with my work. They are saying that, since you have become my apprentice, my healing ability has decreased. They blame you too."

There was no news about the mine, but the small group of people who knew that the white man had discovered it was worried. None of that prevented me from taking my daily walks. Only meditation offered me more relaxation than those walks throughout the forest. Occasionally, Uakaú would come with me, but I'd rather walk alone on these days, musing about my life and thinking of a way to shed some light into my black hole. I used to keep this routine because this helped me forget the gold, the powder keg we were sitting on.

My day started early, with meditation and the Shaman training prescribed by Tsiipré. I was determined to become proficient in Shamanism, to be able to get my memory back. The sooner, the better.

Every day, rain or shine, after meditating for a couple of hours, I would go out for a quick plunge in the lake and a walk in the forest. It usually rained in the afternoon, but sometimes the rain came in the morning, giving the walks a marvelous sensation of freedom. How could I explain this sensation? Unfortunately, no answer from my black hole. Perhaps as a boy, my mother didn't let me play out in the rain.

I would walk for some three hours, stop for a frugal lunch of fruits near the lake, and come back to swimming and relaxing for another couple of hours. These were perfect holidays, except for the black hole that I carried in my head. That was a heavy load to bear. Several months had gone by, and my memory was still a vacuum. Sometimes, I seemed to be making a little progress, on the verge of remembering something significant of my past, but an invisible barrier stood in the way of any advance. Other than that, I was happy.

In my walks, I always opened different paths and explored new areas, so I acquired a good knowledge of the entire surrounding region. Tsiipré was teaching me to work with medicinal plants, and I always used these outings to gather some herbs for his stock.

One day I got lost, but guided by the sun, I walked west as far as the Rio Grande. Then, I started walking downriver, as I was sure that I would find a familiar place to show me the way home.

While on the trek, following the river downstream, I heard a strange noise. I cautiously approached its source. A group of white men was setting up a camp at the side of the Rio Grande. I was about to speak to them, but decided to investigate what they were up to, before exposing myself. What I saw left me worried. It looked as if we would have to face more trouble, besides the gold problem.

I hurried home, looking for Tsiipré. I described what I had seen and asked: "What do you imagine they want to do here?"

"I wonder what it could be. Maybe they are looking for timber."

I couldn't agree with him: "I don't think so. It looked like an expensive operation. If it's timber, it's a big thing, and it will bring problems for us. I'm almost sure that timber is not what they want."

"What makes you think so?"

"They are using well equipped boats, with powerful engines. It's a professional operation. No resemblance to the amateurish John. Those guys won't be stopped easily," I said.

"No use to keep talking. Let us go there tomorrow and take a look."

The next morning Tsiipré, Uakaú and I left early. After a two-hour walk we arrived at the site, and hid ourselves among the trees. We saw seven men, one looking like the boss, and six others working, cutting down trees and bushes, opening up what seemed to be a landing strip. At a sign from Tsiipré, we withdrew quietly to a place we could talk without being overheard.

I said: "The boss speaks Spanish. They may be Colombians, and they would not be coming for timber."

"I agree with you. I have never heard of the need of a landing strip to carry timber. It floats downriver to where it is picked up. I guess we may have big trouble ahead," said Tsiipré.

Tsiipré was right. The problem was serious. Our new neighbors appeared to be in the business of drug refining, setting up a laboratory in a remote place, protected from the police. With the pressure increasing in Colombia, they might be seeking alternative bases of operations. From what we saw, they were trying to start operations in the Brazilian side of the Amazonian forest.

"These people will give us a lot of trouble," Uakaú said.

Tsiipré remarked: "The Government of Colombia, with American help, is fighting against the production of cocaine. The Medellin Cartel has been disbanded. Would they want now to establish a bridgehead in the Brazilian side of the jungle?"

"From what I've seen, there is nothing we can do to stop them. I bet they have modern weapons, and they know how to use them. Our warriors would not be a match for them," I said.

"The economic power of drug traffic," said Tsiipré, "dominates by fear or money a sizable part of the Government and the Justice in Colombia. If they come to Brazil, they will try to do the same here. Brazil will not be the only one to suffer. This country is much bigger than Colombia. The consequences will be terrible. Worldwide. There will be cheap cocaine for the addicts all over the world."

I was really scared, and eager to do something about it. But what could we do? However, we couldn't let those bandits get away with it. I said to Tsiipré: "Don't you think this operation can well be an experience to find out whether it's easier to operate in Brazil than it is in Colombia?"

"I have the same suspicion. The Brazilian forest area is much bigger than the one in Colombia. It is easier to keep out of sight here."

"We have to find a way of showing them that their operation won't be easy on this side."

"You are right, but how can we do it?"

"We can send a messenger to alert the Brazilian Army," I said.

"Not that. You know that the Kauauá do not want to have anything to do with the white men."

"But we cannot confront them without help."

## The Amazon Shaman

"We will see. I am nor discarding the Army's help, if we do not have other options. Anyway, it will take a long time for the army to come. Bureaucracy moves slowly. By then, the Colombians will be well settled and may have already fortified their camp."

"The army will have to do something. Better late than never."

"Will they believe us? They will probably submit the matter to Brasília and await instructions. In the case of the Kauauá´s land demarcation, my experience with the bureaucracy of the capital city is very discouraging."

Tsiipré was right, as always. But I couldn't stand the thought of doing nothing. We simply had to think up something.

I said: "We have to stop this project at its root. If we fail, the drug gang will spread their influence all over Brazil. They can put in their payroll legislators and magistrates, just as in Colombia."

"I agree," said Tsiipré. But to be honest, I have no idea how to deal with them. We will have to meditate and ask Kauaí-Açú for inspiration."

"I'll discuss this with ShuoKua, as soon as I can."

We returned to the village and went to see Kaniuá. After telling him the bad news, we began to discuss what to do.

Kaniuá said: "We have to force the white men out of here. I do not want to see our land full of drug people and the military fighting against them. I will call a meeting of the Council of Wise Old Men to decide what we should do.

Tsiipré said: "Expel the white men? This is easier said than done. This is a very well equipped group. These people are not amateurish like John."

Tsiipré was right. Maybe we could drive out the seven men, but they would come back. If we killed them, their friends would come with enough fury to destroy us. "We have to prepare a plan," I said, "and for this we must take a better look at the situation. After all, I work in strategic planning and can develop a line of action."

After I said this, I became aware, for the second time, of something of my past. So ... I used to work in strategic planning? Where? Again, I made an effort to see if more thoughts emerged from my past, to no avail. Nevertheless, I was happy at the sign that my memory might be back at any moment. With luck, soon.

It was peculiar that the opening of my black hole appeared whenever I was in a critical situation. Now, for example, either I found a way to force the drug gang's exit or all would be ruined. Would the Kauauá survive an encounter with the bandits? Would I be able to continue my lessons with Tsiipré? And my training? Without it I would never be able to find my memory.

Next day, Uakaú and I returned to our observation post. There were now thirteen people. Another boat had brought in these new men, and lots of more equipment of a kind that confirmed our suspicions about their plan to set up a cocaine lab. The construction of the landing strip was pretty advanced.

In addition to the problem of the gold, now we had another big, huge problem to face -- how to deal with the drug gang. Things were really becoming very difficult for the Kauauá and myself.

The only good news of the day was about Pokrã's grandson, who had regained consciousness and was getting better. But many Indians and their mothers still didn't trust Uakaú. Two days later, he invited some boys to go out with us to the forest, and their mothers wouldn't let them. Pinuim had done a good job of poisoning their minds. If the selection of the next chief were to be made now, he certainly would be chosen. Fortunately, Kaniuá was old, but in good health.

## The Amazon Shaman

That night, Tsiipré sat on the floor of his shack and began the preparations to go into trance. I mentally followed his monotonous chanting, and this helped me relax. I also entered into trance, and descended to my inner world, looking for ShuoKua. I wanted to get some advice from him for this new big crisis.

"I'm glad to see you, ShuoKua. I need some guidance. Can you help me with a good idea to solve the problem of the drug gang?"

"I can only help you to help yourself. You told me you do not understand this, but I am a part of you. I am your unconscious, that part of you that knows all because, at this level, there are no barriers to knowledge."

"Then, how shall we deal with the drug gang?"

"Let us think it over together. You have admitted that fighting them is unwise. The Kauauá's arrows are no match for the guns of the drug gang."

"That's true. No chance that we could fight against them and succeed. They can bring up lots of people and enough weaponry to devastate ten villages the size of the Kauauá."

"You have to force them out in a manner that they will not blame the Indians," said ShuoKua.

"This would be ideal. But how?"

"One way to solve a problem is to think about it before going to sleep. You may wake up full of inspiration the next day."

"For God's sake, I never get a direct answer from you."

"This piece of advice is very objective: sleep and dream. Before going to sleep, think about your problem. You have to create a situation that will drive the drug gang away, without involving the Indians. Think, and go to sleep."

"As easy as that?"

"For inspiration, I suggest that, before sleeping, you talk to Tsiipré, and learn about the tales and myths of the Indian tribes in the region. Learn all you can before sleeping, and do not limit yourself to the myths of the Kauauá."

"But ... how can these tales help me with my problem?"

"How? Why? Life doesn't have only a rational side. Wisdom, the principle of all things, encompasses much more than the rational."

"It's only that I don't understand how this may help me."

"Then, do not try to understand. The legends and myths of all peoples are but lessons of life, sometimes disguised as interesting little stories."

"Our situation is serious. Couldn't you be more specific in your instructions?"

"I am giving you precise instructions. Think, meditate, open up to the non-rational and let your intuition work. And do not forget to ask Tsiipré to tell you some of the Indians' legends. Sleep well, relax in your dreams, and leave everything in the hands of God. Goodbye!"

ShuoKua disappeared. I returned to the shack and went to see Tsiipré.

"Tsiipré, I need to know about the Indian tales and legends. Can you tell me the ones you know?"

"Your request makes me glad. A deep knowledge of the legends and the myths of the Indian people is part of a Shaman's initiation process. In one night, I cannot tell you all the tales that I know. We will need several sessions."

"Tell me what you can tonight. My Guide wants me to listen to some legends before going to sleep."

"Then let us start right now."

That night I slept only for a couple of hours because Tsiipré kept telling the Kauauá's legends and of other Indian peoples almost until dawn.

## The Amazon Shaman

Even in a short sleep, I had an important dream. It's amazing how dreams really may help in solving your problems. The following day, I had a clear plan in my mind. Tsiipré was already up and bathing in the lake. I told him my plan and he liked it. We called Uakaú and we went to see Kaniuá.

Tsiipré started: "Kaniuá, we have been discussing the problem of the drug gang and William has a proposal that seems interesting."

"William?"

"That is his real name."

I couldn't hold back my anxiety: "I think that we can expel the outlaws and they'll never know that we are behind all of it."

Kaniuá's face showed doubt. Talking to him was never easy. He seldom agreed with ideas when first presented. He was careful, a good characteristic for a Chief. He was also intelligent and very shrewd, but couldn't be compared to Tsiipré, who had a remarkable intuition. Kaniuá was conservative, and would not accept a crazy idea like mine offhand. He asked for some time to think it over. But at Tsiipré's request, he called a meeting of the Wise Old Men for that same afternoon.

Kaniuá described the plan to the members of the Council. He was not totally convinced, but out of respect for Tsiipré's intelligence, Kaniuá supported the idea in the Council meeting. The initial reaction of the members was far from encouraging.

"The white men will not be fooled easily. They don't know the Indian legends," argued Pokrã.

I had been invited to the meeting, because my idea was being discussed. They didn't expect me to take the floor, as I was neither Indian nor old, but even so, I dared to speak up. "I want to point out that I intend to pay a visit to the drug gang and find a way of telling them the local legends."

"How can you talk to them? They may kill you."

"If we don't do anything, we'll probably be killed just the same. With the help of Kauaí-Açú, I'll work out something to let me get near them."

The reference to their deity fit well and after much discussion, they tentatively approved the plan. Kaniuá had a last recommendation: "I want you to talk to Tsiipré about every step to be taken. If he thinks it necessary, he can bring the matter again to the Council."

"You can be sure that I'll do nothing without Tsiipré's advice. I respect him as much as you do."

The session ended with the Council's authorization to go ahead with our plan. Uakaú and I walked back to Tsiipré's hut. I wanted to talk to him about certain details. To begin with, we had to establish a contact with the outlaws, in such a manner that they would not feel threatened. It was risky, but we had to try.

"Uakaú, how about another visit to the place, so that we can further explore the area?"

We agreed to visit the place in the following morning. I woke up early and Uakaú was already at the door of Tsiipré's shack. We went as far as the Rio Bonito, carrying a boat on our backs. Getting there, we took the boat and started rowing upriver. In about thirty minutes our boat was in front of the lab area.

We were in full view of the bandits, and some men pointed at us. The camp seemed to stir with our appearance. We turned the boat in its direction and approached slowly. That was the moment of danger. Some men with pistols and rifles flanked the man who seemed to be the boss. One of them was aiming his rifle at us. Our boat was approaching the shore. They probably thought it would be better to kill us on land. I asked my Guide for help, and said a silent prayer to Kauaí-Açú.

## The Amazon Shaman

The chief and his henchmen were staring at us. They looked unfriendly. I was scared. With all my meditations, I wasn't prepared to face these bandits. Uakaú, by contrast, seemed to be perfectly calm, showing no fear of death.

**Roberto Lima Netto**

> In all ancient native traditions, the solution to personal problems is closely connected to "power" and to following messages of the spirit in animals and plants and in your dreams and body. Without contact with this power, everyday life is not what it could be. But to find power, you must become a hunter and learn some minimal disciplines.
>
> Arnold Mindell, M.D.
> The Shaman's Body

## Chapter 19 - A dangerous game

As the boat reached the shore, the boss was waiting for us, surrounded by three well-armed bodyguards. The other men had stopped working and were looking at us with curiosity. They were surprised at our arrival. They probably didn't even know about the existence of the Kauauá nearby, let alone of a white man.

I stepped on the shore and offered to shake hands with the boss. He shook mine with caution. In our position, we couldn't represent any threat. Uakaú's bow and arrow were on the bottom of the boat, and all I had was a knife in my belt.

My concern was that they might kill us to prevent the spread of the news about the installation of the drug refining lab, since all that equipment couldn't be disguised. I should talk in a way that would make them feel secure that I wouldn't be a threat to their business.

As we had agreed, Uakaú stayed quietly in the boat, with no indication that he would step out. I started the conversation with greetings.

The chief spoke to me: "Strange thing to see a white man in these wilds. What are you doing in this end of the world?"

"I'm an anthropologist. I came to live among the Indians, because I got tired of the city life. I've been here for several months, and I like it very much. I have no intention of returning to Rio de Janeiro, where I used to live. By the way, let me introduce myself. My name is William, but the Indians call me Eagle, because of my cap. I pointed to my cap, with the most friendly and innocent smile that I could muster.

The boss asked: "Do the other Indians know we are here?"

"Sure. It is difficult to hide an operation as big as yours." I wanted to let them know that killing us would not stop the news of their arrival. It could even be worse, because the others could react against our deaths. It seemed that the man had the same thoughts, because he gestured for his bodyguards to lower their guns.

"My name is Gonzales," he said coldly.

"You must be surprised to find a white man around here."

"Yes. We didn't expect to find even Indians. Don't you have any contact with civilization?"

"It depends on what you call civilization. If you mean the white man, the answer is no. The nearest white settlement is a five-day trip from where we are. I haven't even been there. I'm happier among the Indians, and I intend to live and die here."

After saying that, it occurred to me that I shouldn't mention death at this moment. Why call attention to it? I continued: "I have no family or any other ties whatever with the white civilization."

My fears vanished as if by a miracle of Kauaí-Açú, and I felt quite confident that we were in the right track. I was very calm and lucid, alert to everything around us.

"What we call civilization is destroying itself. It's not possible to live in the midst of so much injustice. The social crisis is getting worse every day, because the wealthy think only of adding to their fortunes. Poverty is increasing, and so is the number of those living in misery. One day, millions of these poor will rise in rebellion, and do away with the wealthy few.

## The Amazon Shaman

I paused for courage, with another silent prayer for help from my Guide, and took the plunge: "I see that you are setting up a lab here to produce cocaine."

When I said that, Gonzales frowned. The objective of the group was clear to us, from all the stuff that was before our eyes. But it seems that putting it into words created a certain tension. Gonzales didn't say anything. He kept looking at me, waiting for what would be coming next.

"In fact, I want to say that I appreciate the work you are doing. One way to help solve the problem of the unfair income distribution of wealth in the world is producing and selling cocaine to the rich. You generate income for the poor farmers, and attenuate the growing inequality between rich and poor in our unjust civilization. I even believe that our countries should not only allow, but also encourage drug production. The richest country in the world, the United States of America, which consumes half of all drugs produced in the planet, be damned."

Gonzales became more relaxed with my rhetoric. His frown disappeared, and he even grinned a little. I was relieved, and concluded: "Since the Americans don't want to use a small portion of their wealth to help the poorest countries, let's take their money."

"Don't you really have any contacts with Brazilians?"

"With Brazilians? Sure I do."

Gonzales showed surprise: "But you said you did not."

"I have no contacts with the white men, the so-called civilized people. With the Brazilians of course I have. The Brazilians are the Indians among whom I live, those that have been living in these forests long before the white men arrived here."

"Aaah!" Gonzales' face showed his relief.

Not only I was not a threat, as I had no contacts with the white man, but I was also a supporter of their cause. For the first time Gonzales opened up a big smile. My plan seemed to be working. Of course, this was just the beginning, and a lot of divine help would be necessary for its success. So far, our gamble was paying off. The throw of the dice was giving me twelve points. Gonzales seemed really much more relaxed. He even offered me a beer and we walked towards the camp. Uakaú remained in the boat.

Gonzales asked me: "Your Indian friend, wouldn't he care for a bottle of beer?"

"He probably would. But he doesn't dare leaving his boat, and stepping on this ground. This is considered cursed land. There was a massacre of Indians in this area long ago."

"Is that a myth, one of these Indians folk tales?"

"Yes, nonsense. I don't believe this myth either. However, living among the Indians, you see certain things that are hard to explain."

"Like what, for example?" asked Gonzales.

"Would you believe that a Shaman could go down to hell, retrieve the soul of a sick person, and cure him?"

"Come on," I can't believe that!"

"There you are! It actually happens. I've seen it happen."

"Seen?

"Well...This cannot be seen. But I've seen the results of it."

"Hey! Are you becoming an Indian too? I don't believe this crap." Gonzales said that with a feigned indifference.

One of his henchmen, who was accompanying us, stretched his ears, listening to our conversation. We went to a giant andiroba tree, and sat down under its shade. It seemed to be the living room of the camp. Quite a few men stopped working, and sought cover from the fiery sun under the long shade of the tree. Many sat around us, listening to my tale.

"You won't convince any Indian to step on this place. My friend didn't want me to leave the boat. When he saw that

## The Amazon Shaman

you had chosen this spot, he said that you were crazy. I'm sure you are not superstitious."

"No, I'm not. I don't believe in this foolishness about ghosts. I've never seen one. I'd sure like to shoot one, just to see if it died twice." He forced a loud laugh as he said that, and I half-laughed too, for company.

Despite that bravado, his voice was a little hesitant, as if he were trying to drive some fear away. The bodyguards also exchanged glances, showing their apprehension. As I expected, this kind of people are impressed by supernatural stories.

"Why do the Indians think this is a haunted land?" asked Gonzales.

"That's a long story. I If you like tales, though, it's a nice one to hear, except that it's not to be believed."

"Let's hear it, man. Everybody likes a good story."

All the workers were around me, listening to what I was saying. The work had stopped dead, because of the scorching midday sun.

"I'm going to tell you a tale in which I don't believe. I'm not superstitious, and I know that you aren't either, because there are thirteen of you here. Whoever is superstitious would never agree to be in a group of thirteen people, like this one."

Some of the men looked at each other. This seemed to be the first time they realized they numbered thirteen. Some of them looked worried. This pushed me to a good start.

"According to what people say, there was an Indian village in this place you chose to set up your camp. A few kilometers to the north, there lived another tribe, and the two tribes had always been good friends. The people who lived here were hard workers; they had their own crops, and were good hunters. The people of the northern village were lazy, often begging the other villagers for food, and always getting what they needed. Then, during a dry period, the local tribe was unable to provide all the food required. So, one night, when most of the local people were asleep, the other tribe came down stealthily and killed everybody. They occupied the huts and appropriated the crops. All the dead were buried right here. After a few days, the Shaman of the occupying tribe received a message in a dream: To be forgiven for having betrayed their friends, every month they would have to perform a ceremony for the souls of the dead.

Everybody was staring at me and listening intently to my tale. The horror of the story seemed more disturbing to them than the heat of the sun. I continued: "For a few years the Indians followed the prescribed rites, but the old Shaman died, and the new one did not think they were important enough. Even so, he didn't want to take the risk of breaking what was becoming a tradition. Part of the rites required that plenty of food be placed on top of the graves, to feed the spirits of the murdered Indians. However, as they disliked working on the land, the food they raised was never enough. The good cultures that existed were deteriorating for lack of proper care. Some started a rumor that the ceremony was foolish, just a waste of good food."

I paused and looked at the faces of my audience. I saw concentration and concern. Nobody said a word. I continued: "The young Shaman of the tribe had not yet won the respect of the Indians, and was not strong enough to be respected. Against the Shaman's will, the Chief of the tribe decided to stop the rites. In the first month after the interruption, the new Shaman dreamed that a jaguar of fire invaded the village, and burned all the huts. In fact, a few days later one hut caught fire, for no apparent reason. However, it was an abandoned hut and nobody got hurt, so the episode was dismissed as unimportant."

I stopped to get a swig of beer, and again looked around at my audience. They seemed even more concerned. It's odd to see these rough men, who wouldn't run away from a shooting, scared of ghosts.

## The Amazon Shaman

"In the second month, again on the very day that the rites should have been performed, the Shaman had another dream. He dreamed that the village had been invaded by flying snakes, each one having the face of one of the Indians that had been killed. These snakes attacked all the people of the village. A few days later, a poisonous snake bit one of the Indians, and he died a terrible death. The Shaman found the body in the forest, a wholly swollen corpse. This time, he was worried. He insisted with the Chief to restore the rites, but his advice was ignored. There was not enough food at the time, and some families were almost starving."

"In the third month, another dream. Heavy rains would flood the village. Everyone would die, except the Shaman, who for the rest of his life should tell this story to all the Indians of the region, to warn them not to step into this area, which now was considered haunted."

I spoke the last word with great emphasis and repeated: HAUNTED. I looked around and saw fear creeping in the faces of the rough men. I went on with my story.

"The night following this dream, the Shaman was awakened by strong thunders and lightning. Warned by his dream, the Shaman left his hut to find protection on higher ground in the forest. A heavy rain flooded the village and dragged all the people and their huts toward the Rio Grande, where all drowned. Only the Shaman came out alive. From where he was, he saw the whole village being carried away by the raging waters. For believing his dream, he was saved."

One of the workers, a strong fellow looking fearless, asked me: "Do you believe this story?"

"Of course not. But... I recall a Spanish adage that says: "No creo en brujas, pero que las hay, las hay" (I don't believe in witches, but that they exist, they exist!). I hope you won't believe this saying."

"Sure we don't," said instantly someone in the audience, too fast to be true.

"This is just another legend, "I said, "like so many others that one hears around here. However, my Indian friends believe. That's why my companion does not get out of the boat, so that he won't have to step on this ground. I'm not superstitious, and I'm sure you aren't either. Indeed, you are braver than me because, although I don't believe these things, I wouldn't dare to live here in this haunted land. And worse, you are exactly thirteen. This is foolish, but there is always some uneasiness, you know. I have to admit that you are really brave."

One of the men turned to Gonzales and said: "Boss, none of us here believes in ghosts, that's Indian folklore. But . . . wouldn't it be better to move the camp elsewhere? Who knows, maybe we can find a better place upriver?"

The looks of the workers under the tree showed clearly that the suggestion had been well received. The whole group was scared, although they would not admit it.

"What's that, man, are you afraid of ghosts?" asked Gonzales.

There was general laughter – not really genuine – at these words from the boss.

The man who made the suggestion hastened to explain: "It's not that, Boss. I'm not afraid of anything. I've faced many men with deadlier guns. It is not a ghost that will scare me. Why would I be afraid of a spirit? It cannot shoot and, anyway, I'm not afraid to die."

"Then, why move our camp?"

"Well ... I've been walking around, and going up the river, I found a much better place. It even has a crystal clear brook where we can all refresh ourselves when the sun is too hot. That's why I think it's a better place. Nothing to do with ghosts, which I don't fear."

Gonzales stood firm, saying that he did not believe in ghosts. What a liar Gonzales was. I sensed that he had also been shaken by the tale.

His man had just provided the justification for the move, but saying he did not fear ghosts Gonzales could not agree about moving.

"I'm not going to be expelled by any wandering soul. Especially an Indian ghost."

Gonzales paused for a minute and then continued: "I think it would be a good idea if we had thought of it in the beginning. I would like to have a better river to refresh myself, instead of the muddy waters of the Rio Grande. But we've already done a lot of work here. Our airstrip is almost finished. If we start all over again, we won't have the installation ready on time."

That was the end of the discussion. Most of the workers didn't like the decision, but no one said anything. They would not admit their fear.

The sky was darkening, announcing the afternoon rainfall. After finishing my beer and some trivial talk, I said good-bye to Gonzales and his group.

"You can be assured that no Indian will come near your camp. But I'll come over to join you for other rounds of beer. The only problem of my living with the Indians is that there is no beer.

"Sure. You are my permanent guest. I like to talk to smart people. Your explanation about how cocaine traffic can help improve the world is very intelligent. I'll have to tell it to my boss, as soon as I see him."

Oh boy! If Gonzales only knew how I hated his trade. I considered drugs the disease of humanity.

**Roberto Lima Netto**

> The old man shook his head disapprovingly. "Life's too short to waste your time on money. The treasure is within you."
>
> In Search of Happiness
> Roberto Lima Netto

## Chapter 20 – It's show time

We went back to the tribe laughing a lot, relaxed after all the tension, under a summer shower that was not as refreshing as I would like it to be because the day was hot and water came already warm from the sky. It didn't last long. The sun returned strong. A bird was singing in a tree nearby. I looked up, and my eyes caught the sun's rays directly. They were never so bright. I trusted Kauaí-Açú.

Arriving at the village, we told the whole story to Kaniuá, and he was happy at the progress of our plan. It had been a fruitful day. The first stage had been very successful. I had planted the seeds of fear in the minds of the bandits. Now, we needed skill, luck, and careful work. We could not make any mistakes, because we were about to begin the most dangerous part of our plan.

The groundwork had been laid. Although the bandits swore not to believe in ghosts, they were concerned. They would be even more worried after the show we were preparing for them, set for midnight of that very day.

Tsiipré and I put the show together with Uakaú's collaboration. We prepared the script and made rehearsals, with the participation of Katú and Perimatú, two good friends of Uakaú. The first and only performance was scheduled for the next night. The Gala Show was ready to go.

We made a scarecrow, a straw man mounted on a bamboo cross frame, and just before midnight we went to the stage, which was a tree near the clearing of the drug gang camp. We hanged the scarecrow on the tree, so that it would be in full view of the people at the camp. A tree branch supported the rope holding the figure, and Uakaú, hidden behind the trunk of the tree, held its tip. Pulling and releasing the rope would make the puppet move in weird movements.

The night was luminous, with a full moon. All was silent in the camp. The men were sleeping after a hard days' work building the landing strip. When everything was ready, the five of us started screaming, beating drums, shaking maracas, and making all kinds of strange sounds. In a few minutes, everybody was awake and looking at the scarecrow jumping up and down, as if possessed by the devil. Some men got their guns and started shooting at the puppet, but no one had the guts to get near.

The climax of the show happened when an arrow with a fire tip, shot by Katú hit the back of the puppet. The straw caught fire immediately, and the figure continued jumping wildly, as Uakaú kept pulling the rope.

The light of the fire on the puppet, the moonlight and a wrong move by Katú caused the only dangerous situation. Katú momentarily became visible to the men, and one of them shouted: "Look at that! Look at that!"

Katú hid himself quickly among the trees, and we screamed louder. As soon as fire consumed the scarecrow, we became completely quiet. We cleaned all signs of our presence and went back home.

We were happy, but Katu's blunder was distressing. In fact, this could be disastrous for me the next time I visited the camp. It could even cause my death. And I had to go, to keep the plan on track.

"Do you think they saw Katú?" I asked Uakaú.

"There wasn't enough time. Only one of them saw him. When the others looked, Katú was already behind the trees. But we will only know for sure tomorrow, when you visit them," answered Tsiipré.

## The Amazon Shaman

Looking at Tsiipré, I could see he was concerned for my life. "If they suspect something, our plan is ruined." I said. "I told them no Indian would step on these grounds."

Tsiipré joined the conversation, saying what I didn't want to hear: "If they are suspicious, next time you go there you won't get out alive."

Despite Katú's blunder, our theatricals seemed to be working well. They'd better be. After all, my life was at stake. Anyhow, I'd find out on my next visit to Gonzales. I would certainly need Kauaí-Açú's help.

I was tired when I got home, but Tsiipré wouldn't let me rest. He wanted to continue his instructions. I couldn't object, since I was so eager to get my memory back.

"The purpose of the fourth stage of your initiation is to increase your personal power. To do that, you must return to the inner world, call your Guiding Spirit, and with his assistance, try to engage animals and birds as your helpers. You may need them, in case the bandits are suspicious about our show."

"Could they save my life?"

"We never know. It's always wise to have them at your side."

"Which animals should I choose?"

"Your intuition will tell you with the aid of your Guide. You'll be looking for those animals which may be your helpers in your future incursions into the inner world. It is very important to have their help. They may be valuable even in our outer world up here."

"Will they bite the drug runners, if they try to kill me?"

Tsiipré laughed. I started my meditation in his hut full of smoke, with his chanting and playing the maraca. I was already well trained and, in a few minutes, I went into a deep trance. I descended to my inner world and called my Guide: "I need your help in my search for animals of power."

"Yes, I will be glad to assist you. However, remember that an entire universe exists within you. You are a part of this whole. You are a rock, a tree, a river, a mountain, an animal, an Indian, and God."

"And God? What do you mean? You want me to find Him inside of me?"

"Exactly. God is everywhere. Therefore, He is within you."

"I'm not sure I understand."

"Think about this later. When you find your animal helpers, you will also be finding parts of yourself. In finding yourself, you will feel more complete. You are in your initiation to become a Shaman, a spiritual warrior. Your struggle is to gain wisdom, to become whole."

"Maybe one of them brings back my memory, my black hole."

"Be patient. It is not that easy."

"I'll have to think thoroughly about what you've said to understand it better. I feel that I am receiving the gift of a deep truth, and I'll have to reflect about it to enjoy its full benefit. The problem is that I never know whether your words are metaphors or reflect a real truth."

"Don't you know that metaphors reflect the real world?

I scratched my head before answering: "I cannot answer before carefully considering your question."

"Yes, do that at ease, later on. Now, let us take a walk. Be on the alert for any animal that shows up. Keep contact with your intuition, to know if it could be a good friend.

We had been walking for a few minutes when, suddenly, a black jaguar with shiny eyes appeared in front of us. It came silently, and I only saw it a few steps away. It was a large animal, but it seemed to be still young. I was frightened and trying to figure out what to do. I looked at ShuoKua, at my side, and found him at ease. I calmed down, as the jaguar looked friendly. When it came closer, ShuoKua said: "Get down on your four and pretend you are a jaguar. Dance like one."

"I don't know how to dance like a jaguar."

"Trust your unconscious and do whatever comes to your mind."

I started to dance, a little awkwardly in the beginning. The jaguar followed me and did likewise.

"Now, speak to him and give him a name. If he accepts the name, this means that he wants to be your friend."

That's what I did, and gave him the name Negro. He waved his tail cheerfully, and kept following me in his royal pace. I patted his back lightly, his hairs were soft and silky, and he seemed to enjoy the touch. My fear was gone.

The next animal to show up was a Royal Hawk, a beautiful, majestic bird, with which I felt a strong tie. I treated it the same way I had treated Negro, I called it Ray, and it joined us.

Then we met a snake, and this complicated my search. Looking at it, I felt really scared. Perhaps, for this reason, Ray jumped on the snake, trying to catch it, but it got away.

At this point, ShuoKua said that our progress was satisfactory for a first day, and suggested that we stop the search. I thanked him and said goodbye to him, to Negro and to Ray.

I returned to the hut and found Tsiipré waiting for me. He was glad when I told him about the results I got.

"I think you were a shaman in another life. Things are happening very fast for you. You have chosen your friends wisely."

"I'm not sure whether I chose them or was chosen by them."

"It makes no difference. They are all part of you. The jaguar symbolizes movement, agility. It is your protection against the power of the enemy, both for attacking and for escaping quickly."

"What about the Royal Hawk?"

"It's the symbol for your vision and spirituality. It hovers in the sky, where it sees everything. And it is near the place where God is said to live."

"God lives in the sky?"

"This is only symbolic. God is everywhere, including the sky. He is also within you. In a way, you are also God."

"That is what my Guide told me. But to be honest, I must admit I cannot fully understand it."

I told Tsiipré about my reaction to the snake, which caused Ray to attack it.

"In the past, you may have had some unpleasant experiences with snakes. Hence, your reaction."

"Does that mean I should avoid them?"

"On the contrary. I guess it would be the most important animal for you to conquer. Without mastering your fears, you cannot be a Shaman."

"So, in spite of my fear, do I have to continue trying to be a friend of a snake?"

"Sure. Through it, you will be free from your fears and will become a whole man. Through it, you will be saved."

"How?"

"It has been said that demons are really angels to whom we do not give psychic space."

> I have seen in my practice how many shamanic abilities appear when you stop doubting the reality of the spirit.
>
> Arnold Mindell, M.D.
> The Shaman's Body

## Chapter 21 – Visiting the lion´s cage

I woke up the next day curious to find out about the reaction of the drug gang to our dramatics. Curious, but afraid. Next visit could be the last action of my life. I checked my curiosity, and showed up at the camp only two days later. I wanted to avoid Gonzales's suspicion that we might be involved.

As usual, I went by the river. Uakaú went with me and waited hidden before the camp, and I rowed alone the last two hundred yards. I was apprehensive. If they´d seen Katú in that puppet scene, my life wouldn´t be worth a penny. After all, I guaranteed that no Indian would step into that area.

As I reached the camp, I felt some tension in the air. The work had not advanced much. Gonzales greeted me with indifference.

I started the conversation: "I came around to talk with an intelligent man. Since we first met, I saw that you are a competent person, and I'm sure that, before long, your boss will give you a promotion, and take you away from here. Meanwhile, I want to take advantage of your presence, and learn from your life's experience."

It's amazing how some people soften with flattery. Gonzales smiled, happy at my words, and didn't remember that, in our last meeting, he had hardly said anything. The lower people feel, the easier they are deceived by flattery.

"You came at the right time. It's too hot, and we are going to stop work for a while. It's a pity that Brazilians have not yet adopted the siesta. With this heat, it's the most sensible thing to do. If you don't want to take a nap, you can at least rest in the shade."

We sat in the shade of the forty meters tall andiroba, the same giant tree that had been elected as the living room of the camp, because the tents were too hot at daytime.

As soon as we sat down, Gonzales brought up the news. "Something incredible happened here: an apparition, a ghostly figure."

"A ghost? You are joking! You don't believe in these things."

"I don't. But I swear I saw one."

"Do you believe or not in ghosts? I can't make that out."

Gonzales scratched his head: "I don't, but all I can say is that I saw a ghost. It jumped up and down in the air, screaming like hell."

One of the men joined the conversation: "It wasn't a ghost, folks, it was a jaguar, a fire jaguar, like the one in the story you told us."

"That was a legend not to be believed," I said.

A heated discussion followed as to whether it was a ghost or a jaguar they had seen, and I interrupted it: "Are you telling me that the Indians are right in saying that this camp area is haunted?"

Gonzales answered: "You know that I'm not superstitious, but I cannot deny that I saw something very strange. No doubt about that."

"Couldn't it be a dream?"

"If I had been the only one to see the thing, it could have been a dream. However, how can you explain the fact that the whole camp saw it? Could everybody have an identical dream?"

## The Amazon Shaman

"I've heard that in the desert; many people swear they have visions of a lake, which turn out to be an optical illusion. They are mirages. Maybe that's what happened here."

"You don't believe it because you haven't seen it yourself. Are the mirages in the desert noisy, too?"

"Well.... not exactly."

"Ah! That's the point. The thing made one hell of a noise."

One of the workers made a comment: "I saw the ghost of an Indian, under the fire jaguar."

"He was the only one who saw it," said Gonzales. "I don't believe him."

"But it's true. I saw it with the same eyes that saw the jaguar."

I pretended I was beginning to believe, but didn't admit it fully, leaving some doubt in the air. The conversation lasted for about two hours, and was quite lively. After drinking a few glasses of beer, I got up and said: "Now I must go. I want to get home before nightfall. If there are ghosts around here, I'd rather be home with the sunlight."

Gonzales seemed not to find my saying funny. He walked with me to the river bank, and helped me push the boat into the water.

"Come back whenever you want to update our chat."

"OK, as long as you don't send your ghosts chasing me. Ciao."

Gonzales forced a laugh: "That's a bad joke, Eagle."

Now I was going downriver, so the return was easier. I just let the current take the boat to where Uakaú was waiting for me.

"The results were terrific," I told him, "better than I expected. The men are convinced they saw a ghost that night!"

"And how about Katú?"

"That's the ghost. Only one of them saw him, and he believes it was an Indian ghost."

We laughed all the way to the village. Now we would have a few days to plan the next episode of our play – "The Land of the Ghosts" – directed and produced by Tsiipré, Uakaú, and William. It was night when we arrived, and Tsiipré had a lot of fun when I gave him a detailed account of our adventure.

Tsiipré wouldn't let me sleep before another task. I had to return to my inner world, and try to get a snake as a helper.

"Tsiipré, the snake is one of the few animals that I don't like. I already told you I'm afraid of it."

"All the more reason for you to learn how to work with it. The snake is a symbol of death and rebirth. Usually, the white man fears death. In addition, the snake is an animal that represents the earth element. You already have the Royal Hawk, which represents the air, and the jaguar, which represents the fire. After the earth, you will only need the animal for the water."

I was tired, but I obeyed Tsiipré's orders. After all, the sooner I was able to fill my black hole, the better. There were days in which my anguish was almost unbearable, and this was one of them. I went into trance, with the help of Tsiipré's chanting and the sound of his maraca, and returned to my inner world. This time, I decided not to call Ray to come with me, but I thought that the jaguar might be useful. If the snake was hostile, it would be good to have Negro with me.

I also called ShuoKua to my help. His presence would make me feel more secure to face the snake, a task that for reasons unknown to me, I was reluctant to accomplish.

I walked through the inner world until I met a snake. My first reaction was one of fear, and the snake noticed it, but I controlled myself. I decided to talk to it: "Mr. Snake, I fear you."

"Like many white men. They think the snake is bad. Your religion turns you against us. But we are not unfriendly to man. We only react when attacked."

"Then, why do we have this fear?"

"Let's say it's a cultural fear. The snake is unfairly blamed for what happened in the Garden of Eden. We have to share the guilt of Adam and Eve."

"You are a very cultured snake."

"We come from the earth. That's where our knowledge comes from. And because we change our skin, people think that we live many lives. I'll tell you a secret: we do."

After this conversation, my fear disappeared. I lowered myself near the ground, and performed a sort of improvised dance, accompanied by the snake. I named it Earth, with its acceptance. Thus, I conquered one more animal of power to help and protect me, and one that could be very useful for its wisdom.

On the way home, I went by a clear-water lake, and thought of the aquatic animal that was needed to complete my fourth stage. I jumped into the lake, and started swimming underwater. I knew now, from my experience in the water tunnel, that in the inner world you need not breathe. I could swim underwater for an indefinite period of time.

Deep in the lake, I found a beautiful red fish, which seemed to be the king of fishes. Many others followed him as if they were its subjects. Swimming like a fish, I got close to it and said: "Your name now is Kingfish. Do you like it?"

"It's a nice name, better than Redfish as I'm called here."

"Go on as Redfish for the others, but for me you are Kingfish. I'm going to be a powerful Shaman, and I want to count on your help."

"Sure, whenever you need me, just call."

"Likewise. You can ask my help if you need it."

Kingfish was happy with our agreement. I said goodbye and promised to visit it often. Now, I had as my helpers the four power animals: Negro, the jaguar, representing the fire element; Ray, the royal hawk, representing the air element; Earth, the snake, the earth animal, and finally, Kingfish, the royal fish, master of the waters.

Going back to Tsiipré's hut, I told him about my progress. He was satisfied and said: "Now you have a good team of friends. The fish, a symbol of peace, the capacity for introversion, to learn from your mistakes. The snake, the very symbol of man's origin. Some Indian legends say that man was born from the snake."

> The question about the meaning of life can only be answered by conjectures or beliefs. However, it does make sense to think that we came to this world in order to become better, so that our essence - we could say *our soul* - learns a few lessons. The religions which believe in many lives, especially the Asian ones, preach that our soul reincarnates many times in this Earth to learn lessons, and this cycle of lives is only interrupted when it reaches a state of illumination.
>
> The Jungian Bible
> Roberto Lima Netto

## Chapter 22 – Tension in the air

I had finished bathing in the lake when Uakaú came to see me. The community was upset. Kaniuá had called a meeting of the Council of Old Men and wanted everybody to be present.

When I arrived at the village, there was already a large group in the central yard. Uakaú found a space for us to seat. The members of the Council were already in the center of the yard. Tsiipré was seated at Kaniuá's right side, forming a circle of ten Indians.

Kaniuá called the Council to order: "Something very serious happened today. An Arakati Indian attacked me."

This immediately aroused the anger of the audience, and enraged shouts of revenge were heard. The Chief asked Pinuim to describe what happened.

"Kaniuá, I and two of our brothers were hunting in the forest, in the area of Rio Bonito, when all of a sudden, a rifle shot was fired in his direction. Fortunately, the bullet missed him, passing close to his head, and hit a tree behind him."

"Who fired the shot?"

"We don't know yet. The Indian who fired it escaped, but we found a bow and some arrows of the Arakati where he was hiding."

"Did he leave his bow?" asked Tsiipré.

"The aggressor escaped so quickly that he left behind his bow and arrows, for fear of being caught."

I looked at Tsiipré and could see in his face that he was uneasy. He was not buying the story.

Tsiipré asked: "Did you see who fired the shot? Was he really an Indian?"

"This outrage must be punished," said one of the Council members.

Shouts of approval. Tsiipré insisted: "I do not understand how this could happen. The Arakati have always been our friends."

Pokrã said: "Friend doesn't shoot at a friend. If they want war, let them have war.

The emotions of the group were getting out of control, and Tsiipré was trying hard to bring common sense back to the discussion.

"How can we be sure that it was an Arakati that shot Kaniuá?"

In spite of their respect for him, Tsiipré's sensible question was unanswered. The people were angry.

Pokrã said: "We've got to give them a lesson, so that they will never again meddle with the Kauauá and try to kill our Chief."

More shouts of approval. Pinuim was the most enthusiastic. They all wanted a declaration of war. The Kauauá had not had the opportunity of a good fight for a long time, and Pinuim and Uakaú's generation had never been in a war. The repressed aggression was trying to find an outlet.

## The Amazon Shaman

Tsiipré spoke again: "It is very strange that the person who shot at our Chief escaped leaving behind his bow and arrows. Even assuming that he was in a rush, an Indian does not leave his bow behind. We have to look into this matter more carefully."

"More carefully into what? Are we turning cowards? Are we not reacting to the aggression to our Chief?" said Pokrã. "They almost killed our Chief! What else do we have to wait for?"

"Can you guarantee that the aggression was done by an Arakati Indian?"

Pokrã continued: "The Arakati deserve a good punishment. The Kauauá are a noble people. We do not want a war, but we do not shirk from a provocation either."

"We have to punish them, for sure," said Tsiipré, "if they are the guilty ones. Is it possible that the chief of the Arakati would order the murder of his friend Kaniuá? Would a member of the tribe do it without the Chief's knowledge? He who fired the shot is the one that must be punished, so that everybody will always respect the Kauauá."

Normally, Tsiipré's words were listened to, and carefully considered. Not this time, though. No one paid any attention to his words because the general feeling was in favor of a war to avenge what the Arakati had done to Chief Kaniuá and all the Kauauá. But Kaniuá was still undecided.

Tsiipré changed his tactics. "The Kauauá are a strong people. We want and we must avenge the affronts from anyone, but we must not be unfair. Who can really swear that an Arakati Indian fired that shot?"

"We found their bow and arrows. Isn't this proof enough?" Pokrã said that, more as a statement than as a question.

Tsiipré went on: "Has anybody seen the shooter? Should we risk tainting the honor of the Kauauá with a hasty judgment, perhaps unfair?"

Turning to Kaniuá, Tsiipré said: "My brother, you know that I am a friend of the Arakati Shaman. He is an honorable old man, and will not lie to me. If we are to have a war, all of us will fight, but you cannot prepare for war in one day. I ask your permission to visit their Shaman tonight, and tomorrow morning we will decide what to do."

"If the Arakati are preparing a war against the Kauauá, they may kill Tsiipré," said Kaniuá. "They know you have a power that would help us in a war."

"The Shaman is my friend. His shack is outside the village. He will not betray me. I will go with great caution, if Kaniuá agrees."

Kaniuá was initially unsure, not wanting to risk Tsiipré's life, but finally approved Tsiipré's suggestion, and called a new meeting for the following morning.

The decision didn't please the majority. Tsiipré wanted to depart immediately, because it would be a three-hour journey and he intended to go before nightfall. Afterwards, he would have only the moonlight. Uakaú and I insisted in going with him, and he agreed on a condition: "When we get to about one hundred yards of the Shaman's shack, I will walk the rest alone. You wait for me in the forest."

We started on our trip immediately. The afternoon was dark, a sign of rain. Uakaú was armed with his bow and arrows, I had my knife, and Tsiipré his amulets. In our position, if the Arakati really wanted a war, the amulets would probably protect us better than Uakaú's bow and my knife. That's why I also carried my amulets in a small pouch tied to a leather collar around my neck.

On the way, before getting close to the Arakati land, we talked to one another. I asked Tsiipré: "Don't you think that we are having too many problems, all at once? John trying to steal our trees, the drug people, the gold problem and, now, this crazy war. We'll be lucky if John doesn't have his finger also in the gold mine. The fellow who died was his employee."

Tsiipré said: "We are indeed involved in a lot of trouble at the same time. I cannot imagine the problems that we would have if there is a gold rush in our lands, let alone having to fight a war. John would be happy, would he not?"

"And we aren't sure that we'll be able to drive the drug gang away," I said.

Tsiipré added: "We have to avoid this silly war. I do not believe that an Arakati Indian fired at Kaniuá."

Uakaú was surprised by this statement. "If it was not an Arakati Indian, who would it be?"

Tsiipré said: "The situation is becoming difficult. I trust that Kauaí-Açú will help and guide us."

"Why would the Arakati attack us?" asked Uakaú.

"That is exactly my question," said Tsiipré, "I have no doubts that the attempted assassination is a ruse to create enmity between the Kauauá and the Arakati. An Indian would never use a rifle to kill Kaniuá. What is more, an Indian would not leave his bow and arrow behind.

"Who could be behind this scheme?" I asked.

"I bet that John planned everything. Either one of his henchmen did the shooting, or he paid an Indian to do it, not necessarily an Arakati Indian."

At the Council meeting, Uakaú had been one of the strong supporters of the war. After listening with attention to Tsiipré's last words, he wasn't so sure.

Tsiipré went on: "The problem of the drug people is the most serious one. If it works as they expect, and they feel safe operating in Brazil, they may try to do in our country what they are doing in Colombia: try to influence the three branches of the government."

"Should this happen, what can we do about it?" I asked.

"If things come to that point, nothing. It would be a disaster for Brazil and the world."

"That's precisely the case in which we rely mostly on luck to solve. I'm not sure that our schemes will be effective to expel them," I said.

"More than luck, we need divine protection," Tsiipré added.

"With so many problems at the same time - the timber, the gold, the drug and now this conflict with the Arakati - Kauaí-Açú will have to work real hard," said Tsiipré.

We started to walk at a faster pace to gain time, and the conversation dwindled. A sudden shower soaked us, but it was hot and we couldn't complain. The rain stopped quickly, and the setting sun came out again.

We arrived at the Arakati village. To avoid getting too close to the village, we approached the Shaman's shack by a circuitous way. We didn't want to be seen by the Arakati. The wind was blowing in our direction, and bringing to our ears some disquieting sounds from the village.

Tsiipré stayed for more than one hour with the Arakati Shaman, and, when he came back, he seemed relieved, but wouldn't tell us anything. He addressed a remark to Uakaú only.

"May this whole episode be a lesson to you, Uakaú. If you want to be a good chief, keep in mind that it is not advisable to let the first impressions influence you. To be right and fair, your must make your decisions only after gathering as much information as possible."

Uakaú's face showed that he didn't understand what Tsiipré was trying to tell him. Tsiipré continued: "If we had made a final decision at yesterday's meeting, today we would start a war that could result in the death of many Kauauá and Arakati Indians."

"But ... what happened? Wasn't it an Arakati that shot at Kaniuá?"

"That is what you think. That is what seemed. Keep in mind that not always what seems to be, really is. Learn this lesson."

Uakaú tried to get more from Tsiipré, but he wouldn't say anything else.

Our way back was harder, because walking at night through the forest, even in the moonlight, is quite difficult. I wouldn't have been able to make the journey alone. However, the orientation ability of the Indians is remarkable.

I suggested to Tsiipré: "Why don't we sleep overnight in the forest and proceed tomorrow morning? We're all tired."

"If you wish, you may stay. I want to be back early, so that I can attend the Council meeting from the beginning, and try to avoid a serious mistake."

Of course we didn't accept the suggestion. Tsiipré was older and should be more tired than us, and we also wanted to be present at the meeting. The return trip took more than five hours. We arrived when the sun was about to rise. As soon as Kaniuá learned that Tsiipré was back in the village, he sent for him. After talking with him, he called the Council.

The whole community sat down in the yard, leaving enough space in the center for the members of the Council. Kaniuá started the session. "Yesterday we discussed the proposal to declare war against the Arakati. Today, Tsiipré has some information that changes everything. He will speak to you."

"I have met with the Shaman of the Arakati. He was glad to see me, as he had a very serious matter to discuss with me. The Arakati wanted to make war against the Kauauá."

The group was confused by this remark. Tsiipré was interrupted by a Council member, who said: "This seems clear enough. Otherwise they would not try to shoot our Chief."

"That is not really the case." Tsiipré answered. "Yesterday, at about the time that we were assembled in this Council, someone fired a rifle shot at an Arakati Indian. The bullet hit his leg. Luckily, it did not kill him. The shooter escaped, but he left behind his bow and a few arrows."

"And what have we got to do with that?" asked Pokrã.

"They were bow and arrows of the Kauauá."

The audience was astonished. A dead silence in the air. Tsiipré continued: "We all know that no Kauauá warrior did that. We were all in the meeting of the Council, here, in this very place. The Arakati Shaman was also quite surprised when I mentioned our suspicion that some Arakati warrior tried to kill Kaniuá. After these two occurrences, I am sure that someone intends to manipulate the two tribes to provoke a war."

"Who might want a war between the Kauauá and the Arakati?" asked Prokrã.

"The drug gang?" ventured another member of the Council.

Tsiipré answered: "Can anybody tell me what the drug people would gain with such a war?"

Since nobody ventured an answer, Tsiipré continued: "I know that they would have a lot to lose. A war will cause much disturbance in the area, and the Army might decide to send their soldiers over here. Will this be good for the drug people? Of course not."

The audience was listening quietly, but they seemed not to understand the arguments. Nobody spoke, so Tsiipré continued: "The only one who is interested in a war is John. He wants to control this area to get timber. After a war, we would be much weaker. The Army could show its presence, but it would not be here forever. When it left, it would be much easier to dominate our people. That is how John could get the timber he wants.

Kaniuá completed the thought: "John knows that Kaniuá does not want the white men around here. Kaniuá does not want to sell the trees. If that shot had killed Kaniuá, John would have been happy."

Tsiipré continued: "In order to bring about a situation where we all can live in peace, I have planned, together with the Shaman of the Arakati, a general meeting of the Chiefs and the Shamans. Kaniuá has already agreed to that, and we want to submit the idea to the Council.

After a pause, met with silence, Tsiipré completed: "Maybe the results of all this will disappoint some young warriors on both sides, but we have done no injustice, and John, the evil man, has not been able to deceive us."

**Roberto Lima Netto**

## Chapter 23 – The divine song

After walking over ten hours without sleep, I was ready to take a good rest. But first I wanted to relax, swimming in our lake. Just a plunge to unwind, then eat something light and take a good nap. But this wasn't Tsiipré's plan for me. When I came back from the lake, he called on me to start the fifth stage of my initiation.

"You are going to get your power song. It is an important weapon for any Shaman. You must have one of your own."

"What is it good for?"

"You will teach it to your helpers, your animals of power, and it will be used to call them when you need help. It will also help you to concentrate more quickly."

"Shouldn't I eat something and rest a little? I didn't sleep or eat anything since we started our trip to the village of the Arakati."

"No! To get your song of power, you must be tired and hungry. This way you divert your ego, and it loses some of its control over you. Your rational side becomes somewhat confused, dormant, and you operate under the control of your emotions."

"All right, I'm resigned. After all, I'm the one who has an urgent need to cover my black hole. What do you want me to do?"

"Go to a quiet place in the forest and meditate. Let your inspiration free, give reins to it. Come back only when your song is born, grows, and fills your head."

I took the boat, crossed the lake, and walked for a few minutes, to arrive at a site where a stream, its bottom lined with little white pebbles, flowed into the lake. I walked upstream, barefoot in the cold waters of the brook, as far as a cave that protected a spring. Large leafy trees and the scent of wild flowers created a magic atmosphere.

A strong conviction invaded my mind: this is the place! I'm sure it's a magical place. I sat on the soft grass and began to relax, in preparation for entering in trance. It was night already, with a full moon. At first, weariness and hunger disturbed me, but in a short time I had transcended the material world and was in trance.

You cannot gauge time in an altered state of consciousness, because measurements do not belong to it. When the sun was beginning to appear on the horizon, I guessed I had meditated for a long time, maybe for about seven hours. A whole night. Then, I heard a flapping of wings and saw Ray, my friend the Royal Hawk, landing on a tree branch right in front of me. It changed forthwith into a beautiful bird, with all the colors of the rainbow, as I had never ever seen before. The bird started singing, repeating a lovely song:

---

Kauaí-Açú
The Divine Spirit
To the true Man
The Power Gives.

Blessed by the Spirit
The true Man

**The Amazon Shaman**

## Goes thru the World Doing Good Deeds

I kept humming the song for a long time, and felt that it gave me inner strength. I didn't want to stop singing, but I had to go back to the village, and tell Tsiipré what had happened. He would be happy. As I got up to walk, I remembered that I had not eaten for the last twenty four hours, and when I thought of it, I felt a weakness in my legs. I brought the song to my mind, and my body was sound again.

The Chiefs' meeting took place two days later, in the village of the Arakati. Kaniuá was accompanied by all his counselors and many young warriors. Uakaú and I were present. The old counselors of the two tribes formed a circle, and in its middle were Kaniuá, Tsiipré, Tiriuá -- the Chief of the Arakati -- and their Shaman.

After the greetings, Kaniuá said: "Brother Tiriuá. This misunderstanding between our sister tribes must never happen again. We are one people, and must live like one. We should never forget our friendship, our common roots, and the customs that unite us."

To this opening, Tiriuá answered: "To avoid situations like this, I propose that whenever common enemies try to incite quarrels between us, we should discuss the matter peacefully, and clear up any misunderstandings."

"I agree with your proposal and submit it to the counselors of my tribe who are present."

All of them signaled agreement with their heads. Tiriuá spoke again: "I propose also that, to foster a closer friendship between our tribes, every year we stage dancing and wrestling festivities, bringing together our two peoples. Each year one tribe will promote the feast."

Full approval again. Kaniuá said: "I propose that the first festivity be organized by the Kauauá, and that it should take place this year."

Tiriuá added: "I further suggest that, in order to unite our peoples even more, a young woman of one tribe is given in marriage to a warrior of the other tribe."

"I think that is a very good idea," said Kaniuá.

"I offer my son and my daughter to be married to a young woman and a warrior of the Kauauá."

"I accept your offer," said Kaniuá. "I have no son to offer, but I can suggest a great warrior."

Kaniuá pointed to Pinuim. The choice was well received, because Pinuim was already known to the Arakati for his feats in wrestling and hunting.

I looked at Tatainim, who had come with us to the village of the Arakati, and was present at the meeting. Her face paled with worry about the probable next words of her father.

Kaniuá continued: "As to the young woman, I would like to name our choice in a few days. Until then, I ask that your son visit us, and let me know any preference he may have.

Tiriuá was surprised at this indecisiveness, perhaps because he was expecting that Kaniuá would offer his daughter. But he said nothing. According to the customs of the Indians, the father made the choice without first asking the youngsters to be married. Kaniuá loved his daughter and probably took a different position because he knew of her preference to follow Tsiipré's footsteps, and become a Shaman.

When the meeting was over, and all visitors went home, Tatainim went to see Tsiipré almost in tears. I was present at their conversation.

"Tsiipré, I'm afraid that my father may still offer me to marry the chief's son. You know I don't want that."

Tsiipré answered: "This is a very difficult situation. Did you notice Tiriuá's disappointment because Kaniuá did not offer you to marry his son? I believe your father wanted only to gain time to convince you that it would be the best thing to do to strengthen the friendship of the two tribes."

"I know that I shouldn't complain. Our customs require that it is the father who chooses her daughter's husband. However, you have given us a somewhat different education. It's hard for me to accept certain outdated customs."

"I noticed the warm looks that Tiriuá's son directed to Atacim. It seems that they already know each other and, if he could choose, Tatainim's problem would be solved."

Tatainim was encouraged by my comment. Atacim was a beautiful sixteen years old girl.

Tsiipré talked to Kaniuá and also with the Chief's son. Atacin was chosen. Maybe the choice was not to Tiriuá's entire satisfaction, but his son was happy and Tatainim was immensely joyful the day this was announced.

**Roberto Lima Netto**

> Man's task is to become conscious of the contents that press upward from the unconscious. Neither should he persist in his unconsciousness nor remain identical with the unconscious elements of his being.
>
> C. G. Jung
> Memories, Dreams, Reflections

## Chapter 24 - Kauaí-Açú

I asked Tsiipré to continue my preparation. He refused because he believed that before moving to the sixth stage, I should practice more the preceding steps.

I insisted: "Tsiipré, you´ve praised my rapid progress saying that I probably had an important development in previous lives."

"That is right, but I do not want to expose you to needless risks. To start a new stage, full mastery of the previous ones is important. All steps must be very cautious and secure, otherwise, instead of filling your black hole, you may lose your mind."

After a pause to let me reflect about his words, Tsiipré continued: "In the next stage, you will seek a direct contact with Kauaí-Açú, introducing yourself and asking permission to operate in the spiritual domains. But before giving you specific instructions for this journey, I want you to learn more about Shamanism."

"Fine. I'm always interested on how and why things work."

"Well, do not expect a rational explanation about how and why. Spiritual phenomena are not explained by reason. What I can tell you is what I know, either through my own experience, or from teachings of my mentor, the old Shaman."

"I'll be glad to learn that much."

"I believe I have already told you that, the methods of Shamanism are essentially similar all over the world."

"How could this method have spread all over the world? Have the civilizations been in contact? How could this cultural manifestation have spread without a meeting among the various groups?"

"That I do not know. But it is a reality. I can only speculate that, in entering the inner world, the world of spirits, you are in an altered state of consciousness. Therefore, there is no time nor space, so the spread of the same methods throughout the world should not be considered so mysterious."

After another pause for his words to sink in, Tsiipré went on: "One of the functions of the Shaman is to heal. Of course, he is not the one that effects the cure, although, in less precise language, the cure is attributed to him. He is only Kauaí-Açú´s instrument of cure. In this role, the Shaman may have to undergo a great mental, emotional, and spiritual adventure, involving both himself and the patient. In his heroic journey, with his efforts, the Shaman helps the patient to transcend ordinary reality, including the condition of a sick person. The Shaman's efforts are the catalyst of the patient´s emotional reaction , feeling obliged to struggle alongside the Shaman in order to be cured by Kauaí-Açú.

"I'm not sure I understood you. Please explain a little further."

"In ordinary reality, in which we live most of our waking life, when someone is sick, he feels unwell, feels a concrete ailment and suffers. In a higher level of consciousness, such a state is an illusion. Hinduism, for example, suggests that our life on earth is only a dream of the Gods. Therefore, concrete reality, the fact that you feel pain when you are hurt by a knife, is an illusion in the world of the spirits."

"How does a Shaman find the power to change the mental and emotional state of a patient?"

## The Amazon Shaman

"Through his initiation, which is not carried out without suffering and anguish, the Shaman gains his power, and learns how to communicate with Kauaí-Açú. In this process, through which you are going now, you secure the support of your Protective Spirit and of your animals of power."

"Can anyone learn from another the Shaman's power?"

"His knowledge, yes. But the Shaman's power can only be acquired by personal experiences. The dismembering proof, which is an experience of death and resurrection, is common among Shamans of the whole world. Your old ego dies for a new man to be born."

"My motivation to learn how to be a Shaman is to get my memory back. What was yours?"

"A motivation is not necessary for someone to become a Shaman. The person is called, and if this call is not heeded, the person's mental health may suffer. A refusal may lead to severe mental problems."

"I haven't received any call yet."

"That is what you think. Your plane's crash near our tribe, your loss of memory – if you had fallen without anybody seeing it, you would have died."

"Do you think this might have been my call?"

"It is more than thinking, it is a fact. Do not forget that it was no coincidence that I was nearby and ready to help you. Also, if you had not lost you memory, you would probably have left us. Your own motivation to retrieve your past and clear out your black hole, makes you work hard to learn how to be a Shaman. Don't you think this is too much just to be a coincidence? Can't this be your call?"

"Well, I hadn't thought of it this way. But you're right. Anyway, I would like to insist that we start the sixth stage."

"We should not rush life. I will tell you a story.

Tatiú was a Shaman's apprentice for several years. He always complained that his training was taking too long, and could be shortened. His mentor used to reply: "You shouldn't be in such haste. A Shaman's apprenticeship is not a question of time."

"Why not? I've been practicing for many years. You told me that you were an apprentice for a much shorter time."

"We carry what we learned in past lives. Those who have had previous training advance more rapidly. Don't let this discourage you."

"But Tatiú was not convinced. He was sure he was prepared, though the Shaman knew he was not. Tatiú thought highly of himself, and his ego was still a problem. After insisting and not obtaining permission from his master, Tatiú decided to go ahead and take matters in his hands.

Already knowing the steps he should take, he presented himself before Kauaí-Açú, without his Shaman's permission. He came near Kauaí-Açú, but couldn't stand the intense light emanating from him. Tatiú lost his mind.

That set me thinking. "Would I also run the risk of such an accident?"

"Nothing can be assured in the spiritual world. This may happen to anyone who tries to rush the process, and run the risk without being prepared," said Tsiipré. "I hope you understand why we have to be careful."

"Well, my case is somewhat different. I wouldn't lose my memory, since I haven't got one at this moment."

"You are making fun of it, but I hope you take my words seriously. Believe me. There are worse things than losing your memory. You could lose your mind."

I didn't have to wait long. A few days after that conversation, Tsiipré called me. He wanted to give me the preliminary instructions for the next stage of my journey.

"The purpose of the meeting with Kauaí-Açú," Tsiipré said, "is to ask for his protection and for your acceptance as a Shaman. This sixth stage is extremely important, because it will give you the strength for the seventh and last stage of your training. You must go out tonight, and look for a protected place in the forest, a place of power. Use your intuition."

"Can it be the same spot where I received my song?"

"Probably yes, if that is where your intuition takes you. You will stay there for three days and three nights, eating nothing, drinking only water. It would be interesting to have a spring nearby. It not only provides you with fresh water, but is a great source of positive energy. Stay in meditation most of the time you are there"

"What if I feel tired?"

"You should not feel tired, because the meditation will refresh you. But if you do, try to sleep a little. At the start of the third day, you will mentally look for a very large tree, which your intuition indicates to be the center of the world. Climb up the tree, as far as the Upper World. That is where Kauaí-Açú symbolically can be found. After the reverences he deserves, ask for his permission to be a Shaman, and also for protection in the seventh and last stage, the most hazardous of your journey. If all goes well, within a short time you will be prepared to seek your memory."

I left at once towards the place I had already chosen in my mind. The journey took a little longer because the night was dark, and after crossing the lake, I had some trouble to climb up the mountain, and find my place. On arriving there, I sat down to meditate. I spent most of the three nights and two days of meditation singing the song of the Spirit or talking with ShuoKua. Finally, on the third day's dawn, I left on a mental journey in search of the Center of the World. I found a huge tree, the biggest one I had ever seen. My intuition agreed that this was the tree I was searching. Climbing it would be hard, but I was convinced I would succeed.

I started the climb. Suddenly, I felt that I had got hold of a snake. I had a strong sensation that this had already happened to me once in my life. This time, I was not dominated by terror. I saw that my snake, Earth, was helping me climb the tree, pushing me upwards.

I tried to recall sometime in the past, when I had a faint idea I was in a situation like this, and the image of a snake that I held and let go for fear came to my mind. This had caused the fall that put me in the hands of Tsiipré. In this true vision, the snake was helping my spiritual growth. My journey came to a critical point, where I was unable to reach the next branch. The distance was too great. I thought for a few seconds, and called Ray to help me. Holding me delicately with its claws, it took me to the Upper World.

I was then above the clouds. Again, I had the impression of having been in a similar situation before. I saw myself for a brief moment, flying in an airplane over the clouds. Was I retrieving my memory? This thought excited me, and the vision vanished.

Ray deposited me in a forest of huge and majestic trees. They irradiated an ethereal, supernatural light, that gave me absolute calm and tranquility. My intuition took me to the east, in the direction of a strong white light.

After walking a few miles, I got to a lake, the bottom covered with golden nuggets, coloring in yellow the transparent water. A high and clear waterfall was descending straight into it, without disturbing the stillness of the lake, as if the falling water weren´t touching its surface.

I had to cross the water curtain. Something was pulling me beyond it. I walked on the surface of the golden lake without wetting my feet. I crossed the curtain and felt the cool water. I looked up and saw a large throne, on which a giant was sitting. He had pure features, a gentle face, and an expression of kindness and peace. On his head, a headset made with large feathers of all colors. My ears were filled with the sounds of thousands of birds, singing a most beautiful symphony coming from above. Together with the music, a delicate scent of wild flowers.

## The Amazon Shaman

I would have liked to get closer, but I didn´t feel strong enough to stand the luminosity that emanated from the being in front of me. I knelt down right there, over the waters, lowered my head and said: "Kauaí-Açú, I humbly ask your permission and protection to become a Shaman."

I felt the deep look of Kauaí-Açú over all my being. After some time, I heard the sound of thunder. I didn't hear words, but I understood clearly.

"You have my permission and protection. But you also have another mission: to save the Amazon forest and the Indians.

The sound of the celestial music increased and filled the whole space. I felt that my prayer had been well received. But I also felt the weight of my mission.

I was kneeling on the water. Suddenly, I submerged in it, as if the lake were baptizing me. I went toward the bottom, and lost the notion of time and depth. I lost conscience. When I awoke, I was near the lake, still kneeling.

I stayed in that posture for a long time, my eyes closed, feeling in my body the heat radiated from the bright light of Kauaí-Açú, and the celestial music in my ears.

Now the music turned into my song. I was at once transported to my place of meditation, where the water from the spring greeted me. I plunged into it, like in a second baptism. Despite the three days without food, I wasn´t hungry. A new energy took possession of me.

It was time to go back. I got down the mountain, got on the boat and rowed to the village. I arrived at Tsiipré's shack, where I met him. He smiled as he saw me. I immediately knew that he had mentally accompanied my pursuit. He seemed to have been really concerned about my safety. I didn´t have to tell him all that happened; my expression showed my satisfaction.

After a few minutes, he broke the silence: "Now, you have to tackle the last part, the hardest and most hazardous. Not that the one you´ve just finished was easy, but the seventh stage is more difficult, and it is where most of the aspiring Shamans give up, or have their egos unstructured. However, with Kauaí-Açú's protection, and some more preparation, you will make it. As I have already said, you probably have been a Shaman in a previous life, and this is speeding your training."

"Why do you think so?"

"Your progress in a few months is the equivalent to years of work of many other aspiring candidates."

> The loss of spiritual values has made men lose their objectives in life. They live without a meaning for their lives. Their lives became empty. Why live? To become richer, to collect more stars, to have vassals, to drink more alcohol, to light up and turn off more lamplights, to own more cars?
>
> Roberto Lima Netto
> The Little Prince for Grown-ups

## Chapter 25 – Gold, Always Gold.

"Hi, John, you around here? I thought that, after having become rich, you wouldn't show your face in Formoso anymore.

I didn't answer. I was not interested in idle talk. It was Monday, and I was near my boat, waiting for my two helpers, Ben and Jake. It was eight o'clock in the morning, temperature in the high nineties with high humidity. No breeze.

I was beginning to get mad at these two guys that were so late. I had been away in Manaus for two months, and the two probably were fooling around all that time. Now that I needed them, they didn't show up.

Jake's wife appears and asks me: "Mister John, have you seen Jake?"

"Jake? You are his wife and you ask me?"

"A week ago, he and Ben left on the motorboat, saying that they were going to fish and swim in a lake nearby. They haven't come back, and I'm worried"

"And Ben, what did he say?"

"He said they went up the river, and that he left Jake a few miles from here."

"Is that all he said?"

"Ben claims that he has not seen Jake since. To tell you the truth, he was a little strange, kind of nervous. When I wanted to know more, he went away. Ben arrived back in Formoso yesterday, with a wounded arm, and went directly to see Joseph in the pharmacy. This was four days after leaving with Jake for this mysterious trip."

"Strange! How was the wound?"

"Joseph said that it was an arrow."

"Humm!"

"I've been making inquiries around, Mister. Some people saw Jake leaving with Ben, but nobody saw him coming back. Ben came back alone. Nobody knows where Jake is. I think that Ben knows more than he's telling me."

Something had happened with Ben and Jake. I waited half an hour more, and none of the two showed up for work. I went to Ben's house. He was asleep. When I woke him up, he said he was sick. I couldn't find Jake.

The following day, Ben left for Manaus, without telling me. He returned three days later. I met him by chance in the corner bar. "Ben, if you go on like this, without working, I'll fire you. Keep in mind that I'm your boss, and you have to let me know when you'll be absent from work. Tell me before you go away to Manaus."

"Mister, I had to see a doctor."

"Doctor? Didn't you see the pharmacist?"

Ben was embarrassed and stammered: "I went by the pharmacy and he put a dressing on my wound. But I had to go to Manaus anyway, to visit an uncle who was ill, and took the opportunity to see a doctor there."

"How did you get hurt?"

"I was in the land of the Kauauá, looking at the trees, as you ordered, and was shot in the left arm."

"Did you fight with the Indians?"

## The Amazon Shaman

"No, sir. When they saw me, they attacked right away. They wanted to kill me, but I escaped."

"That's curious! I know that they don't like us, and always drive out white people they find in their land, but that's the first time they've tried to kill one."

"Yeah, but they've tried to kill me, I can assure you. Look at the scar on my arm."

"Didn't you threaten them before they shot you?"

"No, no! Not at all. They started shooting as soon as they saw us."

"Us? Who was with you?"

"No, no. I was alone. But they know I represent your group."

The story didn't make sense. Ben was concealing something. "Who were the Indians that shot at you?"

"They were three, but I don't know any of them."

"And you didn't fight back?"

"I was wounded and couldn't hold my gun properly. They were three, so I thought it would be better to run away."

Ben showed me, again, his left arm with the arrow scar. He was trying hard to appear convincing. But this story was not believable. His wound, for instance. Whenever he had a problem, he used to go to the pharmacy. What could he be concealing? Was it possible that the wound was not the only problem? What if he was becoming impotent, and didn't want the whole village to know it? This would justify going to a doctor in Manaus. Ahah! If I found it out, I would tell everybody, and people would make fun of him. This would be great.

I continued pressing him for answers. "What about Jake? Where's he hiding?"

"I don't know. His wife asked me the same question."

I looked at him in the eyes. Ben was lying, no doubt about it. He was quite different.

"Many people want your job. If you don't want to work anymore, just say so."

Ben was silent for a moment, and said: "Yeah! I think I'll take some time off and rest. I don't want to meddle with those Indians again. It's too early to die."

There was some mystery in the story. Ben was trying to fool me. I also noticed that he had bought new clothes, and even a pair of new boots in Manaus. Where did the money come from?

I spent a good part of the day thinking about all this, trying to figure out what might have happened. No news of Jake so far, and his wife was worried. In the evening, I ran into Ben, in Rick's bar. He was drinking. I decided to help him get drunk. "Have another one, Ben. The celebration of your leaving the job is on me. After all, you have been a good hand."

"No need, Mister. I'm the one that will pay for you. The feast is on me."

That was all wrong! It didn't make sense. As far as I knew, Ben was always tight for money. He would never turn down a free drink. And now, he wanted to pay for my drink. Hard to believe!

"The pal is indeed in the money, aren't you?"

"An uncle of mine was ill in Manaus, and I went there to visit him, but when I arrived, he had died. With no heirs, he left me all he had. Now, I'm in good shape."

"Why didn't you tell me?"

Ben stopped for more seconds than necessary to answer that simple question. He continued to lie: "Well . . . When I went to Manaus he was still alive. He died when I was there, and when I came back with my inheritance, I didn't want people to know about it... you know."

"I know what? I never knew you had a rich uncle."

"He was my mother's brother. He left everything to me. That's why I went to Manaus."

"I thought you said you had gone to see a doctor."

"He was a doctor."

Quite odd. Ben had never mentioned a rich uncle. I was sure he continued lying.

The following day, Jake still had not appeared. I decided to investigate. I went to see his wife, and found her weeping. "Dona Zinha, Jake hasn't shown up yet?"

"No sign of him, Mister. If he disappears, what shall I do with four children to raise?"

"Did he take any money when he went out with Ben?"

"I don't know. I know nothing about money."

I decided to go back to talk to Ben. He was at home. A new refrigerator and a television were in full view. Very odd indeed!

Ten o'clock in the morning and Ben idle at home, as if he had really become rich. Did that uncle exist? I tried an innocent approach.

"Ben, Jake hasn't come back yet. Are you sure you don't know where he might be?"

"I don't know a thing about him. I already told you that."

"Didn't he go to see the trees with you the other day?"

"No. In the last minute, a friend of his showed up in a motorboat and invited him to go to Manaus. I haven't seen him since."

"Manaus? How come you said to Joseph that you left him a few miles upriver?"

Ben was embarrassed. Before he had time to make up a new lie, I pressed ahead:

"That mysterious uncle of yours, when did he die?"

"Shortly after I arrived in Manaus."

"And his estate? All is in order?"

"Estate? What is that?"

"His will."

"There was a lawyer there who prepared everything."

"In two days? And secured the Judge's approval?"

"I don't know about such things. I believe he had the money in the safe."

"You're lying Ben. This doesn´t work with me. You know that I'm smart. I think you killed and robbed Jake. His wife said that he had earned some money."

"I wasn't the one who killed him."

"Now you're in trouble. How do you know that Jake was killed?"

"I don't know anything. It was a manner of speaking."

Ben was nervous. Some more pressure and he was going to sing. "I think we had better go and talk to the sheriff to clear up this whole mess."

"Not the sheriff, Mister. I have a bad record with him."

"Some time in jail won't hurt a liar. Either you tell me the whole story or we´ll go to the police. By the way, I'll ask the sheriff to check on this story of your rich uncle who died."

Ben kept quiet. He seemed to be pondering what to say. In order not to give him time to reason, I kept on the pressure.

"I'll tell the sheriff about that quarrel you've had with Jake. You´ve threatened to kill him. It seems that your threat has been carried out."

"That's not true. I´ve never quarreled with him. I´ve never threatened to kill him. He was my friend."

"My word against yours. We'll see in whom the sheriff believes. After he finds out that the story of the rich uncle is false, it'll be easy to know who is lying."

Ben finally gave up. He told me the whole story of the gold mine, the encounter with the Indians and Jake's death.

"Are you sure he is dead?"

"I can't be sure. He seemed not to be breathing. I had to escape. No time to check anything."

"How strange! I have never heard any talk about gold in these areas.

Ben opened a closet, and showed me about a dozen gold nuggets, hidden under an old pair of trousers.

He said: "There are lots more in the mine. The nuggets are visible, sticking to the walls. I took only what my pockets could carry."

"Where is the mine?

Ben kept quiet again, thinking. He seemed undecided about the answer. He looked at me, then looked the other way. Finally he asked: "How about a partnership?"

"What do you offer me?"

"Fifty-fifty.

Now it was my turn to think. "What do you want me to do?"

"I need help to exploit the mine. It's location is ….." Ben stopped. He was silent for a while, then he said: "We'll need some men to work on the mine. Do you agree on an equal share?"

"I may, under one condition." Ben gave me a look of curiosity. I continued: "I agree if the deal applies to these nuggets that you have now.

"No," he said quickly. "those are mine."

"They won't be any use to you in jail."

"Now you know that I didn't kill Jake."

"I believe you. And the sheriff? I won't tell him the story of the mine. It would stir the whole city."

Ben finally surrendered. With a broken heart, he separated the nuggets into two equal heaps, and gave me the one on the left. I took one of the nuggets from his heap and said: "The agreement is fifty-fifty. What about the one you sold in Manaus? It's this one here."

It seemed that he would object, but he just shrugged and said nothing. He was defeated. We started then to make plans to exploit the mine.

"First, you have to take me there, so that I can see it, and plan the best way to organize the exploitation. We can go tomorrow.

"I think it would be better to wait a few days. The Indians must be mad at us. I believe Jake's shot hit one of the boys."

It was my turn to reflect. Finally, I made a decision:

"They are probably waiting for your return to fetch more gold. If, within a few days, no one shows up, they will quiet down, and will believe that you also are dead."

"Yeah, I think this is all right."

"Who else knows about the mine?"

"Nobody, not even my wife."

"To whom did you sell the nugget in Manaus?"

"To the Colonel."

"To the Colonel? It had to be to that stinking goat!"

"Well, they told me on the boat that the Colonel liked to buy gold."

"It was a great mistake. Now he is suspicious, and will go out of his way to find this mine. We can't let him do that!"

"He thinks the gold is near the Colombian border."

"Do you think you can trick that scoundrel that easy?"

"What should we do?"

"I think we should wait a few days and go see the mine. As for the Colonel, I will take care of him. I'm going to Manaus, and I'll to talk to him."

**Roberto Lima Netto**

> Look at all the incredible savagery going on in our so called civilized world: it all comes from human beings and the spiritual conditions they are in.
>
> C.G.Jung
> Psychology and Religion – Collected Works 11

## Chapter 26 – Talking to the father

A gold mine! I was really a lucky guy! All my dreams would come true sooner than I expected. After knowing the location of the mine, I would be richer than the Colonel, that old goat. Then my revenge could really start.

A plan came to my mind at that instant. With the money I would have, I could hire an army of mercenaries to take care of the Indians.. Those dirty bastards would finally pay for what they did to my mother. Unfortunately, I would have to involve the Colonel in the exploitation of the mine. I would need his political leverage to secure the mine.

I went to see the scoundrel. "Colonel, I have a good deal to offer you."

"A gold mine?"

I was taken aback. "How do you know?"

"One of your henchmen visited me here and sold me a few nuggets.

"A few?"

"Yes. He has been here twice, bringing the nuggets he said belonged to a friend. I didn't buy this crap. Evidently, the two nuggets were his."

Two nuggets? That swindler had mentioned only one. I went on: He was prospecting some trees for me, and discovered a gold mine. How about exploiting it as a partnership?"

The Colonel looked pleased, but also suspicious. "Why are you inviting me as a partner?"

"The mine is on Indian land. We'll need some political pull, should they want to interfere with the exploitation. It's possible that we may have to be ruthless, and having some backup would help. An association with the most powerful businessman of Amazon would be more than welcome. In addition, I am a grateful man, and cannot forget what you have done for me, when I was a kid."

The Colonel's eyes were shining. He wouldn't miss this opportunity for anything in the world. Gold is irresistible and human greed unlimited.

The colonel said: "If I accept, what would be the division?"

"One third each: you, I, and Ben."

"One third for Ben? Isn't it too much? All he did was to find the mine. And he was working for you, being paid by you."

"You are right. I'll try to persuade him to take twenty percent. But only after he shows me the location of the mine."

"That's better. Don't you already know the mine?"

"Not yet. That is the reason I don't want to raise this matter of sharing the gold. For the time being, Ben expects one third. I'm planning to go see the mine in the next few days."

"I like this kind of deal, but before accepting your proposal, I also want to see the mine."

"I intend to go there with Ben next week. I believe that, the first time you should not go. The Indians are somewhat upset, and I don't believe your presence would help."

"But I want to see the mine. I'd like to go and see it right from the beginning."

"Easy, Colonel. You've got a deal. I won't go back on my word. After all, I owe you everything I've got in my life."

## The Amazon Shaman

The Colonel was calmer after I said that. I was the perfect cynic. The Colonel will come to his doom sooner than he could imagine. My revenge was nearing. I thought of my mother, and of how she would be enjoying it in heaven. I would make the Colonel pay for his filthy behavior with her.

After waiting a few days for the Indians to calm down, I picked Ben up in Formoso, and we went up river in my motorboat to see the mine. As we approached the area of the Kauauá, we pulled the boat to the shore, and hid it in the dense bushes around.

I would feel better if we had brought some bodyguards with us for protection, in case of another incident. However, it was out of question to let others know about the gold, let alone the location of the mine.

That particular day we were out of luck, because there were several Indians around. Once we had to hide from some passing Indians. After walking for quite some time, without locating the mine, I turned to Ben: "I think you are fooling me. We have been walking in circles and there's no sign of the mine."

"The mine is right here, but I can't find it. Those dirty Indians! They probably disguised the opening. But we will find it."

I thought that Ben was really confused. He didn't act like he was trying to deceive me. At any rate, a threat might reinforce his efforts to find the mine. "You know, with no mine, I'll have to suggest to the sheriff that you might have killed Jake."

"I've told you that I have nothing to do with that."

"You've also said that you know where the mine is."

Ben said nothing, but he looked at me with anger. I would have to be careful – he might kill me during the night.

As a sort of protection, I said: "I haven't told you yet, but I've talked to the Colonel and invited him to join us in this exploitation. He knows that I'm here with you."

"Why? One more to share the gold?"

"He has political power. Do you think that it's going to be easy to exploit a mine on Indian land? They already have a decree of delimitation."

"What would be his share?"

"We agreed that he would have one third of the mine. There's lots of money for everybody. It's better to share the gold and become rich than being the only owner and unable to grab any gold."

Ben didn't like the idea to have the Colonel as our partner. At least, now he was aware that the Colonel knew of our trip, and he couldn't kill me and think that nobody would know."

Suddenly, I saw Pinuim coming toward us. I thought he was searching for us and when he saw us, he came to talk to me. There was no way to hide from him.

"John, what are you doing here?"

"I'm just walking around, looking at your trees. Who knows ... maybe Kaniuá changes his mind and accepts my offer."

"Don't bet on that. He thinks that you are responsible for the attempt on his life. Tsiipré convinced him that you want to kill him."

"Me? What attempt? Tsiipré does not like me."

Pinuim told me the whole story, with some details that I didn't know. That worried me. Had Kaniuá discovered my plot or was he only suspicious? It explained why the attempt failed to cause a war between the two tribes. In any event, after I discovered the mine, I would hire paid guns to take care of the Kauauá.

I was tired of so much walking around, and it was getting dark. We went back to where my motorboat was hidden, and set up our tent for the night, on the shore of the Rio Grande. We would resume the search the next day.

"Let's go, Ben. Today we have to find your famous mine."

The sun was rising and we started our search for the mine. Today, we should have better luck.

After we walked around for about two hours, Ben finally found the opening of the mine. It was dark inside and our flashlights were in the boat. Lighting a few matches was enough for me to know that I had quite a treasure in my hands. The Indians had disguised it well, but it didn't fool me. I had discovered the mine, and it would belong to me. I'd be rich! I'd be rich!.

I thought it would be better to exploit the mine on another occasion. There were too many Indians around. My aim in this trip was only to know its location. I looked around slowly, trying to determine some reference points. I marked a big tree by carving a triangle with my knife. On the way to the boat, I marked several other trees and paid careful attention to the surroundings. I would have no difficulty in coming back. My half Indian blood gave me a good sense of orientation in the forest, and my photographic vision was very useful.

I decided that we should not take any nuggets this time. We could have come back to the boat to fetch the flashlights and extracted some nuggets, but I wanted to avoid running into Indians with my pocket full of gold. That mine would make me the richest man in the whole Amazon. I would never forget its location.

**Roberto Lima Netto**

> The story (Parsifal's search for the Holy Grail) mentions that King Arthur's knights were called for the search, but each had to choose their individual path. It was considered dishonorable to follow a path already traveled.
>
> For many centuries, most human beings were following the path opened by the Church. That is not possible anymore. You have to open your own path.
>
> Roberto Lima Netto
> The Little Prince for Grown-ups

## Chapter 27 – The Flood

After encountering John, Pinuim went looking for Kaniuá to inform him of his encounter with John. The Chief called Tsiipré to be present and I went with him.

Pinuim said: "John is walking around our land. I found his motorboat near the Rio Grande, hidden in the bushes. I looked for him, and found him with one of his hired hands. They looked tired, as if they had walked for a long time."

"What were they looking for?"

"He said he was visiting the area, to take a better look at the trees. He hopes that Kaniuá will change his mind about the timber deal."

"And what did you say to him?" asked Kaniuá.

"I said that Kaniuá was mad at him, because of the attempt on his life."

"Did he say anything about that?"

"He said he knew nothing about an attack. He asked me to tell you that."

"What a scoundrel!" said Tsiipré. "Who was the other man?"

"I don't know. I think he is one of John's hired hands. He has been here before with John. He has an ugly arrow scar on his left arm."

Ohh! An arrow scar?"

Tsiipré was clearly concerned, but he did not show his fears in front of Pinuim.

When Pinuim left, Tsiipré said: "This story about looking at the trees is false. John has something else in mind: the gold."

I said: "The man is the one we met in the mine. His friend shot at the boy."

"Do you think he told John about the mine?" asked Kaniuá.

"Sure. John is very shrewd, and may have induced the guy to talk," said Tsiipré.

"If he told John about the mine, he is not being able to locate it. Eagle and Uakaú did a good job disguising it," said Kaniuá.

"We have got to be very careful. Things are becoming complicated. John is not giving up that easy. Eventually, he will find the mine, despite our disguises." Tsiipré said.

Kaniuá agreed. "Now, on top of our problem with the drug runners, we have an emergency. If John finds the mine, we will have a catastrophe in our hands."


When I woke up, Tsiipré had already gone out. I did my meditation and went to the lake for my early morning swim. With all the walking, swimming, and boating, I was physically very fit. When I got to the lake, Tsiipré was sitting on a rock, looking at the water with a serious face. "What's bothering you now, Tsiipré?"

"John and the gold problem. A short time ago, some boys saw John again in our land, with the man with the scar. This means that after Pinuim met him yesterday, he did not go away. He slept around here. He is seeking something, and I am sure it is the gold. It looks like they have not discovered it yet."

"What did he do when he saw the boys?"

"John couldn't see them. They hid themselves, and ran back to warn Kaniuá."

"This may be good news, Tsiipré. They have not been able to find the mine. Our disguise must be working."

"Things are going to get much worse. John is a big problem for us, but I hope we will be able to handle him."

"Since there is nothing yet we can do about John, how about the drug guys? They could turn out to be even more dangerous than John."

"What do you propose to do?" asked Tsiipré.

"We can think about the next step of our plan. Despite the turmoil caused in the camp, the trick of the fire ghost by itself is not going to drive the drug runners away. We have to keep the pressure."

After the conversation with Tsiipré, I went to the mine and checked whether the bandits had found it. I entered the mine with a torch and found everything in place, as Uakaú and I had left it. The hole in which we hid the gold nuggets looked untouched. The veins which we had covered with clay seemed intact."

I hastened to give the good news to Tsiipré. "Tsiipré, our worries were unfounded. So far, John has not discovered the mine."

"How can you tell?"

"I was there and everything seems untouched."

"Did you check for footprints near the opening?"

"No. But I can go and check."

"It is too late now. The heavy rains and your own steps would confuse any signs that we might see."

I realized that I had made a mistake going to the mine alone, though Tsiipré did not blame me. I did not know how to recognize tracks.

"What can we do now?" I asked.

"Just wait and ask Kauaí-Açú for help against John and the drug gang."

The next stage of our struggle with the drug runners was going to be less spectacular, but more difficult to carry out. With the help of several Indians, we caught about two dozen poisonous snakes, and put them into baskets. At nightfall, we went to the drug runners´ camp.

This second presentation of our show had the participation of Tsiipré, Uakaú, Katú, Perimatú, and I . We approached the camp when the night was quite dark. No moonlight, which made our work easier.

I was in charge of the operation: "Let's wait a while, until they turn the lamps off, to make sure they are all asleep. Then we´ll release the snakes near the tents, so that they´ll try to seek refuge inside. But let's be careful not to make any noise. When we are done, we'll meet here again. I repeat: be quiet. If they see us, our whole plan will go down the drain."

As I had said to Gonzales and to all the workers that no Indian would ever set foot on this sinister land, if they found that I was lying, it would be the end of our plan.

All was going well, until I stumbled and fell down with the basket, making a noise that resounded in the silence of the night. A light went on in a tent nearby. A man appeared with a flashlight, and pointed it in my direction.

My God, we are lost! My body was painted black with genipapo, and I stood motionless. Did he see me? Luckily, he did not seem to, but I would be sure only on my next visit to Gonzales.

Tsiipré and Katú went back to the village, but Uakaú, Perimatú and I stayed, to watch the outcome of our show. After a while, flashlights went on and there was an uproar in several tents. The snakes were doing their work, as expected.

We had some trouble again, before leaving. Uakaú inadvertently exposed himself from behind a tree, right when a flashlight beam caught him. Again, we were lucky - the men were afraid to come near the apparition.

We went back to the village at dawn. I was nervous. I looked for Tsiipré and told him about the flashlight episode.

"I'm worried, Tsiipré. The men saw Uakaú in the camp area. I always told them that no Indian would come to that patch of land."

"No use to worry about what you cannot change. Let us wait and see how they will react."

"Well ... To know their reaction I'll have to visit them. And then, it might be too late to worry."

I decided to wait for two days before visiting the drug camp. The flashlight episode was bothering me and I had doubts about the reception I would get there. At least one of the men had seen Uakaú.

Tsiipré called me for the next stage of my initiation. The day of my major test finally arrived. I was feeling a mixture of satisfaction and fear. This would be the final stage, the one that would prepare me to get my past life back.

Tsiipré called me in the evening and said: "This time I will not give you any specific instructions. I just want to warn you that the process involves suffering and pain. Be brave, and all will come out well. Now, get into trance and proceed to the inner world. I will be there, waiting for you.

I did as Tsiipré ordered, and met him at the exit door of my cave, after passing the aquatic tunnel. We walked for several minutes, hearing a beautiful symphony.

The music started fading and changed into dissonant noises. We came to a clearing in the midst of a dark forest.

"Walk in alone," said Tsiipré.

It was a dreadful place. A strong smell of sulphur made breathing almost impossible. The noises were getting louder and louder. The closer I got to the center, the louder the sound. Pain in my ears. Fear. I stopped. I felt like running away from the place. But if I did that, I would never fill my black hole. Only this thought made me keep walking toward hell.

I reached the center. Horrible animals appeared from the air and surrounded me. They looked like demons. I had no chance to escape. They took hold of me and started dismembering me. What an excruciating pain!

I screamed for Tsiipré's help. He had followed me and now was merely watching the scene, unruffled. My suffering reached the limit of my physical resistance. I was desperate, angry at Tsiipré for not helping me.

My soul came out of my body and, despite the great pain and anguish, it seemed to be in peace. This split of body and soul confounded me. I was desperate – my body - and at the same time tranquil – my soul. Which one was I, my real being?

The pain made me faint and I could not feel my body. Now, I was only soul. Through the eyes of my soul, I continued to observe everything. I saw when they spread my body apart, each part in one direction. My head was put in the east, where the sun rises, my legs and arms divided between north and south, the trunk in the west. Of my innards, only the heart was taken out and placed in the center.

Having finished their task, the demons went away. Tsiipré came closer and began to put the pieces of my body together. In a few minutes I was whole again. That is, almost whole, because I felt that something was missing in my head. Unfortunately, it wouldn't still be this time that I would retrieve my memory.

That flaw did not diminish my euphoria. I was feeling in the seventh heaven. I was in ecstasy, fulfilled, and confident that the retrieval of my memory was merely a matter of time.

Two days later, I pulled myself together and went to visit the drug runners' camp. I was met by a worried Gonzales, anxious to see me and talk.

"Oh man, I'm glad to see you. Some strange things have happened around here."

"Like what?"

"A learned man like you, an anthropologist with experience of living among the Indians, do you believe in their creeds?"

After a studied silence, trying to convey a feigned insecurity, I said: "I don't think I do, Gonzales. However, living among these people, you see so many strange things. I'm beginning to have some doubts about the rationality of the white man. I'm losing the certainties of a civilized person. Science cannot explain everything." I made a new planned pause. Gonzales was gazing at me, without a word. I continued: "At least with the scientific knowledge that we have today."

"That story about ghosts in this area ... do you believe it?"

"If I did, I wouldn't set my foot here. After your arrival, have you seen any Indian around?"

"No, I haven't. So many odd things have happened around here that I think the Indians may be right. My men are scared."

I disguised my relief to hear him saying he had not seen any Indian in that area. I said: "Mind you, I'm unable to explain the case of the fire ghost. To be honest, I think you have exaggerated it. If I'd been here, and had seen it with my own eyes, perhaps I would have an explanation. But it's not because of a single and poorly described episode that you'll believe in that Indian myth of a ghost area."

Gonzales was annoyed: "It's because you weren't here on the day of the ghost. I wish you had seen it with your own eyes, so wouldn't doubt. But that's not all. Mysterious things continue to happen."

"Like what, for example?"

"Two nights ago, the camp was invaded by snakes."

"Strange. Usually snakes do not come close to a camp, where there is much activity. Are there rats here? Any food leftovers that might attract rats? The snakes may have come after the rats."

Gonzales scratched his head before answering. "I haven't seen any rats here."

"Which doesn't mean they don't exist. Anyhow, it's all very strange. I agree with you. Thank God I don't live here."

"And there's more. Half of the men swear they saw the ghost of the Shaman of your story, looking at our camp, on the same night of the snakes."

"How come?"

"One of our men is positive that, as he turned his flashlight to that tree, he saw the old Shaman of your story."

Gonzales pointed to the tree behind which Uakaú was hiding and had been caught by the flashlight. I made no comment, but a keen observer would have noticed my repressed smile. Uakaú had become the old Shaman. I'm sure he would laugh at that.

We changed the subject of our conversation and began to talk about the rainy season. Summer would still last for about two months, but winter was already in the minds of people. Winter was really unpleasant, because of the mosquitoes, of the muddy rivers, of the hunting and fishing difficulties . It's said that there are only two seasons in the Amazon: summer and winter. In summer, it rains every day; in winter, the whole day.

A few minutes later I said good-bye, on the excuse that I had to visit some place nearby.

Now was the time for the final blow. The men at the camp were already scared enough, but all the trouble we had created for them did not justify their giving up a practically completed landing strip, plus all the laboratory installations almost finished. Now it would be all or nothing.

In my strolls through the forest, I paid special attention to the discharge system of the creeks in the area. With heavy rains, these streams rapidly become torrential. The campsite was in a lowland area, on the banks of the Rio Grande. Two streams of clear water flowed from a hill about two miles to the north. With heavy rains, they changed their appearance. They would overflow, and carry to the Rio Grande a large amount of muddy water, with lots of rocks.

During one of my walks with Uakaú, we took a look at the hillside and found the source of the two streams. The one that ran on the east side of the camp could be diverted with some effort.

"Our next surprise to our friends will be a bath that they will never forget," I said.

"It will take a lot of work to divert this stream."

"Oh! Don't exaggerate. It´s not that difficult, and we've got to do it. Now, it's all or nothing."

We went back to the village and spoke to Tsiipré. He liked our plan. With his help, we were able to bring together a few Indians to work with us. It could be done in the daytime, with no risk that we would be seen by the drug people because the site we were working on was far from their camp.

Kaniuá also liked the idea and approved our plan. The good results of the previous actions helped the acceptance of our new scheme. The Indians were having fun with our theatricals. Even those who didn't take part in the action enjoyed listening to the stories of how the white men were scared. As I was already respected for being Tsiipré's assistant, I became still more honored.

When my ego was getting inflated with all the praise, Tsiipré called me: "I want to repeat my warning. Be careful with your ego. You are preparing yourself for a difficult struggle, the retrieval of your memory. Your fondness for your ego is harmful to your spiritual way. Never forget that all is the grace of Kauaí-Açú. We are instruments in his hands. Control your ego, instead of letting it control you."

Tsiipré, as always, was right.

The following day, very early, we left the village, taking with us five of Uakaú's friends. We arrived at the site of our work at about ten o'clock. The sun was hot, but we were working in the shadows of big trees. The earthmoving was small, but took three days. The progress was slow, especially on the first day. On the following day, two Indians didn't want to go back and had to be replaced by others. On the third day, the work was practically done by Uakaú, Katú, and me. We finished the job. Now, all we had to do was to wait for a heavy rain, and tear down a small passage in the wall that kept the stream on its original bed. If we made a small hole in this earth wall, the force of the water would enlarge it. This would be a work for Uakaú and me.

Our plan was to block the original river bed with rocks, change the course of the water forcing it to run the way we wanted. With the small opening and the rocks, already prepared on the side, which we would throw down to block the original river bed, the hole would grow larger and direct the water to rush through in force.

We waited two days for a really heavy rain. On the first day the skies were threatening a downpour, Uakaú and I ran to the site of the water diversion. The rain wasn't heavy enough, and we decided to wait for a heavier one. We couldn't make a mistake.

However, the experience was not wasted. In case of a really heavy rain, we would have to start the diversion as quickly as possible. We didn't want to waste water. To improve our chances of success, Uakaú and I decided to set up camp on the site and sleep there.

On the third day, the big rain came. We acted quickly. First, we opened a small hole on the wall that blocked access to the new river bed. Then, we dropped earth and rocks on the original bed. This last operation was almost unnecessary because the alternate course that we offered to the water was steeper. However, our work reinforced the water to flow towards the new bed.

Summer rains in the Amazon are usually heavy, but that particular one was especially heavy. Having done our work, we ran to the observation point we had chosen, to watch the results of our efforts. It took us about fifteen minutes to get there.

What we saw was terrific. The laboratory was totally destroyed by the water. No sign whatever of the tents and the equipment. They were on the bottom of the river or floating downstream. Some boxes were still afloat in the current of the Rio Grande. Practically nothing was left of the camp.

Uakaú and I could hardly contain our joy. We ran to the village to tell the good news.

"Even so, we can't be sure that they will give up," said Kaniuá.

"That, I'll find out tomorrow. I intend to inspect the place," I answered.

The next day, I went to pay a visit to Gonzales. He was already leaving with what remained of the camp, practically only the boats. He was in a hurry and in a bad mood, so that there was almost no talk. Before climbing into the boat, he said: "It's amazing how some people still don't believe in ghosts!"

When we came back to the village, I had to repeat the whole story several times. The Indians keep a tradition of nurturing their stories, passing them on from generation to generation. Their memory is fantastic. The story that Uakaú and I told them was immediately memorized and repeated by the youngsters.

The ejection of the drug runners deserved a feast, in which a little theater replayed the main parts of the action. The fire puppet, the night of the snakes and, finally, the flood. The village had a lot of fun.

My ego was already inflating and trying to take control, but in good time, I remembered Tsiipré's advice and with a mental prayer, I thanked Kauaí-Açú for the successful undertaking.

> My definition of a devil is an angel who has not been recognized. That is to say, it is a power in you to which you have not given expression, and you push it back. And then, like all repressed energy, it builds up and becomes completely dangerous.
>
> Joseph Campbell
> An Open Life

## Chapter 28 - The Enemy

Indians are cheerful, they like to have fun, and the ejection of the drug runners was an excellent reason. The celebration that began soon after the victory was going on with the same enthusiasm. Two days in a row with dancing, singing, flutes, maracas, and drums. I had to tell and retell the story in detail a thousand times.

The Indians have an excellent memory and are capable of repeating every word they hear. In my continuous storytelling, whenever I changed some words, I was promptly corrected amid lots of laughter. They memorized everything, but even so, they liked to hear the stories over and over again. I think that listening to the story, they felt as though they were living it personally. This gave them, particularly to women and children, a special sense of participation.

During the intervals in which neither Uakaú nor I was telling the story for the umpteenth time, groups of boys tried to reproduce the various scenes as in a small theater. There was a dispute for my role as well as for Uakaú's, but no one wanted to act the drug runners. The solution was to repeat the performance a number of times, rotating the actors.

During the festivities, I met Tsiipré by chance. He called me aside and said: "I see that you are the center of attention.

Be careful not to let your ego inflate. True growth requires a distancing from the ego. You must be aware that all the attention and praise may hinder your spiritual growth. Remember that we still have to recover your memory, and the last thing you need is an inflated ego."

"You have already said this. I must say that, in these first days, I am in a state of grace. Not because of driving out the drug people, nor because of the attention bestowed on me by the community, but because of the peace I've been feeling since I've met Kauaí-Açú, and the experience of reuniting my body and soul. The death and resurrection passage is very strong in my mind. After that, the expressions of admiration from the boys can hardly affect me. Anyway, thanks for insisting on your advice."

"That is what everybody thinks. But the ego is subtle. If you are not conscious and alert, it can dominate you again."

Once the festivities were over, the routine of my life continued. Meditation in the morning, swimming at the lake, walking, and sometimes fishing and hunting with Uakaú and his friends. My day always ended with the evening meditation before going to sleep.

My memory hadn't improved, but despite my inner emptiness, I was confident that I would recover this lost piece of myself. I was no longer anxious for this to happen soon. I knew that with Kauaí-Açú and Tsiipré's help, sooner or later I would get it back. For the first time I wasn't anguished about my black hole, nor worried about the day on which I would recover my memory. Everything was in Kauaí-Açú's hands.

I was happy. Our problems were being solved, the drug runners were a thing of the past. The worst problem still worrying us was the gold. But I was confident that, also in this case, Kauaí-Açú would help us.

One night, Tsiipré called me with a surprise. We were going to get my memory back. I was nervous. Since the death and resurrection passage, I succeeded in avoiding my anxiety for this to happen, but now it came back in force. The long expected day of finding my black hole was near. I was eager to move on, but also afraid. The pain involved in the last stage was still vivid in my mind.

Who am I? A good, decent citizen or an outlaw? What was I doing flying an airplane over the jungle, on a route where no airplane ever flies? Am I connected with drug dealers? Now that I was on the verge of being capable to answer questions, all of these thoughts occupied my mind.

Tsiipré began to sing and to prepare for a trance. He asked me to accompany him. His shack was full of smoke. Green leaves of the sacred plants. In a few minutes I reached a deep trance. I went to my inner world through my door: the cave with the aquatic canal.

Tsiipré was waiting for me at the exit.

"What shall we do now? I asked.

"Follow me."

"Where are we going, Tsiipré?"

"To look for the Jurupari that stole your memory. You will fetch it and I am going to help you. We will go to the Center of Hell. Are you afraid?"

"After the last experience of death and resurrection, I thought I would hardly fear anything, but I was wrong. Yet, I feel secure with your presence, and I know that I have Kauaí-Açú's protection."

"From here on, speak only the essential. We are entering the territory of the Juruparis."

We went by a beautiful valley, walking beside a clear brook. In the air, the scent of wild flowers and a celestial music. We walked toward the sunset. As we approached hell, the Juruparis territory, the light started fading, the music turning dissonant, and darkness falling. The fragrance of the flowers mixed with sulphur odor. Suddenly, the music changed into a strong noise, hurting my ears in an increasingly frenetic rhythm.

We came to a heavy gate, guarded by two gloomy creatures that Tsiipré said were Juruparis. I had never seen anything so ugly. I already knew some Juruparis, but these looked much fiercer. Their skin was gray with a jelly texture, and their bodies exhaled a smell of rotten meat.

I thought how horrible it would be to have to fight with one of these creatures. Just the touch of their skins would make me shiver. Tsiipré read my mind, for he whispered in my ear: "You have still a lot to learn about hell. Do not show any fear."

Then, addressing the ogre, he said: "I am Tsiipré, Shaman of the Kauauá, assistant to Kauaí-Açú. I am master of light and darkness. I conquered them in great fights. I came for my friend´s piece of soul that was left behind. My friend is a powerful Shaman, worthy of having back his missing part."

"We are guardians of the gate of the end of the world. No living being crosses this barrier."

"Tsiipré will cross, and so will my friend."

We had to fight the creatures. Tsiipré knocked out his opponent quickly and watched my fight. My first contact with that jelly skin was repugnant. I controlled myself and fought the best I could, concentrating my mind. I managed not to think about the aspect of the creature. I finally immobilized it. Tsiipré liked my performance.

"You still have to learn a lot, but this was an excellent beginning."

"Thank you. I don't have enough experience fighting Juruparis. My initial problem was controlling my repugnance. I really have a lot to learn."

"You are conditioned to fighting with the body, but in the spiritual dimension you have to use your mind. Look right in the middle of your opponent's forehead, and try to gain control over his spirit. Use your willpower and your

## The Amazon Shaman

confidence, knowing that you will win with Kauaí-Açú´s assistance. If you have fear, do not fight before you dominate it. If you are not confident of victory, it will not happen. If you control your opponent's will, you will win. Remember, the enemy is as big as you imagine him to be."

We moved forward, leaving behind the two unconscious Juruparis. We soon came to a lake of dark waters, with a sulphur odor mixed with a strong smell of sewage. On a small beach, we found an abandoned boat.

"Let's take the boat and row to that island in the middle of the lake. But be careful. You will see many drowning souls asking for help. You cannot help them," said Tsiipré.

"Why can't I?"

"If you try to help them, you will be done for. You do not have the strength for that, yet. Your task is to survive. We will collect your memory and get out of here. In time, your strength will increase and you will be able to help others."

We arrived at the island and went to a place which seemed an abandoned prison. In the past, that construction must have been a medieval castle. With the passing of time, the lack of repairs led to these ruins. The roof was gone. Charred wooden pieces indicated that it had burned down.

In the basement, where the dungeons used to be, there was some activity. Shouts, wails, and laments made the place more terrifying. In spite of all my preparations, I was afraid. I followed Tsiipré through the ruins to the basement where the lamentations came from. The basement had many cells, full of suffering souls that were making the sad choir we heard. The cells had no doors.

I asked Tsiipré: "Why don't these souls just leave?"

"They are unable to want that. Their will has been taken away from them. All they can do is to show regret."

"Can't we help them, somehow?"

"They have been here for a long time. There is nothing we can do for them. They are condemned to eternal hell."

"How have they happened to be in such a condition?"

"When still living, they prepared this future. Now, they are paying off what they did on earth."

"Will they ever finish paying?"

"Perhaps in one hundred, one thousand years, they may reincarnate. In this new life, they will have another chance to grow spiritually."

"They will have to wait one thousand years in this hell?"

I didn't have the time to go on feeling sorry for those beings because we soon found the lost part of my own soul in one of the cells. The door was open, but the soul was dispirited, totally without energy.

Tsiipré addressed it: "Let's get out of here. We do not have much time."

The soul seemed not to have heard Tsiipré. It stayed in its corner, moaning and squirming, as if with some affliction. Tsiipré seized it and dragged it away.

We left those dungeons and ruins with great relief. Tsiipré carried the piece of my soul, which seemed heavy.

"Do you want me to help, Tsiipré? After all, that's part of me."

"You would not have the strength to carry it. Your time has not come yet."

We walked toward the lake as fast as Tsiipré's load would allow. When we got there, the boat had disappeared.

"That is the Juruparis' doing. They know that they do not have the power to hold me here, but they believe they can get you."

"I can swim."

"NO! Not in this lake. If you put your foot in it, all your energy will go away. You will be like this piece of soul that I am carrying."

"What should I do then?"

"Concentrate. Call your Protective Spirit."

Following Tsiipré's instructions, I sat on the ground and began to sing my music. In a short time ShuoKua appeared. Seeing him beside Tsiiptré, I perceived how they looked alike.

"I have to cross the lake, ShuoKua. Can you help me?"

"I suggest that you call Ray. This task is easy for it."

I continued singing my music, mentally calling my Royal Hawk. It appeared, held me gently with its claws and we took off.

Flying over the lake, I could see again the great number of drowning souls. I realized, once more, that this was hell. While some souls suffered and wailed in the dungeons, with no will to free themselves, other souls drowned eternally in the lake, waiting their thousand years for a new incarnation, a new chance. Would the living people behave as they do on earth if they were aware of this drama?

In a few minutes we were on the opposite margin of the lake, and from there to Tsiipré's shack it was an easy walk.

**Roberto Lima Netto**

> **"Know thyself"**
> Inscription at the entrance of the Temple of Apollo, in Delphi

## Chapter 29 – Light again

I awoke very tired next day. I was still dizzy, trying to remember where I was. Suddenly, a flash in my mind lit up my black hole: my real name was William, as ShuoKua had told me before.

What an emotion! Light in my black hole. I was struck with joy. What else would I remember? Little by little, new flashes began to come. I saw my life as in a videotape: my childhood, my youth, my graduation, my job. My parents! I remembered them affectionately, but I also remembered that they were dead, and my eyes filled with tears. Other images followed to soften these recollections.

I jumped from my hammock and went out of the shack. The sun was beginning to rise, and the morning was still fresh. I was very happy. Life had never been so beautiful. Now, I remembered Valerie and my friends. I wept. Still excited by so much happiness, I went to tell the news to Tsiipré. "Tsiipré, Tsiipré! I´ve found my past."

He smiled knowingly.

I continued thrilled: "I also know that I'm no drug runner."

"What?"

"You don't know, but I couldn't understand how my airplane came to crash in the middle of the jungle. I was afraid to be a drug dealer, going to Colombia for cocaine. That distressed me."

"How foolish. Even not knowing who you were, I could have assured you that you had a good character."

I was in a state of grace with the return of my memory, and wanted to go home quickly, to see Valerie and my friends. No doubt I would miss my life among the Kauauá. I hoped to come and visit them soon, bringing Valerie with me.

After living in that paradise, how would I get used again to life in a large city, the so-called civilized life? I was worried. I had no motivation to resume my previous lifestyle. I felt an urge to help the Kauauá and a sensation that something pushed me to change my life, to devote myself to the cause of the Indians. I wanted to be an ecological warrior for Brazil and the world. The fight against the drug people was already a good credential, and with Kauaí-Açú's help I felt invincible.

The condition of the Kauauá was of great concern to me. We had won the war against the drug gang, but the gold problem continued to hang over our heads. John had been seen in the area. The man with the scar in the left arm was always with him. They probably hadn't found the mine, but we couldn't hope that John would give up easily. Had the man with the scar told John the location of the mine?

Something had to be done to safeguard and preserve the rights of the Kauauá. The demarcation of their land would be a major feat, and I would fight for it. However, we should go further. My goal was to seek a definitive solution to ensure the survival of the Kauauá, with their beautiful traditions and customs. The success of the Kauauá could serve as a model for other tribes. The Kauauá enjoyed the privilege of having Tsiipré, with his rare intelligence, his wisdom, and his knowledge of the white civilization. I decided to talk to Tsiipré. I wanted to know whether he was as concerned as I was. I found him thinking near the lake. "One thing bothers me, Tsiipré. It's increasingly difficult to keep the tribe completely isolated. The loggers, drug runners, gold seekers; for how long will you be able to keep this isolation?"

"I have also given that a lot of thought. So far, in the case of the drug gang, we had Kauaí-Açú's help, we were competent and we also had good luck."

"Something has to be done, but what?"

"This has been discussed in our Council on several occasions. There is no ideal solution. We can fight, expelling the white man. It is risky, it solves the problem only for a short time and will cost many lives."

"You don't approve this alternative, right?"

"Of course not. But it is the one preferred by the young and by some councilmen. The ideal solution would be the immediate demarcation of our land, for which I have been pleading for years before the Indian Affairs Agency in Brasília."

"I know that the demarcation is very important, but I doubt it will stop a gold rush. I will help you in Brasília, to bring the demarcation process to a conclusion. But in addition to that, couldn't we do something else?"

"The demarcation may take long, and even if the gold situation does not become worse, the conflict with the loggers may continue. It would be good to do something else, in addition to the demarcation. But what could it be?"

"I don't know, yet. We've got to do something to prevent a gold rush. We'll think of a solution."

Tsiipré understood the situation well. To stay away from the white man was impossible in the long run, and very difficult in the medium term. I was debating in my mind how to persuade Tsiipré to accept a controlled involvement, preserving the culture and the customs of the tribe.

A gold rush in the area would endanger the whole plan. For how long would this apparent calm continue? That night I went to sleep with this problem in my head. In my meditation, before falling asleep, I asked Kauaí-Açú and my Guide for inspiration.

While sleep didn't come, I thought about my life among the Kauauá, from the time I came into Tsiipré's shack with a broken leg and my black hole. I remembered my conversation with ShuoKua in the Golden Eagle. At that time, he told me to work on my spiritual development, and I made a great progress with Tsiipré's guidance.

It's remarkable how life teaches its lessons. You have to learn them one way or another. If you are sensitive and attentive enough to perceive the signals, and are able to change your life accordingly, its course will be smoother, with less upheavals and suffering. However, if you don't understand what God expects from you, he will let your airplane crash.

Part of my training under Tsiipré was the knowledge of herbs. Since the beginning of my initiation process, I used to accompany Tsiipré and Tatainim in their walks through the forest, to gather medicinal plants. I was impressed by the bio-diversity wealth of the forest. It's not by chance that many foreign laboratories are interested in the Amazon, promoting expeditions to gather these valuable natural resources.

I woke up very early next day, enthused with a daring idea in my mind. I wondered if Kaniuá would accept it. I was eager to talk to Tsiipré, but he was out. I sat down for my meditation. It was difficult to concentrate. I couldn't get the idea off my mind. After a long time Tsiipré came back and I immediately asked him to listen to my idea. "Tsiipré, I have a plan that I would like to explain to you, and win your support. Because it's rather daring, I fear your initial reaction, so I ask you to take your time before judging it."

"You do not need to go in circles with me. If the idea sounds good to me, of course you will have my support. Let's hear it."

"Wait a minute. First I want to remind you of a story about Black Elk, the Oglala Sioux Shaman, that you told me. Do

## The Amazon Shaman

you remember what he said when he was ninety years old, in an interview that was transcribed in a book?"

"Sure. He had had a vision that could have saved his people, and he blamed himself for not having, at the time, the courage and the strength to carry it out."

"Well, what I'm going to tell you is a vision that I've had in a dream. A strong dream, a Great Dream. I would very much like to put it into practice, so that I won't feel guilty when I'm ninety. But without your support, I can't do it."

"To help you, I must know what your idea is. Stop going around and speak up."

Tsiipré was also showing eagerness, a rare occasion.

"Before going further, I want to stress that it does not require the community's involvement with the white man. At first, only you and I would maintain this contact. In time, we would train other people to carry on the work. Don't you think this makes sense?"

"Let's have your idea. Your going around is leaving me skeptical. First, I want to be acquainted with your Great Dream."

After I described my plan in detail, Tsiipré's eyes shined. His answer was to take me to see Kaniuá. I described again my idea with the enthusiasm and emotion that overpowered me. I was deeply convinced I had found a wonderful solution for the problem of the Kauauá, one that would be helpful to other Brazilian Indians too. What's more, my plan could prevent further deterioration of the Amazonian forest, and save the region from destruction. It would be the great ecological venture to protect the whole Amazon.

On this occasion, I remembered with my recovered memory, a conversation at Gordon's party, about the risk of the Amazonian forest being transformed into an Amazonian desert. My plan would prevent this. I felt that my enthusiasm was justified.

It took some time for Kaniuá to grasp the concept. He realized what was at stake, but his great conservatism was an obstacle:

"This will bring us again into contact with the white man."

I held back my enthusiasm to let Tsiipré speak, because Kaniuá respected his opinion.

"My brother, I am not sure how long it will take for the demarcation to occur. Remember that at least one white man knows about our gold mine. John does not seem to know yet its exact location, but he is searching it. And, eventually, he will find it.

"We are in the hands of Kauaí-Açú," said Kaniuá.

"Yes, we are. But we have to do our part. If John finds the gold, our problems may return in force," Tsiipré replied.

He paused to watch Kaniuá's reaction and continued: "William has an idea that can be very good for our people and also for the Arakati. Never again shall we have to worry about Johns, Gonzales or gold rushes. And if our project is successful, there will be a great pressure for the demarcation of our land, which could occur earlier than we imagine."

I couldn't keep quiet: "It's a very limited contact. Practically only with Tsiipré."

Kaniuá finally approved the idea and called a Council meeting. As we left, Tsiipré pointed out that this was Kaniuá's usual posture, very careful, not showing outright enthusiasm for any idea.

I was invited to the Council meeting, and noted that Kaniuá had already accepted the idea, although he tried not to show his enthusiasm. He strongly supported my proposal in his presentation to the elders, and succeeded in overcoming their natural resistance. The plan was approved. Now, making it happen depended only on our work. I was greatly excited, eager to start the action. For that purpose, I had to return to Rio.

## The Amazon Shaman

I spent two days saying farewell to that paradise. A temporary farewell, as I intended to come back soon with Valerie. In those two days, I talked at length with Tsiipré, walked around leisurely, hunted and fished with Uakaú and our friends. When I got tired, I would sit down and listen to the birds and to the noises of the jungle, trying to keep them all in my memory, so that I could evoke them in the big city.

On the day of my departure, I woke up early. The first leg of the trip would be a long one, five days. That is the time it takes to go downriver, as far as the Indian Agency station, in the village of Formoso.

I spent the whole trip thinking about my project, expanding and improving it. Even when it was my turn at rowing, I would still keep thinking about the plan. I thought also about Valerie and my friends, my job, which, if my plan succeeded, soon would be a thing of the past. I was going to devote myself entirely to the Indian cause and to the success of the new idea.

I enjoyed the trip. To be sure, I wouldn't call it a trip, but rather a leisure tour, so pleasant were the days. Everywhere I looked, I would see a natural picture of great beauty, which I tried to file in my memory. The weather helped, despite the regular tropical showers.

Arriving at the settlement, it was time to say good-bye. Uakaú wanted to go back immediately. He wouldn't stay even one day to rest. He´d rather sleep in the forest than stay in the city, in contact with the white man. He would face a double effort in rowing upriver.

I introduced myself to the chief of the Agency station, Mr. Peter Anthony. He seemed to be a good person, knowledgeable about the Indians, but disillusioned with the bureaucracy in Brasília. He had been in that station for many years, and was respected by his chiefs in the capital.

Anthony had his family, his wife, a four year old son and a three year old daughter, and he liked to live in Formoso. When his children reached school age, he would have to move. An attraction of the big city is that it offers more opportunities for employment. Anthony already had his job, and didn't want to lose Formoso's peace. If one thinks of the ills of the big city, he might be right. On the other hand, the cultural life of a great metropolis, the possibilities of relationships with people of different philosophies of life, the opportunity to be informed up-to-date on what goes on in the world, all of these aspects favor life in a big city. If my project succeeds, I would have the best of the two worlds, living part of the year among the Kauauá and part in Rio de Janeiro.

I told my story to Anthony, how I happened to be among the Indians. He showed much interest and promptly spoke on the radio with Brasília, asking them to inform Valerie that I was alive. Surely this would be quite a surprise, after so many months of my disappearance.

He also asked, in his radio contact, whether it would be possible to arrange transportation to Rio for me. There was no regular transport in that area. I would have to wait for an Army boat which once in a while went by there, or take a boat of John's FSTC. I'd rather avoid this last option.

Anthony offered me a small room in his modest but hospitable house, to wait for the Army boat. Of course, Formoso had no hotel. But the treatment he and his wife gave me, as their guest, was perfect. Anthony's house was the social center of the settlement. In a city where nothing much happened, I was the new attraction of the moment. I had to repeat my story many times, but I didn't mind. They were all very nice people.

I waited one week for the Army boat. I devoted my free time to improve my great dream. I wanted to be well prepared to develop the plan as soon as I arrived in Rio. The more I thought about the plan, the more I liked it. It would be the redemption of the Kauauá, who I now called my people. If the plan worked well as I was confident it would, the solution for the entire Amazon area would be assured. Because of my fondness for the Kauauá, but also out of ecological consciousness, I was determined to move ahead with the plan as fast as possible, with total dedication.

The trip from Formoso to Manaus was uneventful. It was slower than I would like, but for a good reason. The Brazilian Army is one of the few government bodies that performs social work in the region. Its boat carries physicians and medicines, offering the only means of medical attention to the people in the settlements along the rivers. The stops in each village delayed our arrival in Manaus. In spite of my urgency, I couldn't complain. It was a good cause. The trip was also a lesson to me. The contrast between the kind of life of the population of those villages on the margin of the Amazon River and that of the poor sections near the big cities struck me. I saw the difficult conditions in which the so-called civilized man lives. On the other hand, the Indians who have not been exposed to acculturation, like the Kauauá, considered primitives, live in decent conditions and are happy. Changing their way of life is wicked.

After five days, we arrived in Manaus, where I was taking an airplane to Rio. From Manaus, I called Valerie, talking to her for the first time in months. Our conversation was full of emotion, with a lot of weeping.

I boarded the Varig plane in Manaus. There were no direct flights to Rio. I chose flight RG 2205, a five hour trip, leaving Manaus at 2:25 pm., and arriving in Rio at 8:30 pm local time, with a stopover in Brasília. During the trip, Valerie occupied my mind, but I also gave some thoughts to my idea. I could hardly wait to meet Valerie again. Now that my memory had returned, I missed her every day, every hour, every minute. After long hours, the plane arrived in the Tom Jobim airport, in Rio. My anxiety was at a maximum. I had no luggage. I rushed through the corridor, following the exit signs, passed the baggage claim area in a run and got to the lobby. I found Valerie. I embraced her I kissed and kissed her. In between our kisses, I asked her to marry me.

**Roberto Lima Netto**

> Terrorism is a manifestation of the psyche. It's time we recognize it as an autonomous factor in world affairs. The psychological root of terrorism is a fanatical resentment - a quasi-psychotic hatred originating in the depths of the archetypal psyche and therefore carried by religious (archetypal) energies. A classical literary example is Melville's Moby-Dick. Captain Ahab with his fanatical hatred of the White Whale is a paradigm of the modern terrorist.
>
> Edward F. Edinger
>
> Letter quoted in Archetype of the Apocalypse

## Chapter 30 - The Gates of Hell

A meeting was being held in Zurich, in Monycar's office, an important reunion of the president with all the directors. He was saying: "We have to take some action. We are operating in the red, and our medical products are becoming outdated. As the president, I am responsible to turn this company around, and you can be sure that I will do it, whatever means I have to use."

"Mr. President, we have to be careful not to allow our actions to break some laws," said one of the directors.

I looked around from my position at the head of the table. "I don't give a damn about laws. Without profits we cannot survive." My ten other directors, sitting around, in our office, listened to my words as if what happened to Monycar was not their responsibility. They were older officers chosen by my father, and had become expert at doing nothing under his tenure. Now, my father was dead, and with the company in my hands, the situation of these directors would change drastically. Whoever did not produce profits fast would be fired, no matter how long he had worked for my father.

Negative results were an understatement because the situation of the company was really bad. Monycar was losing a lot of money and if something wasn't done fast, it would shut its doors in less than a year.

One of the directors asked me: "Among the options available to us to improve our sales and profits, which one do you favor?"

"The launch of new lines of products. Our research department has studied the market, and we have concluded that natural products constitute the most promising field for us. There is an increasing worldwide awareness of the advantages of natural medical products as compared to the conventional ones."

"But our company has never had access to the basic elements of such products. How can we expect to enter this market?"

"We have been trying for several months to establish contacts with people who study this area. Our representatives in Brazil are talking to professors at the University of Manaus, who have a good knowledge of the medicinal herbs of the region. We may be able to buy the technology to produce our new lines."

"Would the University transfer the technology to us?"

"Well ... We have to try. But keep in mind that whatever we cannot buy, we will get somehow."

"Might not that be illegal?"

"Would you prefer to go broke, to lose your job? We would merely be doing what several of our competitors are doing. When we get to know the secret formulations, we will apply for patents."

"Would this mean that only our company could market the products?"

"Exactly. Not even the Brazilians who will provide the information will be able to commercialize them."

## The Amazon Shaman

"Isn't that some kind of robbery?"

"Name it as you please. That's real life and several of our competitors have successfully done it. By the way, I am ready to accept the resignation of whoever objects to this practice."

I waited a few minutes to see the reactions of the board. No one was prepared to lose his directorship. All of them agreed to the proposed strategy. I continued: "The New York Times recently had the story of a Brazilian engineer whose plane crashed in the jungle. He became friends with an Indian Shaman who is said to be a great expert on natural medicines."

"Mr. President, what are your plans?"

"Our representatives in Brazil already have my instructions to hire this engineer for our company."

"That is a great idea. Should we be successful, we will gain an enormous lead time."

The meeting ended with enthusiastic approval for my action. I went to my office and asked my secretary to call Brazil. It was 1 p.m. in Zurich, 9 a.m. in Rio.

"Klaus, any success at the meeting with the engineer?"

"I'm having dinner with him this evening. Mark has arranged it. I think we'll get what we want."

\*\*\*

"Valerie, I think that today I'll be able to finish our business plan."

"When you are ready, I want to summarize it in a Powerpoint presentation."

The day following my arrival in Rio, I started working feverishly with Valerie's assistance, in the preparation of our plan. From the very moment I told her of my idea, she was enthusiastic about it. Our first task was the preparation of a full presentation of our idea. With such a report in hand, we would start an intensive program of contacts with various non-governmental organizations (NGOs), both in Brazil and overseas, interested either in the Indians or in the ecology of the Amazon Forest.

As soon as the study was ready, we started our visits. The project met with great interest and approval in all of our presentations to local institutions, and it was equally successful with foreign organizations. In a few months we had received enough support to go ahead with the project. However, all parties wanted to meet Tsiipré, since the execution of the plan depended largely on him. We prepared a meeting in Manaus, inviting all interested organizations and some government institutions as well. A good number of foreign NGOs also planned to be present.

The talks with various organizations produced some side effects. I received a telephone call from someone requesting an interview.

"Mr. William Forrest, my name is Markus Brumel. Call me Mark, please. You do not know me, but I have heard the story of your adventure in the Amazon. I would like very much to have your company for dinner. This invitation includes your girlfriend."

Mark had a strong foreign accent. Even allowing for that, I didn't like his intonation. His voice sounded sort of false. With my new sensitivity given by the shamanic training, I could sense some hidden motives. I wondered what could be his intentions to invite me for dinner. I had a feeling that his real name was not the one he used. Nevertheless, I was curious. If you have enemies, it is better to know them.

"Mr. Brumel, I'll be glad to meet you, but I'd like to know the subject you want to talk with me about."

"Of course. I should have said that before the invitation. I represent a California producer of TV and movie films, and I have a great interest in talking with you about your adventure among the Indians. My company could be interested in producing a movie with you."

## The Amazon Shaman

A film about the Kauauá! It might be a big help in spreading my idea. I accepted the invitation. The dinner was set for Monday, 8 pm, at the Sheraton Hotel.

Mr. Brumel must have had my description because when we arrived at the hotel, he came toward us without hesitation and introduced himself:

"I am Mark. This is my friend and associate Klaus Huber, who also wants to have the pleasure of meeting you, and is joining us for dinner if that is all right with you."

"No problem. This is Valerie, my fiancée."

Mark spoke good Portuguese, with a strong German accent. He should be German or Swiss. He was tall and blond, around thirty, with the looks of a playboy. Maybe he was really a Hollywood type. He tried to be pleasing, but in general, he didn't impress me.

Klaus was older, short, thin, dark hair, probably dyed, around sixty. He was quiet and said practically nothing after the greetings. I didn't like Mark, and Klaus even less. The bad feelings I had in their presence made me wonder if I was right in accepting their invitation.

We were having dinner at a private room of the restaurant. When the four of us were seated, Mark said: "I learned from friends about your great adventure in the forest. I think we can make a film out of it. You know how interested the whole world is in the Amazon region."

It was an excellent idea, but not with those fellows. I didn't trust them in the least. Feigning interest, I answered: "This may be a great idea. Tell me more about it."

Mark spoke at length about his plan. I couldn't put my finger on it, but my intuition, now highly developed by Tsiipré's training, gave me signals that something didn't make sense. Even so, I continued to show interest, to see what Mark was driving at. The dinner proceeded in a lukewarm atmosphere which was offset by my curiosity. What did these guys really want from me? The talk about Hollywood was hard to believe.

At dessert, Klaus spoke for the first time. The way that Mark drew back in his chair, showed that Klaus was the boss. "I represent the Swiss Monycar Laboratory in Brazil. As you undoubtedly know, it is one the biggest labs in the world. My company has a great concern for the well being of mankind. Without neglecting the need of an industry to be profitable, our major objective is to develop medicines that will enable the human race to improve the quality of life.

I thought to myself: idle talk. What's this fellow leading to?

Klaus continued: "To work better for mankind, Monycar is always seeking new ideas, and we realize that the knowledge of the Amazonian Shamans could be extremely useful. We are informed of your training, and of your excellent relationship with the Kauauá."

Soon after my arrival, I was a subject of much interest for the media. My adventure in the jungle stirred the imagination of many people: my appearance after being lost for several months, my life among the Indians, and my being trained as a Shaman, all of this made news that reached overseas. Even the New York Times devoted a good space to it. I was happy with this, because I intended to use all that exposure for the benefit of the project I was trying to develop.

Klaus continued: "I am sure that you can become a great benefactor to humanity if you join your knowledge with the economic and technological power of Monycar. We have the best research facilities in the world, and with the knowledge you have acquired, as well as your friendship with the Shaman of the Kauauá, you will be very important for Monycar. We want to offer you a position of consultant to our company. You name your salary."

Now the game was clear. Nothing to do with a movie. The business was much bigger. Medicines. Monycar was famed, not only as one of the biggest labs in the world, but also as one of the most active pirates of native plants.

I felt like telling them to go to hell. I knew that Monycar was one of the greediest labs on earth. Formulations of medicines that they developed, but for which the market was small, were kept unavailable. Talk of helping mankind! Haha! But it's always wise to keep your opponent in the dark, and try to get as much information from them as possible. I decided to play the game.

"Mr. Huber, I'm greatly honored by your offer. I'm sure I can be useful to Monycar. The wealth of the medicinal herbs to which I have had access is fabulous. The economic and technical resources of Monycar can transform them into extraordinary benefits for humanity."

"I am glad that you also think that way. This makes me believe that you are accepting our offer. And, as I have said, you name your salary."

"Before giving you my answer, I would like to become better acquainted with Monycar and its plans for medicinal herbs. Please, let me have all of your publications on this subject."

Klaus and Mark seemed satisfied with my answer. They probably didn't expect it would be so easy to involve me. They were more relaxed during the desserts, and were even pleasant. Two days later, I received abundant material, articles and publications about herb medicines and their expanding market.

**Roberto Lima Netto**

> The truth of the myth is greater than the truth of facts. The myth has a symbolic language, metaphorical, and thus accepted, is essential for the development of human beings, making their lives meaningful. The mythological images of the Bible symbolize spiritual powers that all humans carry within their psyche, even those who believe themselves atheist. This is why the myths do not refer to facts; they cast their light beyond them, as greater truths, which transcend the facts.
>
> Roberto Lima Netto
> The Jungian Bible

## Chapter 31 – Victory thwarted

In our conversations in Rio and S. Paulo, we felt the strong interest for our conference in Manaus. I received the suggestion to involve not only all the potential partners, but also the media. This would ensure a good worldwide coverage. It was all set for the critical meeting.

At my request, an interested institution took over the organization of the event, allowing me free time to go to the Amazon a few days in advance. I wanted to show Valerie the area, and she was eager to get acquainted with the Kauauá. I traveled to the area with her, to meet Tsiipré and bring him to Manaus. We hired a fast motorboat. Leaving Manaus, we went up the Amazon River, the Rio Grande and the Rio Bonito, to a point near the Kauauá village.

With her adventurous nature, Valerie marveled at everything she saw. Our arrival at the Kauauá tribe was a feast. It was unexpected, as there was no way of announcing our visit. Valerie was a sensation. Everybody wanted to meet Eagle's white woman. As soon as I could, I went to see Tsiipré. "I came here to take you to Manaus. Our plan was very well received by Brazilian and foreign organizations. We're going to have an important meeting for the official presentation of the project, and you must participate."

Tsiipré was very happy with our progress, and promptly agreed to come with us. I invited also Kaniuá and Uakaú. The chief was glad at the news, but did not accept my invitation, even when I pointed out that Tsiipré was also coming.

"Tsiipré will represent the Kauauá people," he said.

"But Kaniuá, your company will be a pleasure for us, and will strengthen the Kauauá's presence at the meeting."

No way. Not even Tsiipré could convince him. But Uakaú was glad to come. Several young people wanted to join us, but there was no room in the boat, except the space reserved for Kaniuá. So we took Katú.

The trip to Manaus was very nice. On the boat, now going faster downriver, Valerie was never tired to show her delight at the landscape, the birds, the animals, and the fishes that she could see all the time. Although she had seen many of these sights when coming up, this was a new world to her. Last weeks' emotions, finding me alive, having friendly talks with the Indians, and the beauty of the scenario, made her weep with no other reason than that she was living through these rich experiences.

As we had plenty of time, I decided to make a break and stay overnight in Formoso. I wanted to introduce Valerie to the good people of the village: Anthony, his family and all the friends I had made there.

We pulled our motorboat out of the river and tied it down securely, near two other boats already there. One belonged to Joseph, the pharmacist, and the other to a visitor who was also staying in Formoso for the night.

Valerie and I would be Anthony's guests. Tsiipré, Uakaú, and Katú preferred to sleep in the woods. Our evening meeting was in Anthony's home.

He asked: "Did you, by any chance, see John's boat, when coming down the river? It seems he is very much interested in that area of the Kauauá."

I hesitated for a moment. The least I talked, the smaller the chances of their knowing that John was looking for gold. If this were known, the Kauauá´s life would turn out to be quite impossible. A gold rush would be the last thing they would want.

Anthony continued: "The people that work for John said he had gone with one of his men to that region and should have been back by now."

We planned to leave very early the following day. That would enable us to arrive in Manaus late afternoon. With some luck, we could avoid crossing with John. We had made reservations at the Tropical Hotel, where we would spend the night in preparation for the great day ahead, when all our hopes to save the Indians and the Amazon forest would be at stake.

I got up early. I hadn´t slept well because we´d been talking with my friends in Formoso until late. Also, I was under much strain, waiting for the great occasion. Anthony and many friends joined us as we walked to the harbor.

As we arrived there, a surprise! Our boat had been sabotaged. Its hull had various holes, its engine dismantled, some parts removed and stolen. Of the two other boats that were nearby. one had also been destructed. The other was gone.

Whoever did that dirty job - probably the owner of the missing boat - knew what was needed to block our chances of arriving in Manaus in time for the conference.

Tsiipré was silent beside me. I asked: "Who may be behind this?"

"Who would be interested in your failure?" he answered.

"I have really no idea."

"You told me about the foreign laboratory. They wouldn't be happy with the success of our project. You would create a formidable competition for them."

"You may be right. S.O Bs. Only they would benefit from disrupting our meeting."

"No use cursing now. We are in deep trouble. Would it be possible to postpone the meeting?"

"Very unlikely. There are many prominent people who confirmed their attendance. Many are coming from Brasília, some from overseas. I doubt they would stay in Manaus for another day."

> The purpose of human life is the creation of consciousness.
>
> Edward. F. Edinger
> The Creation of Consciousness

## Chapter 32 - Saving the forest

"Let's think of a solution," said Tsiipré.

"What can we do?" I asked him.

"I think that we should go to a quiet place and meditate."

I was not so sure this was best thing to do at the moment. "Going into meditation when we need rapid transportation to Manaus? Is it the way to solve our problem?"

"Perhaps because you've spent some time in Rio, you are turning back to be the old William, the rational man." Tsiipré joked.

"Sorry, Tsiipré. You are right."

The whole village already knew what had happened, and many people came to the harbor to be with us. I excused myself and went with Tsiipré to the nearest forest, leaving Valerie with Uakau and Anthony.

Tsiipré had brought his maraca. He began to shake it and to chant his mantra, with my accompaniment.

In a few minutes I reached a reasonable level of concentration and called my Guide. "ShuoKua, you already know of our embarrassing situation. What can I do?"

"The superior man stands firm and does not change his direction."

"ShuoKua, please, metaphors again! I need an objective advice. What must I do?"

"Just because you have recovered your memory, you have become the old William again. Have you forgotten that you are a Shaman now?"

"But I don't understand your advice."

"Send your problem to heaven."

"Again! I still don't get it. Can't you be more objective?"

"More objective? Yes. Talk to Tsiipré. He will understand my message. I'm being very objective."

When Tsiipré finished his meditation, I said to him: "My Guide suggested that I should send our problem to heaven. I didn't understand what he meant by that."

"Radio waves roll in the skies. Anthony has a radio. Let us ask him to help send our problem to heaven. Simple, no?"

"After Columbus made the egg stand, it is very simple to do it."

Through Anthony's radio, we explained our situation to his friend in the Indian Agency, asking him to contact the person in charge of the event in Manaus.

The rest of the day we did nothing. In the evening, we received a message that the man had been contacted, and said there was nothing he could do, except cancel the whole show. I spent the night in great sorrow, seeing all my dreams go up in smoke, rising to the skies.

I couldn't sleep, neither could Valerie. The next day would have been our great day, and we were miles away from where we should be. Having nothing to do, I went out with Valerie for a walk along the river, where we met Tsiipré. He wasn't feeling down like me. I was envious of his high spirits.

"I don't understand how you can be cheerful in a situation like this. We had everything in our hands to save the Indians and suddenly, it all escapes like water between our fingers."

"You're still a man of little faith. Always remember that Kauaí-Açú knows what he is doing. If your well-conceived plans are not working, he certainly has his reasons. You must learn to leave everything in the hands of God."

"If I leave everything to him and do nothing… "

"That is not it. You have to do your part. Then let him do the rest."

"Even so, I can't help being sad."

When the sun rose, I was in a dark mood. Ten o'clock in the morning. I heard a noise and looked up. A seaplane was circling to land in the river. I jumped up, shouted, hugged Valerie and wept. The solution came from the skies, as ShuoKua said. In a few hours we would be in Manaus, in time for our meeting.

The small plane could not take all of us, so Tsiipré and I went first. To my regret, I had to leave Valerie behind. She wouldn't be present at the great event.

I was tense. That would be the day of the big decision. During the trip, I decided to meditate and talk to my Guide. ShuoKua came with his calm smile, and his presence was enough to soothe me.

"ShuoKua, good morning. First I must thank you for your saving suggestion, though I needed an interpreter for it."

"With time, you will learn not to be so rational."

"I'm desperately interested in what's going to happen today. Will our project be approved?"

"When one is in harmony with the divine, success is assured. If there has been no success yet, it is because the process is not complete."

"This doesn't answer my question. Will the project be approved?"

"Have you had a relapse? Having been just a short time in the big city, you reverted to the super-rational William that wants precise answers to everything. Listen carefully: man is as great as his dreams. What is important is that you give yourself wholly to what you are doing."

"You're right again. I'll put it differently. How should I act in today's meeting?"

"Act naturally. No sophistication. Be simple and spontaneous. This way you will assure sublime success."

"Thank you, ShuoKua. Your words soothe me."

"They are not my words. They are the wisdom of thousands of years of your unconscious, which is also mankind's. If you look it up, you can find it in the I Ching, the Chinese book of wisdom."

"I have the greatest respect for the I Ching, but I feel better with your support. When I begin my presentation, I'll think of you. I want your inspiration."

"And you will have it. Remember that I am within you. I am part of your unconscious. Whenever you are in need, look for me inside yourself."


The meeting would take place in the afternoon, in time for the newspapers and television news. We expected to have a good coverage by the Brazilian media. There was also a growing interest worldwide. My personal story of crashing over the jungle, the miraculous rescue, the retrieval of my memory, and the Shamanic training were an extra attraction to our project. The auditorium was full. Representatives of various foreign entities, some of which I hadn't even contacted, were present. The New York Times correspondent in Brazil was attending. There would be simultaneous translation into English.

One of the organizations that was most enthusiastic about the idea had leaked to the media that the meeting might change the economic and social fabric of the whole Amazon region. The media - newspapers, radio, and television - were all present. We had invited the Governor of the State

## The Amazon Shaman

for reasons of protocol, but to our satisfaction, he was present.

I was sitting at the head table, to the right of the Governor. As my name was announced, I got up and walked to the podium, at the left of the table. After greeting the audience, I started the session with a general description of the plan. I could feel the audience's expectation.

"It's a great pleasure for me to bring to your attention an idea that may be a revolution in the life of the entire Amazon region. We are all aware of the severe ecological problems caused by the destruction of the Amazon forest. The seriousness of this situation is unquestionable, but if we don't create viable economic alternatives to replace timber logging, there is little hope in our lifetime for the required dramatic improvement. Laws, regulations, inspections, and the tree removal banning are impotent in the face of the financial rewards offered by that activity. The solution, the only solution, lies in finding some other activities, compatible with the preservation of the environment, and offering greater economic return. So far, this has not been achieved."

I made a pause to drink water. I could sense the expectation in the air

"We also know that many of our Indians live in misery, as a result of totally mistaken acculturation programs. Despite the Indian Statute, many Indian areas have not been demarcated yet. This is the case of the land of the Kauauá, and the support of all of us for the urgent demarcation of that area is a basic requisite for the plan that I shall present to you."

I made a pause, and I could feel the interested tension in the room: "Even the non-indigenous population, the poor people who live in the riverside, survive in pitiful conditions, outside the market economy. But now we shall present an idea that will preserve the ecology of the entire Amazon Region, and also meet the problems of the Indian people and of the riverside population."

At this point I noticed a stir in the press section. Cell phones were busy. Some radios were transmitting the event live.

I continued: We all know the great interest in the world for natural medical products, especially in European countries. This sector of the pharmaceutical industry is having an explosive growth. The traditional industry is a highly profitable business, yet the production of natural medicines is still more lucrative. Also, we all know the great wealth of medicinal herbs in our tropical forest. Still better, we know that the extractive activity is not harmful to the environment, and helps the preservation of the forest. If we can coordinate the interest of the market with the availability of herbs from our forests, we shall be able to prevent the destruction of our great ecological wealth."

I paused to drink some more water and could feel an electrical current involving the audience. I thought that the Governor had come for the exposure to the media, but I noticed that he was listening intently to my words.

"Enough of ecological piracy. The big companies see the Amazon as an inexhaustible source of raw materials for their pharmaceutical products, which they protect with international patents, with no benefits to the Indian tribes, who are the true owners of these rights. We must put an end to that. The Amazonian region, at least the part which is in our territory, is Brazilian, and should be cared by our Indians. They are the right owners of a large part of it."

I was interrupted by applause. That showed that all presents were aware of the harm that bio-piracy caused to Brazil and to the indigenous communities.

"But not only to Brazil. The whole world is being affected by the destruction of the forest. The exploration of the region's herbs can be an extremely important economic alternative to the destruction of the forest."

I made another pause. "Well, I have here with me the person who is probably the greatest expert on herbs in the world. Tsiipré, here at my side. To all the theoretical

## The Amazon Shaman

knowledge he gained in his western education, he added his experience as Shaman of the Kauauá tribe to the knowledge of the Shamans of previous generations, transmitted to him by his predecessor."

Tsiipré instantly became the center of attention, with the flashes of several photographers, and the television cameras focusing on him.

I continued: "The project we propose, using the valuable cooperation of the national and international entities present here, is to open the world market to the medicinal herbs of the Amazon. Initially, we would undertake a pilot project, involving only the areas of the Kauauá and of their relatives, the Arakati. Afterwards, with the expansion of the market - which our studies show can be very large and offer a strong potential for growth - we would develop the project to include other indigenous peoples and the waterside populations. Gathering herbs would provide them with an income, thus enabling them to leave the subsistence economy and improve their living condition. In the pilot project, Tsiipré would train instructors for other native communities. For those who may be interested in details of the project, copies of the feasibility study are available on the table in front of the stage. Tsiipré and I are at your disposal for any questions and clarifications. We'll be happy to provide any further information and for those who may wish to have private meetings, please call on us."

I paused to feel the vibrations of the audience. "Gentlemen, I am sure that this project will represent the redemption of our indigenous populations, the suffering waterside communities, and in short, of the entire Amazon. Moreover, you can be sure that the whole world will also benefit by having better medicines, and by having the ecology of the Amazon region preserved. Thank you for your attention."

The applause was long enough to be gratifying. The Governor congratulated me and Tsiipré, and the press rapidly surrounded us. No doubt our project had made an impact. I was euphoric, but I didn't forget Tsiipré's advice about the ego´s inflation. I mentally expressed my gratitude to Kauaí-Açú.

> They have sown the wind and they shall reap the whirlwind.
> Hosea 8:7 - The Old Testament

## Chapter 33 – The Last Battle

The project was now ready to go ahead. I decided to return to the Kauauá tribe to share our success with the whole tribe, and to enjoy with Valerie a few more days in that paradise. We were eager to meet our friends and share our happiness with them. We hired a motorboat to speed up our trip, and departed the next day.

After staying about a week with the Kauauá, we decided to go to Rio. Without us, the project was stuck. The preparations were ready for our departure the following day. I wanted to use our last day for one more walk with Valerie through the forest. We got up early, and started our morning bathing in the lake. Then, I called Uakaú, and the three of us went for a walk to the Rio Grande. It was a very pleasant day.

Late in the afternoon, the weather changed, and a rain storm was approaching. We were on our way back when near the entrance of the gold mine, we saw a white man. He saw us too, and immediately aimed his rifle and fired at us. Fortunately he missed. Uakaú was more accurate, and the man dropped with an arrow in his chest.

We waited a while, but as the man didn't move, Uakaú went around, and approached him carefully from behind. When he came closer, he saw that the man was dead. The arrow had hit his heart. His pockets and his knapsack were full of gold. His arm had the scar of another arrow. That was quite a relief, and I wanted to run to the village and tell Tsiipré.

I said: "This is the robber that was missing. Now we don't have to worry about him anymore. The only question is what John knows about the mine. He won't be able to answer."

How wrong I was. When I finished speaking, I heard a guttural voice growling behind us: "Quiet, everybody. Drop your bow, you dirty Indian."

We couldn't recognize the voice. Uakaú dropped his bow.

"Now, turn slowly," said the voice.

As we turned around, we were face to face with John, holding a 45 Colt Automatic pointed at us. A man of about sixty was with him, armed, with a 38 Smith & Weston.

I looked at John, and what I saw made me shiver. John had a satanic look on his face, with a contemptuous grin of utter hostile malevolence. Looking at him, I knew that Satan existed.

John said: "I want to thank you the favor you've done to me. I didn't intend to share the money with this fool anyway. You saved me the trouble of killing him."

On saying this, John turned his Colt to the man at his side, and shot him in the head, right between the eyes.

"You should have done a more complete service, killing this other one for me, too. Now, the entire mine belongs to me."

That brutal murder increased Valerie's shock. She yelled at John:

"You animal! How can you kill a man in cold blood like that?"

"The young lady is shocked? Well, you'll be more shocked. This dirty old man is the famous Colonel Casemiro. And he happens to be my father. I should have killed him long ago."

Valerie was going to answer, but he interrupted her:

"You can say whatever you want, you bitch. But you are under my control. For a short time because I'll deliver you all to hell, too. Just wait a bit."

John's eyes were wide open, with a blazing hatred. Looking at him I saw that the devil was in front of me. We were astounded.

"You are too confident too soon, John. The shots will attract other Indians to where we are, and you will be caught," I said.

"Is that so? We'll see. In any case, let's hurry. You are going to help me carry a lot of gold to my boat. And if you try any funny tricks, the young lady will be the first to get it."

John picked the Smith & Wesson lying at the side of the Colonel's corpse, but left the other man's rifle lying on the ground. He motioned us to move. We lifted John's knapsack and those of the other two dead men, full of gold, and started walking towards the river.

John was behind us with his pistol. I had no doubt that he would kill us as soon as we were no longer needed. I was watching his every move, to try something, even a desperate gesture. Exactly now that everything seemed to be going so well for the Kauauá and my great dream for the Amazon was almost becoming a reality. Would John destroy it all?

Uakaú seemed to be sharing my thoughts, for he walked very slowly, trying to gain time.

"If you don't walk faster, I may decide to kill you right here. I don't do it because I would have more work to do, carrying the gold."

John needed us to load the gold into the boat. We would have at most half an hour to save our lives. A downpour began.

I was very nervous. It was not only the fear of dying. I was sad at the collapse of my dream to save the Amazonian Indians; that was taking me to despair. Suddenly, all my training with Tsiipré came to my mind. I calmed down. I thought of Kauaí-Açú and asked for help. I also called my Guide: "Help me, ShuoKua."

We were moving slowly under a heavy rain for over half an hour already. The ground was slippery, and we were watching for John's misstep as the opportunity for our reaction. Now there was very little time left. We were reaching the Rio Grande and probably the end of our lives. John hadn't shown any careless moment. Maybe we would have five minutes more, enough time to put all the gold on his boat. Only a miracle could save us.

Getting to the river, John ordered us to load his boat; with the job finished and ready to go, he aimed his gun at Uakaú.

Kauaí-Açú, help us! I began my last prayer to Kauaí-Açú, and perhaps for the last time in my life, a plea to my Guide. John was going to shoot Uakaú. Suddenly, I saw a snake ready to spring at John. I recognized Earth.

John reacted fast. He aimed his gun at the snake and fired. Like a flash, Uakaú jumped over John. They fell to the ground. Uakaú was much stronger.

I heard a shot. Blood spilled from the tangled bodies. Uakaú got up and John was lying on the ground with a bullet wound in his left shoulder. Uakaú had John's Colt, and pointed it at him. I grabbed the Smith & Wesson.

Unarmed and wounded, John was defeated. Even so, he pulled himself together and tried to escape. He got up, dashed to the river and jumped into the boat. This unbalanced the boat and John fell into the water. With pocketfuls of gold and bleeding from the wound, John began to sink.

Uakaú was going to help him, but attracted by the blood, a shoal of piranhas attacked John's body, which was sinking with the weight of the gold. On the surface of the water, a bloodstain marked the spot where John submerged. The stain grew and was rapidly diluted by the river current. That was our last view of John, the greedy logger, the murderer of his own father. The man who devoted his life to amassing wealth was leaving this world with pocketfuls of gold. Would he be able to use it on the other side?

All of that action took place in a few minutes. Valerie, who had kept herself under absolute control in our walk towards the river, now broke into convulsive weeping. I hugged her and tried to soothe her. The snake was still on the ground. Earth, my animal helper, had saved us, but paid with her life.

I closed my eyes and made a silent prayer for her. I got her answer: "Don't be sad. I told you I have many lives."

Under the white men's logic, this episode could be viewed as a great coincidence. Others would call it a miracle, without any concern for a rational explanation. In the beginning of my journey, I certainly would explain everything by using logic. But now, after my initiation, I have no need of rational explanations for what happens in this world.

I believe that God lives inside and outside each one of us, although few are aware of this. When you know the God that is within you, the so-called miracles happen.

We walked back in silence, in a profound calm. Maybe later we would talk about those events, but now it seemed that all the three of us preferred an inner quietude.

We carried the gold to the mine cave, buried the two dead men and returned to the village. In my evening meditation, I expressed my gratitude to my Guide, to my protective animals, especially Earth, my snake, and to Tsiipré, my master, who had showed me the way.

I was grateful to God, whatever the name you may give him, Kauaí-Açú, Brahma, Allah, Yahweh, or any other of your choice.

> Know that, by nature, every creature seeks to become like God. Nature's intent is neither food, nor drinking, nor clothing, nor comfort or anything else in which God is left out. Whether you like it or not, whether you know it or not, secretly nature seeks, hunts, tries to discover the path on which God may be found.
>
> Meister Johannes Eckhart
> Quoted from "The Choice is Always Ours."

# Books by Roberto Lima Netto

www.amazon.com/author/rlimanetto

**The Little Prince for Grownups**

This book, already in its fourth edition in Brazil, brings light into some important insights hidden in Saint Exupéry's masterpiece . The inspiration to write a work of art arises from the unconscious, full of ideas that the very author may have been unaware of. "The Little Prince for Grown-ups" gets to the roots of some of Antoine Saint-Exupéry's Little Prince, using mythology and Jungian psychology concepts to expose some of its buried treasures. As in the book of Saint-Exupéry, the crash that leads the pilot to land in the Sahara desert becomes the beginning of a self-knowledge journey. Exupéry himself, or rather, Antoine, is the protagonist of this journey, and his companions are the blonde boy with the scarf around his neck and the Wise Old Man. In addition, there are many stories from the Bible as well as Gnostic texts, and Greek mythology.. Despite being based on Jungian ideas, no psychology knowledge is required to the read the book.

**The Jungian Bible**

Life explained through biblical stories and world myths from Jung's perspective.

**In Search of Happiness**

A metaphor for the eternal struggle between good and evil, and between light and darkness. The book tells Peter's story, a warrior of light, and his struggle to avoid the dimming of the last sparks of light after Atlantis destruction. Peter is captured by criminals and has to use all his creativity to escape alive and to avoid the killing of a presidential candidate.

## Easy Guide to Jungian Psychology

An easy guide to Carl G. Jung's main ideas and concepts. Do you want to understand the Jungian concept of archetypes? What was Jung's view on the meaning of life? Do you want to be introduced to active imagination, one of the most powerful tools to talk to your angels? Or demons? Would you like to know about the Jungian concept of neuroses and complexes? What was Jung's view on the existence of God? What is behind the break up between Jung and Freud? And much more. No psychology knowledge required.

## The Boy's Journey

The story of a boy, born with a physical defect, that has to win the battle against his demons. A Jungian journey of individuation.

**Contact the author**
**Roberto Lima Netto**
rlimanetto@hotmail.com
www.amazon.com/author/rlimanetto
www.HappinessAcademyOnline.com

Printed in Great Britain
by Amazon.co.uk, Ltd.,
Marston Gate.